Mar X
Marcuse, Irene,
Consider the alternative
$ 24.95

CONSIDER THE ALTERNATIVE

CONSIDER THE ALTERNATIVE

Irene Marcuse

Walker & Company ❀ *New York*

All the characters and events portrayed in this work are fictitious.

First published in the United States of America in 2002 by Walker Publishing Company, Inc.

Published simultaneously in Canada by Fitzhenry and Whiteside, Markham, Ontario L3R 4T8

For information about permission to reproduce selections from this book, write to Permissions, Walker & Company, 435 Hudson Street, New York, New York 10014

Library of Congress Cataloging-in-Publication Data

Marcuse, Irene, 1953–
   Consider the alternative / Irene Marcuse.
      p.   cm.
   ISBN 0-8027-3377-8
   1. Women social workers—Fiction.   2. New York (N.Y.)—Fiction.
I. Title.

PS3563.A6433 C66   2002
813'.6—dc21   2002016770

Series design by M. J. DiMassi

Visit Walker & Company's Web site at www.walkerbooks.com

Printed in the United States of America

2 4 6 8 10 9 7 5 3 1

For Brenda Hinds Taylor
1947–2001

Acknowledgments

Thanks to my readers, Philip Silver, Janet Jaffe, Leigh Henderson, Joyce Willis, Peter Marcuse, Harold Marcuse, and Aaron Kubitza-Marcuse. Because of your copious notes, comments, criticisms, and the discussions and brainstorming sessions they caused, this book and its characters underwent major revisions. Philip, especially, no amount of acknowledgment can do justice to all the ways I rely on you.

I consulted several experts along the way. Marina Stajic, Ph.D., Barbara Greenwald-Davis, RN, and Beth Labush, RN, MSN, all provided information that I have attempted to use accurately.

Tomoe Arai helped with entry to the New York Buddhist Church, and Ellen Pall gave me the last line.

I have had many people on my mind through the writing of this book. Inge Marcuse, who died a good death too early, and John Wiseman, Lew Cetta, Mario Vigezzi, Eddie Elner, Sylvia Muldavin, Erica Sherover; having known you is part of who I am. Most of all, Brenda Taylor. Nothing I write could do you justice.

I didn't know, when I began this book, that it would be among the last of the mystery line for Walker & Company. I've been fortunate to have gotten my start under the editorial guidance of Michael Seidman, and crime fiction as a whole will be poorer without his vision.

Tabitha, as always, you are the light of my life.

CONSIDER THE ALTERNATIVE

1

I⊤ has its moments, being out of a job. Regardless of whether you've quit, been laid off, or gotten fired, if you can manage to set aside the financial worries for a few minutes—no small feat—you notice a kind of elation lurking in your breast. The rest of the world is tied to the clock, busy doing things they'd rather not, while you've got an unplanned day stretching ahead of you. Free time!

Of course, it's a lot simpler when you're young and unattached. I spent my twenties picking up and discarding waitress jobs while I nurtured the hope that someday I'd make a living painting watercolors. Uh-huh. As my mother says, You live long enough, you get smart. I finally woke up to the realization that it was one thing to be waiting tables at thirty, but I sure didn't want to be doing it at forty.

So I moved across the continent from California to New York City, where I nursed my grandmother through her final year. After she died, I put the small inheritance she left me to use and got a master's degree in social work. Since then, I've also acquired a husband and a foster daughter whose adoption we have every reason to think might actually be on the eve of finalization.

Until six weeks ago I'd had a good job, working with the elderly population of my Upper West Side neighborhood. On September 1, the Cathedral of St. John the Divine pulled the plug on funding for my agency, Senior Services. Call me optimistic; I was confident that social work jobs with good benefits, in walking distance of where I live, with hours that could flex enough to allow for the demands of a family, would not be hard to locate or land.

By the middle of October I was getting nervous about money. My husband, Benno, is a self-employed cabinetmaker, which means we carry the major overhead of a woodworking shop whether he's busy or not. Our health insurance disappeared with my job, and our monthly premium as private payers is $18.42 less than a month's maintenance payment on our apartment.

Not that I hadn't managed to occupy my time. I filled two photo albums, bringing our family history up to Clea's sixth birthday—only three years to go. With any luck, the sweater I was knitting would still fit her by the time I got it finished. Not to mention washing all seven windows in our apartment, repotting my grandmother's collection of African violets, and cooking dinners that actually required recipes.

Nevertheless, the joys of unemployment were beginning to tarnish.

While the New York Jets were well on their way to a winning season, I became a devotee of the Help Wanted section of Sunday's *Times*. Monday mornings were occupied with composing hopeful cover letters to accompany my résumé. In an average week, I applied for a dozen jobs that all sounded more appealing in their advertisements than at the handful of interviews I'd landed.

New York—it's who you know, and the connections work in ways mysterious and strange. The best of my job prospects came through Benno, one of those six-degrees kinds of things.

For years, he's been easing the stress on his lower back with a monthly shiatsu session. As he got to know the masseur, Katsu Kajiwara, it emerged that he'd trained as a woodworker before turning to the less strenuous art of massage. When Benno needed an occasional hand on a large project, he'd hire Katsu to work with him.

In one of those odd coincidences New York throws at its residents, Katsu's wife was also a social worker at a small nonprofit agency serving the elderly in Morningside Heights. Benno told me that at the moment of realization, he'd joked to Katsu that maybe they were married to the same woman.

Susan Wu and I had actually met, in a professional way, before our husbands did. Susan was the executive director of NAN, Neighbors Aiding Neighbors, and Senior Services had done money management for several of her clients. NAN's second social worker had quit abruptly two weeks ago. The connection through our husbands meant that I knew about the opening before it was advertised, and Susan had expedited my application and interview. I was more than qualified; I knew the age group, their needs, and the services available to them. Careerwise, it would be a lateral move for me—walking ten blocks farther north was the main difference in what I'd be doing.

We'd discussed salary, schedule, job title, responsibilities. The upshot was that, pending approval of NAN's board of directors, I was hired. They'd met last night, and I expected a formal offer this morning.

Which meant this was my last Saturday of freedom. Walking through the flurry of yellow leaves from the trees in Sakura Park at 10:00 A.M., I was feeling virtuous and full of hope: I'd volunteered the morning to my new job.

It helped that lending some muscle to schlepp boxes for NAN's fall flea market meant that I'd have a chance to check out the donated treasures.

I know, this is a lot of explanation, but be patient. I'm

telling a story, a story about death. Not a topic you can just jump into.

I work with people who are near the end of their natural life spans, so I get to see death up close. It can come quickly, or as a drawn-out misery. I've learned that a lingering death is not always a bad thing, nor a fast death a mercy.

There's comfort in simply sitting with a person on the threshold. I know; when it came time for my grandmother, I wanted her with me as long as possible. Maybe it would have been different if she'd been in pain, but she wasn't.

Some people never recover from a sudden loss. Unfinished business is the greater part of grief, according to my mother, and it's regret that salts the tears. Death without warning steals more than the future; it also takes away any chance of reconciling the past.

Morbid thoughts for a sunlit morning.

October is the month that makes winter worthwhile, that won me over to seasons. Benno has his mother's Mediterranean climate in his blood, and summer is his season. He'd do well in my hometown, Berkeley, where the Pacific air is mild all year long. Me, I relish the days when summer's humid pall has evaporated and the leaves turn from their oppressive, omnipresent green to blaze gold and red against a sky as close as the East Coast ever gets to the crisp blue of northern California.

The seasons actually change later in the city than in the rest of the state. The concrete holds the heat, and leaves linger longer on the trees. Mid-October, the piles were deep enough to shuffle under my feet. Going down the steps from Convent Avenue, the Virginia creeper that clung to the high brick retaining wall was a splatter painting of scarlet and green. It felt good to be up and out in the world.

Just as I got to Broadway, a northbound train came screeching out of its underground lair for the brief stretch where the subway soars over the valley of 125th Street. Caught by the Don't Walk light, I had to wait under the stone arch supporting the track while the ultimate sound of the city clanked above my head. Back to reality.

The brakes squealed into the station. The light changed. I crossed over to Monument Estates, home of NAN.

The office was located in one of the ten buildings that make up the Estates complex. The brick high-rises, erected in the 1950s by a consortium of area educational institutions including Columbia University, Union and Jewish Theological Seminaries, and Manhattan School of Music, served as a bulwark against the encroachments of Harlem. Since it provided subsidized middle-income housing, the Estates also became a haven for an integrated population of mid-level professionals.

As I walked up the steps, a bass drone of movie-actor voices seeped through the crack between open office windows and drawn venetian blinds. NAN sponsored a Saturday video program, and Susan had warned me that a volunteer might be in early to prescreen the movie. It sounded like she was right.

I rang the bell four times before the sound track went silent. An elderly white woman with hair sparse as dandelion fluff opened the door.

"You're early. The movie doesn't start until two."

"I know." I smiled into her unwelcoming face and told her I was meeting Susan Wu.

"I don't know anything about that. Maybe she's in her office." The woman jerked her head at a closed door behind and to her left. "Well, you'd better come in. I'm Addie Collins."

It was grudging, but I'd take it. "Anita Servi." I offered her a hand, which she looked at like it was an unacceptable piece of meat at the butcher's, and didn't take.

"I've been here for half an hour. I suppose she"—another jerk toward the door—"came in earlier. At least she hasn't come out to bother me. I don't expect anyone to be here Saturday morning. I like to watch the movie straight through without interruptions. I'm the one who lets people in, you know, and I have to open the door and take the money. We say two o'clock sharp on the signs, but people always come late, and then they take their time getting settled. With all that going on, I can't concentrate on the show."

"I won't keep you, then." I'd almost forgotten how it was, working with the elderly—you got the whole story, whether you wanted it or not.

Addie wasn't ready to let me go. She gave the inner door two sharp raps with a backhanded fist. "Susan! Your friend is here!"

There was no response.

"Where is she?" Addie knocked again. "I thought that darn alarm wasn't set when I let myself in, but this door was closed, so I didn't worry about the alarm. I assumed Susan was in her office."

"Maybe." I tried a knock myself, and then the knob. It didn't turn.

"I suppose she could have slipped out, and I wouldn't have noticed. This *Henry the Eighth* is rather loud." Addie considered me. "Would you like to watch it with me while you wait?"

At the other end of the short hall were two open doors, one to the bathroom, the other to a second office.

"No, thanks, I don't want to intrude," I told Addie. "I'll wait in the other room."

"Suit yourself." Addie shrugged and went back to the movie.

NAN's home is actually a converted two-bedroom apartment. The wall between kitchen and living room was removed to make a single open space for group events like the videos, shown on a large-screen TV. The former bedrooms serve as functional if cramped offices. Susan had the larger; the other, now packed with flea market donations, would be mine.

I pushed open the door and flipped on the overhead light.

The floor area, except for a small space in front of a pair of file cabinets, was piled with boxes. The desk and both chairs held an assortment of plastic shopping bags that spewed yarn, stuffed animals, baskets, a painted metal tray, empty picture frames. A toaster oven wearing two straw hats occupied the windowsill. It was obvious why Susan needed help carting it all down to the storage unit in the basement.

An orange tiger perched on a shopping cart loaded with jigsaw-puzzle boxes glared at me with a baleful glass eye. I stepped cautiously past him to open the blinds. I thought a little real daylight might help me figure out what I could do while I waited. I surveyed the jumble, trying to organize it mentally. The one cart was already full; any box that could be closed was, and stacked chest-high against the wall.

I kicked myself for not stopping at the Bread Shop to pick up coffee on my way in. Well, maybe that was where Susan had gone. I reached for the tiger, intending to turn him around so he'd stop staring at me, when I realized the cart stood in front of a connecting door between the two offices.

I figured what the hell, and gave it a knock. Still no answer; no surprise there. I tried that knob, too. At least in Susan's office there'd be room to sit while I waited.

It didn't turn. Nor was there a slot for a key. So if Susan wasn't in there, how did both doors get locked?

Right, they were bedroom doors. Maybe it had one of those little buttons, and she kept it locked for privacy. The sound track from the living room provided the kind of menacing, atmospheric music that signals the approach of a bad guy.

I knocked again, louder. The thin walls were perfect for the conduction of noise. If she was there, no way Susan didn't hear me. And if she wasn't, how did she plan to get back in?

I rattled the knob, frustrated.

It took me a minute. If the door had inadvertently been locked when Susan, not realizing it, closed the door behind her as she left, she'd have locked herself out. Maybe she'd gone to find someone from maintenance to help her get back in?

Anything's possible.

I knew an easier way to get past these flimsy locks. I opened my wallet. Visa was everywhere I wanted to be. I used the stiff plastic card to hold the latch back while I pushed the door open.

Thin bars of sun angled through the drawn blinds and fell on a gawky figure in the client's chair beside the desk.

2

THOUGHT it was a joke, a mannequin donated to the flea market. The legs stuck straight out, the feet in low-heeled navy pumps pointing in opposite directions. It was dressed in a dark skirt and a powder-pink twin set, sleeves pushed up to the elbows. A tan plastic bag over the head protected its wig and plaster face.

Even as I hit the light switch, the pungent, oddly sweet smell alerted me that I was wrong. In the harsh fluorescent illumination I noticed a down of real hair on the faintly bluish skin. I touched the arm, hoping for the feel of smooth plaster, ready to laugh at myself for being spooked by a doll.

She was stiff and cold as marble. Up close, I realized that the plastic bag was closed tightly around the figure's neck, held in place by a thick rubber band. The bag was just translucent enough that I could see what appeared to be con-densed beads of water on the inside.

The temperature and rigidity of the skin told me she was already dead, but when I saw those drops of moisture, the thought that automatically followed was that there might still be a faint respiration.

I knew it was the wrong thing to do, but I couldn't stop myself. If there was any chance she was still alive—

I put two fingers of each hand under the rubber band and stretched it until I was able to peel the bag up over the head. A soggy white paper painter's mask covered the mouth and nose. I pulled it down.

This wasn't Susan but a fright mask of the woman I'd known. Her face was a ghoulish blue, her lipstick-smeared mouth frozen, half-open, straining for air. Released from the bag, a trickle of water dribbled onto her chest. I watched, fascinated, as it was absorbed by the fuzzy pink sweater.

I realized my hands were wet. I held them out in front of me, horrified, unable to think where to wipe them.

I looked around the office, panicked by my hands, my inability to touch anything. On a low table beside the body was a glass tumbler with what looked like the dregs of red wine, a book titled *Final Exit*, and, thank heaven, a box of tissues. I wiped my hands with the compulsion of Lady Macbeth, long past clean.

Then I made my second mistake and dabbed at Susan's face, willing her to wake up, to open her eyes.

I knew she wasn't going to, as well as I knew I shouldn't have touched her. It just seemed like the human thing to do, clear the fluid from her chin. Maybe if she wasn't embarrassed by how she looked, she'd open her eyes.

An argument broke out on the video in the other room. For a second I thought the yelling was directed at me. I dropped the wad of tissues and backed away from the body. It took a moment of deliberately deep breaths before my heart settled down.

I was ashamed to admit it, but the first thought in my head was, Why me? I was starting to feel like Typhoid Mary— I'd had a few too many mornings that started with dead bodies in the past several years. Well, even one would have been too many. What weird kink of fate was threading its way through my life?

Yes, I work with old people, and death is a given. Clients are one thing, but Susan was in her early forties, slightly younger than I am. Then there'd been Clea's baby-sitter two years ago, and a street hustler a few years before that.

I closed my eyes and let the movie voices murmur over me.

I don't know how long I stood there, trying to forget those other deaths, before the significance of what Susan had been reading occurred to me. I opened my eyes and picked up the book. Although I hadn't read it, I was familiar with the title, the black capitals of *FINAL EXIT*, a square of blue around the subtitle, *The Practicalities of Self-Deliverance and Assisted Suicide for the Dying*. My mother had given me a copy of the so-called suicide manual years ago, when the Hemlock Society first printed it. Intended to aid the terminally ill in achieving a dignified death, the book was criticized as being open to misuse by otherwise healthy people who for whatever reason wanted to end their lives.

From what I knew about Susan, she had absolutely no reason to kill herself. Not only that, but suicide in her office seemed extremely out of character. In my experiences with her, I'd found Susan to be professional, competent, empathetic, reticent yet capable of dry humor, and unfailingly polite. How could she not have considered the risk of shocking an elderly volunteer, not to mention the cloud such an act would cast over NAN and its clients?

Susan's choice of time and place had certainly spared Katsu, though. I found myself wondering if she'd arranged our meeting for just this purpose, so I'd be the one who found her body. She might've thought I stood at just the right distance—close enough so that I knew her husband, but not so close that— Yeah, right. How can you stay at a professional remove when *anyone* you know dies, and you're the one who finds her body?

God *damn* it. I wasn't going to cry.

Across the room, a red screen-saver message floated across the computer monitor, disappeared, drifted back again from the other side: "Welcome to Neighbors Aiding Neighbors."

Some welcome I was getting. I nudged the mouse. A gray screen with a few lines of text appeared.

"I'm sorry," it read. "I want you all to know this is not your fault. It's my decision, mine alone. I couldn't keep on anymore, so I've chosen the alternative. It's such an easy, peaceful path. Please forgive me."

I tapped the Page Down key. There was nothing else in the document, which I saw from the title bar at the top of the screen had been named, prosaically, "Note."

That was it? "I'm sorry" was all she had to say? "You all"— no personal message for Katsu? She couldn't keep on with *what? Forgive* her?

I was so angry I could've shaken her.

Yes, anger is the first stage of grief, but this was beyond social-work speak. Dying is one thing. Suicide, okay, kill yourself—but to do it where you worked, to leave no word for your husband . . . easy peaceful path, my foot.

I turned back to the body. Susan's eyes were closed, and where at first I'd thought her mouth was half-open in an agonized protest, now it seemed to me to be simply slack, gaping a bit, maybe about to say something that had seemed important at the time but no longer mattered.

What did I know about Susan's life, anyway? Her marriage? Just because Katsu had extraordinary hands and the ability to locate every tense spot on a person's body didn't mean he was an ideal husband. Just because Vivian Brownell, NAN's president and Susan's boss, had come across as enlightened, fair, and compassionate the first time I'd met her, it didn't necessarily make her easy to work for, and heaven knew the clients themselves could drive a person around the bend.

Still, committing suicide in the office seemed like a pretty extreme form of passive-aggressive acting out.

And then I was thinking about Katsu. I might, with effort, be able to suspend judgment and take Susan's suicide at face value, but would he? If Susan had left any other indication of her reasons, surely her husband deserved to know about it. Once the police came, it would be out of my hands, and into the realm of just-the-facts bureaucracy. A few more minutes wouldn't make any difference to Susan, but it might help me to help Katsu understand why she'd done what she had.

I was computer savvy enough to know that as long as all I did was look without opening any files, I could see what Susan had been working on and not leave any footprints in the machine.

I covered the mouse with a tissue and aimed it at the Window menu. A click showed me that there was a second document open, with my name on it: "ServiHire." I brought it up and read the screen. A standard job-offer letter, complete with starting salary, a three-month probationary period, benefits to start immediately, dated the coming Monday.

Great. A job offer written by a dead woman. What was I getting myself into here?

I went for the File menu, with the drop-down list of the last nine documents Susan had worked on. Mostly the file names were self-explanatory, with logical prefixes like "newsletter" and "video" before dates. The two most recent, after the letter for me, started with "minutes," dated September and October; she'd probably sat down to catch up on paperwork after the board meeting last night, entered the minutes, and then typed up the letter for me.

At the bottom of the list was a file that had been worked on from the disc drive rather than the hard drive. It was called, ominously, "Deaths."

There was no disc in the A drive.

There were no stray discs, other than backup software, anywhere. Not around the computer, or on the bookshelves, or in the unlocked desk drawers.

Deaths. What kind of file name was that? And the plural

bothered me—why not simply "Death," if that was what was on her mind?

I stared at the monitor until the screen saver flickered on and released me.

Okay, what about her purse? Which wasn't anywhere in plain sight.

I opened the closet door. A stack of cardboard boxes in one corner, a navy blazer on a hanger, a pair of black flats and two umbrellas on the floor—but no handbag.

In the silence, I realized the movie voices had been replaced by the bang and squeak of folding chairs being taken out and set up. I supposed the afternoon video program would have to be canceled. It was time to get the wheels rolling.

Careful not to look at Susan's face again, I stepped around her stiff legs to get to the phone. When I rolled the chair back from the desk, I noticed a slim brown leather bag leaning against the side of the bookshelf.

The top zipper was open. I used the tissue method again, to avoid leaving fingerprints. I had no idea how carefully the police would examine the office, but things would be simpler if they didn't know I'd been snooping.

There was nothing out of the ordinary. Wallet, keys, a small hairbrush, two tubes of lipstick, a leather-bound address book, pocket calculator, roll of wintergreen LifeSavers, white cotton handkerchief with a spray of pink flowers embroidered in one corner. No computer discs.

I put the bag back where I'd found it and started on the phone calls. While 911 had me on hold, I did a more careful scan of the surface of Susan's desk. She had one of those calendar blotters, the boxes for each day filled with appointments. The weekends were basically empty, except for today's box. In the top right corner, it said "Katsu, Mt. Tremper" with an arrow across to Sunday. Underneath was my name and "10 A.M."

I picked up a lacquer-framed photograph of Katsu. He was

very handsome, with black hair and high cheekbones. He looked directly into the camera, and from the slight, sexy curve of his lips, I deduced that Susan herself had taken the shot. Oh, Lord, how *would* Katsu react? They'd been married more than ten years. I couldn't begin to imagine how it would feel to lose a spouse like this.

The 911 dispatcher came back on the line and told me not to touch anything. Too late for that, I thought, and hung up. A list of phone numbers for the NAN board was taped next to the phone. Vivian Brownell, my future boss should I still have a job on offer, was my next call.

The rest of the morning was an ordeal. I wasn't familiar with any of the four cops who responded to the 911, and they predictably gave me six kinds of grief over having interfered with Susan's body.

Not that anyone called it a crime scene, but—"Unnatural death, lady, you shoulda known better!"

Addie Collins turned out to be an ace, the kind of person who reacts to a crisis by getting busy. Shocked she certainly was, but after pushing past me to see with her own eyes, Addie sat at the volunteer desk in the hall and telephoned the twenty-odd people with reservations for the afternoon show to notify them that the movie would be canceled due to an unspecified emergency.

She also handled the police questioning more patiently than I did.

Easy for her. No one pressured or criticized Addie for not being positive whether or not the alarm had been turned on when she came in. It was a pretty low-tech affair, a motion sensor that was set by the turn of a circular key from outside. Addie seemed to regard it as some kind of magic, something she stuck her key into and hoped for the best.

The detective who showed up a half hour later, in a tailored navy wool overcoat that proved he was one of New York's finest in sartorial terms at least, introduced himself as Donald Graffo. After listening to Addie's confused story, Graffo thanked her as courteously as if she were his own grandmother, and sent her home. Me, it was all the bored young detective could do to nod in my direction.

The information Graffo was most curious about was Susan's ethnicity. I told him what I knew—her father was Chinese, her mother American. He made a remark to the effect that suicide was a badge of honor among Asians. I bit my tongue to keep from pointing out that stereotypes don't always hold water. Graffo would have appreciated that even less than he appreciated being told that Susan's husband was out of town—even though it meant he'd get to spend the afternoon admiring fall foliage on his way up to Mt. Tremper.

Knowing that Katsu was at a Buddhist retreat complicated things. Buddhism, it turns out, is one of the religions whose believers can be legally exempted from a routine autopsy. The crime scene investigator, a beefy woman with bleached blond hair tipped in purple, printed Susan's message from the computer, slid *Final Exit* into a plastic bag, emptied the wastebasket with my crumpled tissues into another bag, and took lots of photographs. No autopsy was fine with her; she took a blood sample and headed back to the medical examiner's office. Susan's body would also be going to the morgue, but no cutting would be done until Katsu's wishes were known.

To judge from outer appearances, Vivian Brownell, president of NAN's board of directors, coped with Susan's death as well as Addie had. A svelte black woman in her late seventies, Vivian had a good six inches of perfect posture over my five-two, and the pleasing yet firm persona of the professional fund-raiser she'd been during her career in Congressman Charles Rangel's office. Whatever personal sense of loss she felt, Vivian hid it with polite responses to Detective Graffo, and concern for my state of mind.

For all the years I've spent working with the elderly, I'm

still surprised by the reserves of strength they have to draw on. Stereotypes again; shows you how deep our prejudices about incompetent, childlike old people run. Vivian handled Susan's unexpected death as though she dealt with suicides on a regular basis.

But what did I know about Vivian's experiences? You live long enough, you not only get smart, you get competent. Vivian's main anxiety was for NAN's clients, those frail elders who relied on Susan and NAN.

While the crime scene investigator went about her business, Vivian made lists on a pad of yellow paper. Of course, keeping busy is also a coping mechanism. If there are things to do, emotions that might be paralyzingly overwhelming can take a back seat. Vivian declined my offer to come in on Sunday and help out; Monday would be soon enough for me to start.

By the time I got home that afternoon, I'd been hired to do a lot more of a job than I'd bargained for.

3

N OT for the first time, I thought that if I'd known having a child meant I was signing up for eighteen years of waking up by 7:00 A.M., I might not have done it. Job or no job, I still had to get up, fix Clea's breakfast, pack her lunch, throw on a pair of sweats, and walk her to school. Monday morning, however, brought home to me how much I'd savored not having to dress for work. Slacks and a silk blouse, not to mention applying a quick layer of makeup in honor of my newly employed status, meant I had to be up a full half hour earlier than I'd become accustomed to.

The day had a déjà vu feeling all over it—familiar yet different. I was starting a new job; Clea was attending a new school. Once I was no longer working under the umbrella of St. John the Divine, the tuition break we'd gotten at the Cathedral School had evaporated along with our health insurance. Our neighborhood, the upper left side of Manhattan, is lousy with good private—or, as they refer to themselves, "independent"—schools. We'd chosen St. Hilda's and St. Hugh's, three blocks away, for its traditional approach, racially integrated student body, and unpretentious parents.

This was the first day of winter uniforms—dark plaid skirt, white turtleneck, navy blazer. I'd spent Sunday afternoon cornrowing Clea's hair, and she'd chosen bead colors to match the stripes in her skirt, navy, green, red, a scattering of yellow.

"My daughter the preppy," Benno teased. I thought she looked quite studious, myself.

Although it takes maybe all of ten minutes, elevator to elevator, I enjoy the walk to school with Clea. It's a brief, intimate moment, the only time she'll still let me hold her hand. Nine years old is a big girl.

Nine years, and the adoption still isn't finalized. Last night, filling out the medical forms for the after-school program, I was reminded that Clea is still a foster child. The Agency for Children's Services, to call it by its latest incarnation, has ultimate say over her welfare; we can't take her out of the state without letting them know. Another unpleasant thought I tried not to dwell on.

It was one of those thick foggy mornings that come in fall. I don't have seasons in my blood, and the first days of changed weather always take me by surprise. When I see it out the window, the fog seems like a friend, familiar Bay Area weather that will burn to blue by early afternoon. It takes walking out into it to remind me that this East Coast fog will more likely turn to a drizzle that will curl itself in my bones for the rest of the day. No matter how warmly I dress, the damp sneaks its chilly little feet in at my collar.

Clea was not in a good mood. I hadn't got the winter jacket thing together yet, so I'd made her wear last year's—a perfectly decent navy duffel coat from Brooks Brothers, a hand-me-down from one of Benno's myriad cousins. Last winter, it had been her favorite garment. This year, she pitched a fit about it.

"It's too small!" Clea flapped her arms. "I can't move my arms right!"

So, the sleeves were a tad short. Clea grows like a' weed, only faster; she's already within a few inches of me. Benno swears he's going to stop talking to her if she ever gets taller than his five-feet-six, which is bound to happen.

"Well, then, don't lift your arms up like that. We'll get you a new coat this weekend, but it's cold today."

"No, it isn't!" Half a block, and she had the toggle buttons undone. "See, I'm not a bit cold."

The other thing I wasn't prepared for about parenthood is how it turns you into a nag. Button your jacket, put your hat on, finish your juice, bagel, vegetables, chicken—everything but ice cream seems to get left with two bites on the plate. Not to mention brush your teeth, wash your face, put your laundry in the basket, do your homework, practice your cornet. I let it go, and by the time we'd gone another block she was holding the front of the coat closed across her chest.

Neon orange and yellow dots of marigolds popped out at us from the fenced tree pits along the way. Sunflowers nodded through the fog in the triangular island between 113th and 114th. The stop sign at the corner was wreathed in morning glories, deep violet trumpets whose crimson centers echoed the red of the sign.

"How come I have to go to the after-school?"

"Because I have a job, remember?" We'd been over it at dinner last night, twice.

"Do I have to go every day?"

They call it Whiney Monday in our house. Clea knew that the sudden start to my job was due to Susan's death. I was worried that her reluctance to be with the new friends in her class rather than home with me was a result of the death of her baby-sitter two years ago. I'd had flashbacks, myself; it was only natural for Clea, too, especially the association of death with after-school arrangements. I went through the whole explanation again, as patiently as I could manage. Clea appeared to be ignoring me.

She allowed me a brief kiss in the lobby before chattering

off with her new best friend, Tamika. Clea would be fine, I reassured myself. Children are resilient.

I could've continued on to my new place of employment through Riverside Park, but I chose the business route down Broadway. Well, up, actually, as Benno reminds me when I head north—that is, uptown. But Broadway slopes steeply after 116th, and to me, down means down; my internal compass still responds to the physical contours of the landscape. I'm not quite New Yorker enough to have uptown and downtown imprinted on my brain.

I passed the high iron gates of the main entrance to Columbia at 116th Street, where a tall Greek couple stood guard over a stream of undergraduates entering the heart of the campus. The stone woman held an open book, its words eroded to illegibility. The globe in her companion's hand was as smooth as his laurel-circled pate, with a single carved word: *Sciencia.* A phrase from some long-ago Latin class swam into my head: "The words of women are as if written on water."

Or on a computer disc, I thought, reminded of Susan's missing "Deaths" file. Either way, ephemeral.

As Broadway heads downhill, the walls of the university rise higher and the architectural face Columbia turns to the community reveals its true sense of itself as a city on a hill. The pink granite walls change from rough, sun-faded stone to precise, highly polished rectangles rising four windowless stories to enclose the gym, excuse me, "athletic facility." The warmer brownstone of Teacher's College, sheathed in semipermanent scaffolding, came as a relief, even with the two vagrants stretched out on the unused steps of the Broadway entrance.

It was impossible to tell anything about the sleepers—age, gender, race, all hidden by a black nylon sleeping bag for the luckier one, an improvisation of plaid and dirty yellow blanket for the other, both of them lying on flattened cardboard boxes as protection from the cold stone steps. Sticking out from the blanket-shrouded figure was a hand in a red wool glove, clutching a paper cup. Call me a bleeding heart; I contributed two quarters. Nobody should have to spend a night like this, and if they do, they at least deserve a hot cup of coffee when they wake up.

It's like entering an oasis, Monument Estates. What sets it apart from Grant Houses, the public housing project that borders it to the north and east, are the gardens, tended by a horticulturist who keeps the trees pruned and the perennial beds bordered in seasonal bloomers. Knee-high coleuses gathered like bright green and magenta socks around a flowering plum whose leaves had gone dark purple in the chill. I'd forgotten my own hat, and I raised a hand to see how my personal humidity meter was doing in the fog. The ends of hair that had escaped from the bun on top of my head were tightly curled in the damp.

"You're early."

It seemed to be the standard greeting at NAN, at least for me. I hadn't minded it from Addie; from my new boss, however, I'd expected a bit warmer welcome.

Vivian must've had the same thought. "I'm glad to see you, Anita. This whole situation has been such a shock, and I'm very grateful that you're able to start work on such short notice. I hope you will keep in mind how much I appreciate your being here, in the days to come, if I seem a bit short-tempered. There are so many things to take care of! I've been in the office since six-thirty this morning, and I miss Susan dreadfully. She really did everything for us." Vivian's polite façade relaxed, allowing me to see how exhausted she really was.

"I'll do my best to try and fill her shoes," I said.

Trite, I know, and Vivian's expression let me know how inadequate my words were. "I will never understand how Susan could do this to NAN." She stared at me as if I might have an explanation.

I didn't.

Vivian turned her back on my mumbled platitude about the incomprehensibility of suicide and led me into Susan's office.

"If you don't object, I think it will be best for you to use this room for the time being. There hasn't been time to clear the flea market donations from the other room, although I did arrange for one of the maintenance people to give the rest of the office a thorough cleaning and airing out yesterday. I hope the thought of Saturday's events won't trouble you unduly."

After a brief assessment of my reaction—I nodded reassuringly to indicate I'd do whatever she thought necessary—Vivian gestured at a carton on the floor. "I've packed up Susan's personal belongings."

Right down to business, indeed. I'd have plenty of space to work, with the framed photographs of Katsu packed away, along with the carved animals that had decorated Susan's desk.

"I spoke with Mr. Cadgey-wahrah yesterday to extend my condolences. It's a tragic shock for him, of course, but he offered to stop by later today to collect his wife's things." Vivian paused. "It may seem as though I'm in a rush to remove all traces of Susan, but I want you to feel at home here, Anita. To make the place your own."

I still had my jacket on.

The doorbell gave its single chime, and Vivian excused herself to answer it.

I was relieved to have a moment alone. Mornings, in particular Monday mornings, have never been my favorite time of day. I opened the closet. The metal hangers clinked together on the empty rod. Vivian was back before I'd done more than notice that the chair where Susan's body had sat was now gone.

"There will be a lot of information for you to absorb, Anita, and I want you to remember that you don't have to handle everything on your own. Our wonderful nurse, Diane McClellan, will assist you with client needs. NAN also has three dedicated office volunteers who come in on Tuesdays, Wednesdays, and Thursdays to answer the phones and the door. They'll be available to help out with the weekly activities and programs as well. Unfortunately, I must leave by eleven-thirty for an appointment I was unable to reschedule, so I've asked our Thursday volunteer to come in this afternoon. I expect you'll be glad to have her here, especially on your first day."

She was right—it was all coming at me at once. The best I could do was to take in as much as possible and hope to sort out the rest later.

I was saved from having to make more of a response than nodding by the sound of a key in the lock.

4

T HAT will be our nurse, Diane McClellan." Vivian nodded at the door.

What I knew about Diane, from my job interview with Susan, was that her office was in a different building and she spent only three days a week at NAN. At least initially, I'd need to rely heavily on her knowledge of NAN's clients. In spite of my responsibilities for the various programs, providing direct services was the real meat of the job.

Diane McClellan's handshake was firm and brief. So was her assessment of me, a glance that went from my face to my shoes and back up again. I had no doubt that she'd taken in the fact that my purple silk blouse was three years old and slightly worn around the cuffs, nor that she'd noticed the charcoal wool pants and vest I was wearing had not started life as a set.

When Diane took off her leather coat, it was equally clear to me that her royal blue pleated skirt and black cashmere sweater had set her back more than I spent in six months on clothes. Not to mention the Arche shoes, as expensive as they were comfortable. Her straightened hair was pulled back in a French twist, which allowed the ruby studs in her ears to catch the light and shoot red glints announcing that they were the real things.

I was relieved to see that her skin, a few shades darker than Vivian's milky coffee, was uncomplicated by any makeup other than a deep burgundy lipstick. I might be okay in the face paint department, but my wardrobe was going to need an upgrade.

Whatever she thought of my attire, Diane kept it to herself.

She made the usual pleasantries, considering the situation. I appreciated the cordiality, and as for the trite words, well, death is an event that by its awesomeness turns every response into a cliché.

Vivian seemed to be watching Diane with the same assessing gaze Diane had given me. I had the sense of some unspoken apprehension on Vivian's part, a wariness, as though there were questions she was afraid to be asked.

"You saw the note I left on your office door?" Vivian didn't allow whatever she was feeling to stop her.

"Yes, thank you, Vivian, but I had already been informed of Susan's death. A detective visited me on Saturday." There was a hint of British in Diane's accent, mixed with an island cadence. Jamaican, probably.

"It was a shock to find out in that way. Someone from NAN should have let me know before the policeman arrived at my door." With a manicured fingernail the same shade as her lipstick, Diane stabbed at a sheet of paper taped to Susan's desk. It was the list of names and numbers I'd used to notify Vivian. "Here is my pager number."

I was surprised by the accusation in Diane's tone. Vivian seemed taken aback as well.

"I am sorry, Diane. It never crossed my mind that the police would—that they would disturb you at home. They insisted on interviewing the board members who'd attended the Friday night meeting, and I had all those calls to make.

I wasn't thinking. You're right, I should have called you as well."

Diane seemed to accept the apology, but it did nothing to dispel the unspoken tension in the room.

"The detective asked if Susan and I had ever discussed the suicide method outlined in *Final Exit*. He was also interested in how she might have accessed the medication she ingested."

Vivian's eyes took on a guarded expression, as if she were prepared for bad news.

"I said yes, she and I discussed the book. We talked about it regarding several of our clients, but never about our own selves." Diane watched for Vivian's reaction. "I also told him that if he didn't tell me exactly what Susan took, I couldn't say where she might have gotten it from."

Vivian's shoulders lowered a good inch. "No, of course not. How could any of us have known what Susan would do?"

Whatever was going on, it evaporated.

If I'd paid more attention then to the careful way Diane phrased her answer, I might have gone looking for what she'd left out a lot sooner.

Would it have made a difference? It's hard to say if any of the subsequent deaths could have been prevented. Monday-morning quarterback is the only way I get to play the position, but I don't think hindsight would have changed how I reacted. It was all too new for me—the place, the people, the responsibilities.

"I'm sure you two want to discuss client-related matters. Anita, let me just show you how to set the alarm and lock the front door." Vivian handed me a ring of keys. "The two smaller ones are for the filing cabinets. Many people come in and out of this office, so it's vital that we ensure the confidentiality of our clients and our financial records by keeping the files locked at all times. Now, this round key is for the alarm. Let me demonstrate."

She walked me through the alarm system, which was so

easy I thought I had a good shot at still remembering it by the end of the day.

"If you have other questions, I'll be right here at the volunteer desk, working on the death notices to be posted in the lobbies. According to Mr. Cadgey-wahrah, Susan's body will be cremated and a private funeral service held at the Buddhist temple."

The exaggerated way she pronounced *Kajiwara* annoyed me, but I wasn't about to correct my new boss.

Vivian picked up a pad of lined paper from the computer table. It shook in her hands. "We'll also need a notice to introduce you as our new social worker, Anita. I'll write that up as well. You do know how to use the computer?"

"Yes." Of that, at least, I was sure.

Vivian took herself off to the volunteer desk, closing the door behind her. I thought the greater challenge to confidentiality would be keeping one's voice low; she was sitting a mere three feet from the flimsy door. It was better than hovering, though, and a bit of my self-confidence returned.

What I wanted was to talk to Diane about Susan's death, but I didn't have a chance.

Diane had been studying the appointments on the desk calendar. She took me through the week as Susan had planned it, providing thumbnail assessments of the people I'd need to contact. I made notes on my own pad of paper, in case I didn't have time to consult the client files before doing a home visit. It was mostly routine, monitoring services already in place. The few cases that looked to be more complicated, Diane added to her own schedule.

I thanked her, and was the recipient of a searching look. From her enigmatic expression, I figured my social work abilities were harder to assess than my clothing budget had been.

When Diane put her jacket on, I got a good look at it: supple black leather that rolled easily into a shawl collar and was probably as soft as Clea's cheek. Diane's lips curved in a slight, involuntary smile as she wrapped the coat closed and cinched the belt around her waist.

Alone in Susan's office, I began to feel like I was on solid ground. The issues faced by the older Estates residents were familiar to me; the referrals would be easy to make.

I'd brought the most valuable tool of my trade with me: my Rolodex, a gold mine of names and direct numbers for contacts at bureaucracies all over the system. When Senior Services had closed, I couldn't bear to part with the information it took me years to compile. I didn't know if I'd be working with the elderly again, but you don't consign a living database like that to a storage unit. I set the card file on Susan's desk. Just seeing it there in its squat beige glory reminded me that I knew what I was doing, and I could handle whatever came at me.

Which was Vivian again. I was almost desperate for coffee, but I typed and printed out for her like a good employee. We spent another half hour going through items from an auxiliary to-do list Susan had kept on a yellow legal pad. Most of NAN's activities, like the video program, were run by volunteers who needed little more than regular support and direction. Others, like the flea market, would require more active involvement on my part.

By the time we finished, Vivian looked as drained as I felt, the lines around her mouth drawing her smile into a caricature of cordiality. She might well be tired. Thanks to her sense of duty, I'd spent my Sunday watching football while she'd been organizing all the responsibilities that were now on my shoulders.

I think we were both relieved when the door closed behind her.

I loaded Mr. Coffee with a double dose of what Maxwell House referred to as French Roast but smelled more like wood shavings.

Along with lunch and the Rolodex, the other thing I'd brought to NAN was a smudge stick, an item my mother never left home without. The wrapped bundle of sage leaves was supposed to smoke out bad vibes and promote healing. I waved it at the four corners of each room in the office. I'm not all that big on religion, alternative or otherwise, but I was alone in an apartment where a woman had died, and a little purification never hurt anyone.

5

was halfway through a tuna sandwich, with my feet up on the coffee table, when the doorbell bonged. The man who stood there could have knocked me over with a strong breath of air. It must have shown on my face.

"Ah, Mrs. Servi, I see you remember me."

"Detective Neville. I thought you retired." It came out sounding ruder than I'd intended, but the last thing I needed was another round of questioning by this particular representative of New York's finest. I held the door open for him to enter.

"It's Mr. Neville now. I am the head of security here in Monument Estates."

So he *had* retired. And head of Estates security was a logical position for Neville to have landed. The apartment complex took up an entire square block smack in the heart of Neville's old precinct, the Twenty-sixth.

He hadn't changed a bit in the years since I'd last seen him—still tall, barrel-chested, with mocha skin and short hair with barely a trace of gray.

Mine, on the other hand, was considerably grayer than when we'd first met.

"Mrs. Servi, it's a pleasure to see you again." Neville's smile was as warm as his accent. "Although once again not, ah, not in the most pleasant of circumstances."

He had that right. Several years ago, when he'd been on the job, a homeless woman had died in my building.

"No hard feelings, I hope?" He held out a hand.

I shook it, remembering the strength of his grip. In my opinion, it was he who might be expected to harbor hard feelings. He'd declined to investigate the woman's death as a homicide, and I'd shown him up. I was also the one who'd wound up in the Hudson River.

"No," I lied. "None at all. Would you like some coffee?"

A trace of sage lingered in the air, and Neville was sniffing curiously. I wanted to get a different aroma into his nostrils before he got the idea I'd been smoking grass.

"Thank you, yes, thank you. I see I've interrupted your lunch. Please, finish your meal. I won't stay long."

He took a chair opposite mine. In spite of his urging, I didn't pick up my sandwich. He had me feeling awkward enough, and I wasn't about to add to my disadvantage by chewing while he asked me benign-sounding questions with barbs in them.

We made small talk about career changes until he got to the point of his visit, which sure enough was more than introducing himself to the new social worker.

"I, ah, I understand a copy of the book *Final Exit* was found with Ms. Wu's body? You're familiar with it? A note was also found?"

I answered yes to each question.

"This note, Mrs. Servi, did you happen to read it?"

Since Mr. Neville knew my Nosey Parker proclivities, I didn't see any reason not to admit having seen Susan's suicide note.

"It referred to the book *Final Exit,* and made clear that

she was acting of her own volition? It was what you expected a healthy young woman to say prior to taking her own life?"

"Sort of. The note seemed a little on the terse side to me, but it did say no one else was to blame. Why?"

I got the assessing look from Neville this time. He raised his mug. I raised mine. We took sips of the nasty, machine-brewed coffee. It was his show.

"I'm going to be frank with you, Mrs. Servi. Since January, there have been eleven deaths here in the Estates. Seven of them have occurred since May, and of those seven, three have involved the plastic bag method of suicide. In all of those cases, the same book was found with the bodies. Only one of the three, however, left an explicit note. The circumstances of the other two deaths, that they were suicides, is not widely known in the Estates.

"And now we have Ms. Wu to make four." Neville stared into his mug and decided against another taste. "I find it curious that so many similar deaths should occur in this small community. Death, yes, death is a rather frequent visitor here, with so many elderly residents. It is the method, the manner, that concerns me, as well as the number."

"You don't think it's just a coincidence?"

"In my twenty-five years on the job, I investigated precisely three such 'plastic bag' cases of suicide. I've been at the Estates ten months, and already there have been four such deaths. No, I would not call this coincidence. Two thousand people live in these buildings. We are a small town, not unlike the village where I grew up, on Dominica. Two and three generations own apartments here. People know their neighbors, and each other's business. Regardless of the information posted in the lobbies, they will be aware of the circumstances of Ms. Wu's death, and that the book was found with her.

"Are you, ah, aware that when it was published, *Final Exit* was on the best-seller list for some years? Many people considered it to be a beacon of hope, promising relief from a painful end. For some, I suppose, it was." Neville looked past me, as if the ghosts of his suicides were perched on the counter. He shook them off. "The medical examiner's office conducted a study to determine if the book had instigated an increase in the rate of suicides. The conclusion, I believe, was that overall, both the death rate and the suicide rate remained unchanged. The number of suicides who chose to deliver themselves by means of the method outlined did, however, rise."

What I might have expected; where there's a will, there's always a way.

"What we have had here in the past six months is an increase in the death rate and also an increase in the suicide rate. Until May of this year, there had been only two cases of self-inflicted death in the Estates in thirty years. In both of those instances, death was achieved by jumping from a high floor." Neville went for the coffee again.

"You think there's something not right about these suicides." I stated the obvious.

"You are an, ah, an astute woman, Mrs. Servi."

High praise, considering the source.

"Is there something particular you'd like me to do?"

"You are also, allow me to say, inquisitive."

His smile was ironic; mine, embarrassed. I put my mug down. Better nothing than this swill.

"Ms. Wu was a young woman, and her death was a shock to me. I, ah, I would not have thought her the type of person who would take such a step. And that she would—here . . ." Neville spread his hands, unwilling to use plain words. "The most recent death, prior to Ms. Wu, was an elderly gentleman, found by a neighbor with a bag over his head and that book, *Final Exit*, next to his body. In his case, the note was quite explicit. Copied, evidently, directly from the book. He was suffering, I believe, from pancreatic cancer. A terminal diagnosis.

"I have no quarrel with those who choose to hasten the inevitable." Neville set his mug down. "What I had hoped, when I saw it was you who would be taking over the agency, is that we might be able to assist each other."

That I'd be able to help him, more like. I had a pretty fair idea where this was going, but I'll admit he'd gotten my curiosity up.

"Of course."

"I don't want to taint you, Mrs. Servi, with my suspicions. Perhaps there is nothing more at work here than the despair of the very ill and the very old. It would set my mind at rest, however, to be certain that all who have died here have done so by their own choice. Death comes for all of us, in his own good time. I have seen too many who were claimed against their will, and I do not think that Death needs us to go to him."

"You'd like me to read through these people's case files?"

He couldn't come right out and say it himself, but Neville was clearly relieved that I had. "Yes, ah, yes. Perhaps from their records you will be able to determine whether any of these individuals indicated in advance the steps they intended to take."

Not that prying into old case files was on the top of my priority list, but— "If you bring me the names, I'll see what I can do."

Now I had more than whole-grain bread to chew on. New job, new attitude—for Mr. Neville as well as me, apparently. I'd never given much thought to suicide as an end-of-life issue, in spite of working with the elderly. Although there's a lot of grumbling about death being a good alternative to a life restricted by infirmities and indignities, my clients are usually too busy staying alive and making it through another day to seriously court death.

6

I WENT back to the computer for a more thorough look at what Susan might have been working on. Sitting in her chair was unsettling. The suicide note had vanished, but I could still sense its presence, like a ghost in the machine. Whatever effects the smudge stick was supposed to have obviously didn't extend to the electronic realm.

I got up and started rearranging furniture. I turned the computer table to face the window, so I'd have a view of the chrysanthemums planted along the walkway outside. Then I shifted the desk forty-five degrees, and appropriated an armchair from the living room for clients to use. It wasn't much, but it helped erase the memory of Susan's sprawled figure.

"Hello? Hello? Is anyone here?" A head of white hair poked itself around the door.

I jumped back and hit the desk with my butt.

"Oh, my dear, I didn't mean to startle you. You must be the new social worker. I'm Muriel Dodge, the Thursday-afternoon Girl Friday, here on Monday." She giggled.

My heart was still in my throat. I was not amused.

Muriel walked to the middle of the room and sniffed the air. "Sage? Someone already did a cleansing ceremony?"

I gaped at her. Your basic little old lady, five feet tall, papery white skin, hair cut short and straight, glasses, a navy raincoat with an enamel pin on the collar—what did she know about sage sticks? She shrugged off the coat to reveal a Guatemalan shirt, blue cotton with a faint white stripe and an embroidered yoke.

I should have known better than to judge by appearances. It turned out Muriel had brought her own incense to purify the place. I let her have at it, complete with chanting rhythmic syllables that for all I knew could have been Sanskrit or some American Indian language. Maybe her approach would be more effective at smoking out the ghosts.

I'd just hung up the phone, a request for Meals-on-Wheels, when I heard the ding of the doorbell. I paused to eavesdrop on Muriel doing her job.

"Is there a trip today?" The voice was raised, querulous.

"No, Olive, not today. In two weeks." Muriel, impatient.

They went through it again.

Multi-infarct dementia, I thought. A layperson's diagnosis, to be sure, but the repetitive questioning was a good indication. It can be the most annoying of the dementias, once it's gotten as far as this woman's apparently had. The sufferer will ask the same question every few minutes, totally forgetting that it's already been answered.

It took one more round before Olive murmured, "Sorry to bother you," and the door closed.

I counted two seconds before Muriel's head appeared. "That Olive Patterson. I'm surprised she remembers her own name from one minute to the next!"

I started with an explanation of dementia. Muriel held up a hand.

"Oh, I know she can't help it. Olive never was the sharpest knife in the drawer, and she gets on my nerves. You wait, she'll be back within the hour."

The next time the bell rang, it wasn't Olive.

"You must be the husband."

Well, Muriel got to the point, if a bit abruptly. Katsu's answer was too soft for me to make out his response.

I got the head-in-the-door treatment again. "Susan's husband is here for her things." The head disappeared.

It was an awkward moment, seeing each other out of our usual context. Mostly I knew Katsu as a masseur; he had wonderful hands, hands that knew precisely how hard to press a tense muscle and stop just short of pain. Those hands had been everywhere on my body, head to foot—through my clothing, of course. It was an intimate, physical relationship, but in all that time I'd never touched him back.

One look at the grief in Katsu's face, however, and I reached out to embrace him. He shouldn't have had to be there, in the room where his wife had taken her own life.

Katsu's body was rigid, surprised by my gesture, but after a moment his arms went around my back. I felt a slight trembling in his shoulders. He was crying, and then I was too.

There's something terrible about a man's tears, especially those of a reserved man. I guided him to the armchair, yanked a handful of tissues from the box, and put them in his hand. Katsu dabbed at his eyes. He held his head up while the tears kept coming, simple as water flowing over smooth stones.

I sat across from him and took his empty hand in both of mine.

"I'm so sorry, Katsu. She was a wonderful person."

Katsu's eyes were black, deep with sadness. He looked straight at me, but what he was seeing wasn't me, it was loneliness.

I didn't try to offer up platitudes, or to speak at all. We sat like that for a long time.

* * *

Katsu was no sooner out the door than Muriel's whole body appeared in Susan's office. My office. I was going to have to change my way of thinking.

"So is it true Susan took the final exit?"

"Excuse me?" I couldn't help it, I barked at her.

"You were here, you found her body." Muriel was not offended. "I'd just like to know if she used the method of suicide that that book recommends."

"Who told you she committed suicide?"

"Everyone knows. They say she had one of those bags they cook turkeys in over her head. I wonder why she did it here?" I got her dotty giggle before she answered her own question. "Easier on the husband, I suppose. I gather you know him? Seems like a quiet duck, don't you think?"

What I thought was that she was too nosy by half, and not very tactful. The attempt to negotiate around all the people I'd met that day, all their various instructions, needs, and emotions, had been about as much as I could take. Now here was Muriel, the cherry on the sundae.

Patience, Anita. You just have to get out of this conversation without adding any grist to the rumor mill.

"I believe the police are considering her death a suicide, yes."

Muriel didn't let me off the hook. "I'm not one for beating around the bush about death. At my age, there's no point. Do you know what she had?"

"Had?" She lost me there.

"What disease she was suffering from. One of the female cancers? Not breast, we would have known about that. Ovarian? Uterine? Did the husband say?"

"What makes you think she had cancer?"

"She's been taking herbs for most of the last year."

"Herbs?" I felt like an idiot.

"Medicinal herbs. Tea. I know a little something about herbal remedies, and what Susan brewed up was serious medicine. You could tell by the way it smelled. She had a special glass pot to steep it, some sort of Chinese potion she drank three times a day. Of course, I asked her what it was. She *said* it was a tonic to help her get pregnant." Muriel paused to see if this was sinking into my thick skull.

It was. I nodded for her to continue.

"I liked Susan Wu. Seemed a levelheaded young woman. I find it hard to credit that she would take her own life out of despondency over an inability to conceive. Therefore, I assume the herbal remedy was actually a treatment for some sort of cancer. All I'm asking is whether or not you know what it was. I thought you might be sensible about things."

"If she had cancer, I didn't know about it," I answered truthfully. It would be nice, I thought, if that was the reason she'd killed herself.

Muriel sat down in the armchair Katsu had vacated. "She wouldn't be the first in the Estates to do it, you know. Just last week, a man in my building used the plastic bag method to deliver himself from pancreatic cancer."

"How do you know that's what happened?"

Muriel tutted at me. "It's common knowledge. Also, he discussed his intentions with me when he got his initial diagnosis. We read the book together. *Final Exit*."

"Did you help him?" I figured there was no point mincing words with Muriel.

But I'd gone too far. "If I had had anything to do with Ira's death, I certainly wouldn't have left his body to rot for three days until the smell alerted poor Fannie Donovan across the hall!" She huffed out.

I looked at my watch. It was 4:30—only 4:30, 4:30 already. The day seemed to have lasted a week, to have gone by in an hour.

I knew I was having a reentry problem with the world of work, compounded by delayed reaction to the stress of Susan's death. Vivian, Diane, Mr. Neville—my guides, despite their good intentions, hadn't made the ride a smooth one.

Well, what did I expect? It had to be harder on them than on me; they'd worked with Susan on a daily basis, and surely they felt her absence and my relative deficiencies in a basic, practical way.

Muriel popped in again, with her coat on this time. She cut off my thanks with a nod. "I'll be back on Thursday. It's my regular day, you know, but I won't be able to stay this late again."

She wouldn't hear my apologies for keeping her, either.

"No need to mention it. In these kinds of situations, we all do what we can. It's a good thing NAN was able to hire you right away. Did someone show you how to lock up?"

"Yes, thank you."

"Good. I'll see you Thursday, then." And she was gone.

7

A MAJOR downside of being employed again was my schedule. Clea's unhappiness at having to go to the after-school program at St. Hilda's was only part of the problem. What I realized as I trudged up the hill of Broadway was that there was no way in hell I was going to be able to summon the energy to cook. Not tonight, and the way things were going at NAN, not any night soon.

This being New York City, where takeout is a way of life, I stopped at Ollie's Noodle Shop to pick up supper, then University Food to get bialys for breakfast and some sliced ham for Clea's lunch.

Life in a student neighborhood: the two stud muffins in front of me were paying for a half-dozen bottles of imported beer, even at New York prices well under $20, with a credit card. Probably their father's. It took forever to run the card, and I realized I'd been spoiled by doing my grocery shopping in the morning, when the students were in class, the aisles empty, the cashiers in good moods.

Seeing the carryout bag from Ollie's in my hand made

Clea's day. It's the melting pot in action; she may love Benno's pasta sauce and my roast organic chicken, but being a child of the city, spareribs, cold sesame noodles, and Little Bit of Everything Noodle Soup are her real comfort foods.

The rain had paused, leaving the skies as downcast as my spirits. The scarlet and magenta impatiens along Riverside Drive looked as bedraggled as I felt. Clea slipped her hand into mine for warmth, and I summoned the energy to ask how her day had gone. She was in a chatty mood, and I let her talk, grateful that she was adjusting to the new schedule.

"Mama!" Clea bumped me with her shoulder. "You're not listening to me. How come you ask a question and you don't pay attention to the answer?"

I raised my eyebrows to let her know she might be right but I was still her mother, and her tone of voice was not cutting it with me.

"I've had a long day, Bops. Can we just be quiet until we get home?"

"Fine." She flounced ahead, asserting her independence.

I noticed, however, that the toggles on her coat were buttoned.

My thoughts had been somewhere out over the Hudson, the slate gray water just visible through the leafless branches of the elms in Riverside Park. I was trying to grasp what I'd taken on with this job, and for the first time feeling the enormity of Susan's absence.

I'd spent the weekend focused on the practicalities of organizing the household, not to mention my wardrobe, for my return to work. Benno had spoken with Katsu briefly on Sunday, but we hadn't talked about Susan with each other. Until now, I'd managed to keep full acknowledgment of her death at an emotional remove.

Denial is a powerful thing. When what you've been avoiding eventually hits, there's no ducking it. The last thing I expected, on what should have been a normal evening walk home with my daughter, was the overwhelming sadness I felt for Susan's passing. It was a good thing Clea kept her distance; I didn't want her to see the tears on my face.

There was no mail in the box, which meant either the carrier was having as bad a day as I was, or Benno had come home early. I switched the bag of carryout to my other hand and opened the elevator door. Well, there'd be trouble if Benno had cooked us supper; knowing Clea, she'd prefer Chinese.

Sure enough, it was Benno on the couch with the *Times*. Light from the lamp at his elbow gilded his hair with a blue-black sheen. Just the sight of him meant home to me, a safe harbor. I had an inkling of how a 1950s suburban husband must've felt when he saw his wife waiting for his train in the family station wagon.

Clea made short work of the paper by plopping herself in his lap, backpack and all.

"Hi, honey, you're home early." I bent to kiss his cheek.

"I just got here," Benno said. "About ten minutes ago."

"We're having Chinese food!" Clea announced.

I was about to ask, irritated, why he hadn't let me know he'd be home in time to cook, when I caught myself. We're back on track after a bad spell in our marriage that started three years ago, on our seventh anniversary, and there's a certain tone of marital annoyance we've both been trying to avoid.

Benno picked up on it anyway. "I called you at work. The woman who answered the phone said she'd tell you."

Minus one for Muriel's competence; there hadn't been any message from Benno in the pink slips she'd given me. I sighed.

Benno poured us each a glass of wine and got Clea settled at her desk to finish homework while I changed from work clothes straight into my nightgown.

"So how's the new job?" Benno folded the paper so I could join him on the couch.

I stretched my legs onto the footstool and offered up an extremely abbreviated synopsis of my day. I hadn't processed it all yet myself, and I didn't want to dump the unedited version on him.

Benno slid an arm under my waist and pulled me close. I nuzzled under his chin and sniffed. By the end of the day, Benno's skin takes on the faint aroma of sawdust. Usually it's a generic, dusty smell mixed with lavender bath soap. Tonight I thought I could identify the wood he'd been working with.

"Cedar?"

"Yup. This project, the people have a walk-in closet bigger than Clea's bedroom. All the drawers are dovetailed, and lined with aromatic cedar. That was Katsu's department, cutting the joints, so I had to work on them today. God, dovetails are a pain. I knocked off early so I could stop by and see him on the way home. He's got a great apartment, Ninety-sixth and Amsterdam."

New Yorkers; real estate is always a hot topic of conversation.

"Tenth floor, south and west exposures, but not as good a river view as we've got. Two real bedrooms, though, and an eat-in kitchen." Benno sounded envious. At under seven hundred square feet, our apartment is smaller than your average one-bedroom.

"How was he doing?"

"I thought you saw him this afternoon? He said he picked up a carton of Susan's stuff from NAN, and you'd been very kind to him. His own words."

"Yeah, well." I sighed. "I wish there was something we could do."

"There isn't." Benno stroked my arm. "Not unless you've got the power of resurrection."

"Do you know if Susan had some kind of cancer?" I sat up and turned to face him.

"Katsu never said anything about it. Why?"

I told him that Susan had been drinking some kind of herbal brew, and Muriel's cancer theory.

"See, that's how rumors get started. Katsu would've told me if his wife was sick. Susan was probably taking the stuff to get pregnant!" Benno laughed. "I know they were trying, then a few months ago, he told me they were applying to adopt a baby from China. Remember, I told you he was using the shop to build a crib?"

I didn't, but I nodded. Maybe he'd mentioned something about it, and it hadn't really registered.

Benno shrugged. "He only brought it home last week, to surprise Susan. It's an incredible piece."

"Why would she kill herself if they were about to adopt?"

"They hadn't actually done the paperwork yet. Katsu said—" Benno paused for a sip of wine. "He said he shouldn't have brought the crib home. He was afraid it was his fault because he pushed the adoption, and Susan didn't have any other way to tell him it wasn't what she wanted."

Knowing that it's normal for someone close to a suicide to feel it's his fault does nothing to mitigate the guilt.

"What took him the hardest was how unexpected it was. Losing your wife, especially like that . . ."

There were no words for the specter of loss hovering in the air around us. Benno pulled me back onto his lap. I closed my eyes and breathed in the cedary, sweaty scent of him.

"Hey, I just remembered, Barbara wants you to call her," Benno told me. "It was on the machine. She sounded kind of upset."

Barbara is my best friend, the Super of the building, the woman who taught me to cornrow Clea's hair. I was even deeper into denial about her situation than I was about Susan's death.

Last August, Barbara had noticed a swelling and pain in her right side. The doctor ordered a massive round of tests, including a CAT scan and several biopsies. I'd gone with her to receive the diagnosis. The image of Dr. Andras's face when he broke the news rose unbidden in my memory. We'd sat across from his desk, two nervous women facing a well-groomed man in a starched white shirt with a fine blue pinstripe.

Dr. Andras took his glasses off to face Barbara. His eyes were serious, concerned. I could see every unruly gray hair in his eyebrows.

He'd given it to her straight. "I'm sorry, Mrs. Baker. The exact diagnosis is inoperable liver cancer. The tumors are malignant, and appear to be quite aggressive. There is one large growth on the left lobe, while on the right there are many smaller ones. Due to the location of the tumors and the nature of the liver itself, there is no treatment."

We none of us had anything to say to that. Dr. Andras let a few minutes pass in silence before offering, "There is one thing we might try. Your liver is not healthy enough to handle more than a very low dose of chemotherapy, which would be administered orally. There is perhaps a fifteen percent chance that it will shrink the tumors somewhat."

Dr. Andras looked at the papers on his desk. "At that dose, you will not lose your hair, but you will experience other side effects. Nausea, and so forth. What you must weigh is the quality of your time. This treatment may prolong your life by no more than several weeks at best, and it will not be pleasant. I suggest you take some time to think about what it is you really want. If you'd like to take a trip, for example, we could wait several weeks before starting chemotherapy. As I said, I don't hold much hope of success."

Barbara agreed to think about it, but she was more concerned about diet—what she could and couldn't eat. Whatever she was able to keep down, the doctor told her, was fine. Drinking, naturally, was not a good idea.

Barbara laughed. It wasn't a happy noise. "Some deal, huh. All the drugs I want, but not the one I like best."

Dr. Andras's eyes got darker and sadder. "Yes. It's hard news."

This time I couldn't keep still. Modern medicine, out of tricks? No way.

"Wait a minute. What about a liver transplant?" As in, if this were a wealthy patient with private insurance and money to burn, what options would you be offering? "Or isn't there some experimental treatment being tried somewhere?"

I got raised eyebrows, along with a patient explanation of why none of the alternatives I'd mentioned were valid.

Starting with transplant lists are long, organ availability short, and Barbara's type of cancer fast-growing, but if we wanted to try, we could call the transplant center ourselves.

As to experimental, he thought there might be a program where they injected the chemo directly into the tumor, but he didn't think Barbara would meet their criteria . . . and again, we could call ourselves.

I took notes. Barbara twisted the rings on her left hand and listened without comment.

Dr. Andras had written out a prescription for OxyContin, a time-release synthetic morphine, and a stool softener, since constipation was a common side effect. As he rose to usher us out, he handed Barbara a card. "You can call me at any time. If the pain increases, please let me know, and we will adjust the dosage."

The OxyContin had been a miracle drug, allowing Barbara to go on a Caribbean cruise with her beau, Lewis. Meanwhile the tumors grew and her weight dropped. Two weeks ago, she'd decided to give the chemo pills a shot. So far, loss of appetite was the only effect they'd had on her. I was hoping she'd finally have some good news to share.

Whatever it was, Barbara didn't want to talk about it on the phone. I invited her up for Chinese. She didn't want that either, so I figured there could be only one other reason she needed to see me. I pulled a pair of sweatpants on under my nightgown, made up a little packet from the stash I kept in a tampon box in the back of my underwear drawer, put my overcoat on, and went down to the basement.

8

BARBARA was waiting for me at the elevator, with her own coat on. I handed her what I'd brought and she slipped it into her pocket. "Thanks, Anita."

"Don't mention it." Every time I saw her, Barbara looked more gaunt to me. It had only been two days, but the lines around her mouth seemed to have become permanently chiseled into her dark skin.

"Okay, I won't." She could still be flip. "Let's go sit in the yard. I want a cigarette."

"I thought you quit?"

"Well, now I started again. What's it going to do, kill me?" She set her mouth, the corners turned down in a you-got-something-to-say-to-me? grimace.

I shut up and followed her down the long hallway and around the corner to the door that opened onto the outside areaway.

It's a major perk of the Super's job, this backyard. In summer, Barbara manages to grow a crop of shade-loving flowers and vegetables in spite of the surrounding buildings that keep all but a few hours of direct sun from her garden. Most weekends, Lewis presides over drop-in barbecues that feed a revolving cast of Barbara's three daughters, his two sons, various spouses, grandchildren, nieces, cousins, siblings, and friends.

This October evening, the garden wasn't much to look at. Barbara hadn't turned on the outside spot, but in New York it's rarely dark. Her windows and those of the building behind ours gave enough light to see that the last of the spinach and lettuce were still doing their thing in spite of an early frost. The late planting of peas was finished, and a small wind rattled the dried vines against their supporting strings.

Barbara had brought a dish towel to wipe the residue of the afternoon rain from two metal lawn chairs. We sat down, and she offered me a cigarette.

"Will I need it?"

"Yeah." There was no humor in Barbara's laugh.

The ashtray on the round table between us already had a half-dozen butts soaking in it.

I let her take her time. We finished smoking, and she shook out another Winston.

"That bad, huh?" I couldn't bear the not knowing; I had to say something.

She slid the cigarette back into its pack.

"The chemo isn't working, Anita."

Her voice was flat, matter-of-fact. I made mine the same way. "How do you know?"

Barbara rested a hand on her swollen abdomen. "See for yourself."

"You been back to the doctor?"

"Went to the lab on Friday so they could test my blood. Waste of time. These tumors aren't shrinking."

In the twilight, I could just make out the look in her eyes, and it stopped whatever response I was about to make. I reached across the table to touch her arm. It was no more than bone wrapped loosely in flesh. What do you say to someone who's under a death sentence? What Barbara wanted was neither my pity nor my protests. I held her hand and waited.

Barbara shifted her gaze to the grapevines threaded along the Cyclone fence and started talking again.

"I called today for the results. Andras said it's still early in the treatment, I should keep taking the stuff. Easy for him, it's not his stomach that gets upset." She patted her pocket. "Good thing I've got you, girlfriend."

"I always knew being a dope-smoking hippie had its redeeming qualities."

That earned me a slight lift at the corners of her mouth.

"Doctor also told me I should settle my affairs." She slid her hand out from under mine. This time when she took the cigarette out of the pack, she lit it. "I thought they only used that line in movies, 'settle your affairs.'"

Her laugh was bitter. I pulled my chair around to face her and laid my hand on her other arm. "How long have you been on the chemo? A few weeks? Like Dr. Andras said, just give it more time."

"Yeah, time is all I've got." Barbara exhaled a sardonic puff of air and tilted her head to look up at the night sky. "You ever notice how even from down here, you can still see the stars?"

"Stars, *schmars*. You need to make an appointment and see him in person. Doctors don't treat you the same on the phone as they do when you're sitting right in front of them. I'll go with you again if you want, or you could take one of the girls?" Barbara's three grown daughters are scattered around the five boroughs—far enough to be out of range of her motherly eye, close enough for emergencies.

She shrugged. "The girls got lives of their own."

I raised my eyebrows at that one. Let Tabitha make a decision Barbara didn't agree with, and whose life was it then?

Barbara heard the comment as clearly as if I'd spoken. She turned an acknowledging smile my way, and we laughed at each other.

Still, I didn't let her get away with changing the subject. "Please, Barbara. Go see Dr. Andras."

Even as I said it, I realized that he wouldn't have any new hope to offer. I'd made the calls Dr. Andras had suggested, and he'd been right—the tumors were too aggressive for the length of the transplant list, too complicated for the experimental protocols.

Barbara shrugged me off. "I don't like taking this morphine stuff, but he says I shouldn't worry about getting addicted. I guess I'm not going to last that long!" She dropped the cigarette and ground it out.

No, not if you keep smoking, I thought. But she was right about one thing—what harm would nicotine do now? Just another addiction she wouldn't live long enough to have to quit.

"One thing I know." She picked up the pack of cigarettes, looked at it, put it down again. "When it comes to the end, I don't want my kids wiping my behind."

There she was, back to a darker reality than I was ready to admit.

Death with dignity. From the day I'd heard Barbara's diagnosis, the premises of *Final Exit* had been trying to get my attention, and I had kept shoving them away. Yeah, I knew Barbara might find some comfort from reading the damn thing. Just tell me how you hand a book like that to someone you love. I was suddenly furious with Susan Wu.

A light flicked on in a first-floor apartment and caught the gray in Barbara's braided extensions.

"I'm sure it won't come to that, Barbara, and if it does—"

"Yeah, Andras said I could go on hospice any time I'm ready." The savage tone was back. "Strangers in my house doing the same shitty job."

"Don't even go there yet. Let's see how the chemo does."

I was placating to cover all the things I could've said. Like that when it comes down to wiping butts, it's no longer a big deal. I did it for my grandmother, and after the first time, neither of us paid it any more attention than we did when I spooned the food into her mouth. Or that toward the end, there's very little that comes out.

"Getting cold out here." She stood up.

"Barbara. Whatever you want, you know I'm here." That's what Benno said: Whatever Barbara wants. He never begrudged me a minute of the time I spent with her.

She nodded, tucking my words away someplace deep inside, stored until she needed them.

Back in the bright basement, I pushed for the elevator. Barbara waited with me. I put my arms around her, and she returned the hug, a strong, quick embrace interrupted by the elevator chiming its arrival. When I let go, it was all I could do to meet her eyes, but if she wasn't going to cry, I wasn't either.

Riding up in the elevator, I put on numbness like a sweater. I'd met Barbara the day I moved into my grandmother's apartment in the building, more than a dozen years ago. Her husband, George, was still alive then, and the Super's job was his. Barbara'd seen me through my grandmother's death, my marriage to Benno. When Clea arrived in our lives as an infant, on an August day so humid the doors didn't close properly, Barbara's welcome gift was a box of cornstarch. By the time she was done powdering her, Clea looked like a gingerbread baby dusted with confectioner's sugar.

After her husband died, I'd shared vigil with Barbara's daughters, staying overnight for the better part of a month, until we were sure Barbara wasn't going to join him.

I blinked back tears and concentrated on denial. What I got instead was another wave of anger at Susan. So much to live for! While Barbara—

Good thing it was a short elevator ride.

Benno had the Chinese food unpacked. I managed to swallow some soup while Clea and Benno dissected the personalities of the college students who staffed the after-school. It was a good thing these young adults had no idea of the attention with which they were observed by the nine-year-olds in their charge.

I contributed enough appropriate grunts that Clea didn't notice my mind was elsewhere. Benno, however, was more astute. Not too long ago, he might have interpreted my reticence as an unpredictable resurfacing of old tensions, but tonight he knew it was about Barbara. He squeezed my hand under the table, a gesture so comforting I had to get up before Clea saw the tears.

"Telling the day," my bedtime ritual with Clea, almost put me to sleep along with her. Lying beside her solid body in the dark room, it took the sounds of kickoff on *Monday Night Football* to rouse me. The first play was as far as we made it; neither Benno nor I was interested in the game.

I waited to tell him about Barbara's dim opinion of the chemo until we were in bed, under the covers in the dark, where it was safe to talk about things too scary for the living room. Then we held on so closely that the thought of losing each other couldn't sneak in between us, and did what people do to keep death at bay.

9

THAT NAN was badly in need of two social workers was abundantly clear to me by the end of my second day. Tuesday, the heavy day for activities, began with a knitting group at ten, which merged into a brown-bag lunch at noon followed by a music therapist with a guitar who led a sing-along hour. Olive, the sorry-to-bother-you woman with multi-infarct dementia, stayed for all the groups, but at two-thirty, she drifted off. Not surprising, since the book group was discussing, of all things, *The Family in the Western World, from the Black Death to the Industrial Age.* It had been written by an Estates resident, which explained why such an esoteric book had been chosen.

The average level of education among the Estates' elderly residents, as I was learning, had to be master's degree at least. Librarians, professors, social workers, mathematicians, engineers, administrators, a retired judge or two—the educated middle class of the 1950s had flocked to this island of affordable housing.

I'd greeted every person who'd entered NAN's door that

day, introducing myself, being available for whatever feelings they needed to express. My arm had been clutched by people whose welcomes were tempered by dismay at Susan's death. I'd held each hand, the bones brittle as sticks, amazed by the strength with which my hand was gripped back. Some of the women got teary, and I took to carrying a few tissues tucked in my sleeve. Death may become a familiar companion to those who grow old, but when it hits someone as young as Susan, everyone is outraged.

Being on the receiving end of so much emotion would have been enough to handle without the infinite paperwork that also cried for attention. Then there were the demands on my time that would never appear in any formal job description, like the chore that pulled me away from the office during the book group: prospecting for flea market donations in the apartment of a recently deceased client who'd willed her apartment and its contents to NAN, in gratitude for services rendered.

The management office would deal with the sale; Vivian had asked me to take a shopping cart and salvage whatever portable items I thought might be suitable for the flea.

"Don't worry if what you find is in need of washing. We have volunteers who will take glassware and dishes home to clean. We often receive donations in need of a bit of care," Vivian had said. It was no preparation at all for what I found in the studio apartment.

I stood in the single room, totally nonplussed by the conditions this woman I'd never met had lived in. A narrow path wound between piles of newspapers and cardboard cartons, stacked in heights ranging up to shoulder level, and ended in the far corner at a bare mattress with ripped ticking and no signs of bedding other than a pillow.

Every surface in the kitchen—sink, table, chairs, both shelves of the open oven—was covered with glass jars. Empty glass jars, apparently once washed but now coated with grime, waiting for God knows what use. The advance scouts of what I knew was a hidden army of cockroaches searched the counters for anything edible.

I honestly could not imagine what services NAN had provided to the apartment's occupant, if she'd been living like this. It was beyond appalling.

I opened the kitchen cabinets, more from morbid curiosity than in hope of finding anything that might please Vivian. To my relief, the shelves over the sink held neither roach-infested food items nor empty jars. Unfortunately, what they did contain were neat ranks of crystal glasses. Wine, champagne, sherry—proud on their slender stems in spite of the grime that coated them. I moved as quickly as I could, keeping an eye out for the cockroach platoons while I wrapped each glass in newspaper.

When the doorbell rang, I almost jumped out of my skin. It was Diane McClellan, on a mission of her own.

She took the state of the apartment calmly, although I read distaste in the pinch of her mouth. "You just can't tell about people, can you? I was not here when they found Ms. Norris. Now I understand why she would never let me in."

"What was wrong with her?" I asked.

"In her mind? I have really no idea." Diane picked her way across the room to the mattress and scanned the floor area around it. "She died from lung cancer. Right here on this bed."

The apartment was creepy enough without knowing its occupant had died there, but hey, Diane in her leather jacket was unruffled and going about her business. I packed the glasses into a big Macy's shopping bag and loaded it into the cart.

"I'll just check the bathroom for any medications that should be disposed of." With the delicacy of a cat walking across a table of China figurines, Diane avoided contact with the slanting, dusty piles. "Ms. Norris took OxyContin for pain. That drug is not something to leave lying around."

I pulled the cart into the hall and waited for Diane. It took her less than a minute.

"Did you find what you were looking for?"

"The medical examiner or the police may have taken it when they came for her." Diane stabbed the elevator button with one of her elegant red nails and nodded at my full cart. "I see you succeeded."

I was so relieved to be out of Dorothy Norris's squalid apartment that it didn't occur to me to wonder why Diane was settling the flap of her bag as if she'd just put something into it.

After a second morning of being greeted by Vivian with "You're early," I got the message. If she wanted to start the day alone in the office, fine with me. I dropped Clea off at eight-twenty, which left plenty of time for a second cup of coffee before work.

The Bread Shop, a neighborhood anachronism started in the 1960s by a collective of hippies, is down to one owner now, a large-bellied man with a receding hairline and a long white ponytail. He presides over a wonderful blend of granola, pizza with exotic toppings like basil and gorgonzola, and the best apple-rhubarb crisp I've ever had.

It's also small enough to be exempt from the city ordinance that bans smoking in restaurants. Between that and the fact that Barbara had started up again, I knew it wouldn't be long before my bumming habit kicked back into action. I can go months without a smoke, but put me in a bar or anywhere close to temptation, and that's it.

Wednesday morning, my resistance was in working order. That, abetted by the fact that the Bread Shop hires people from halfway houses to work the counter. The guy on duty looked like a skinhead who'd toned down his appearance for the job; he had only two safety pins in each ear and a ring through his nose, like an ox, which turned my stomach. Coffee was all I could manage.

I sat at a table in the window and stared at the cars parked under the subway overpass. The day had come on clear and sharp. Sun reflections bounced off windshields and landed in my lap. If I have to be up in the morning, I like a little peace to space out in.

Rather than planning my schedule at NAN, I was thinking that my refrigerator might already contain the ingredients for a quick lentil soup for supper. If I didn't need to stop at the store, I might also have the energy to cook it. I watched an elderly woman at the bus stop across the street as she took something out of her purse, inspected it, put it back, looked up the hill for the bus, and went through the routine with the purse again. It was Olive, in the same plaid wool coat she'd refused to take off during Tuesday's activities. I inhaled the last of my coffee and went to see if she'd let me walk her home.

While I waited for the Walk light so I could cross Broadway, an M104 pulled up to the curb. I swore. Elderly woman with dementia on the loose in northern Manhattan. Sorry to bother you, but that's one more thing for your to-do list. I headed across the street to see if I could find out who, if anyone, was responsible for Olive's whereabouts.

And that was how the week went: not a moment to reflect, only react.

It turned out Olive regularly rode the bus two stops to the library at the end of the line. When she discovered it was closed, Vivian assured me, she'd find her way back to the Estates and be ringing NAN's bell.

Wednesday was blood pressure day. A pair of gray-haired muscle men cleared the second office of the accumulated flea market junk so it could be taken over by a team of volunteers trained by the Department for the Aging to monitor pulses and pressures. Ten o'clock brought them a steady stream of clients—including me.

My pressure was reassuringly normal, considering Wednesday was also the day Vivian asked if I was interested in being considered for Susan's job. The board had met in emergency session Tuesday night to form a search committee and draft an ad for Sunday's paper, but there were some who felt I should be offered the position first. I was flattered enough to consider it for all of maybe twenty minutes.

Until I remembered the fund-raising aspect of the job. I'd never written a grant proposal, and had no interest in starting. I'd seen my previous boss struggle with asking for money, and it didn't look like something I'd enjoy.

The increased salary would have been nice, though, not to mention the prestige of the executive director's title. I had a pang of temptation, almost enough to call Benno for a consultation. Then the phone rang under my hand—Mr. Neville, to report an elderly Chinese gentleman overturning garbage cans—and I dismissed the idea. You can keep your titles and your funders; give me a difficult client any day. At least when you help an individual, the task is clear, the results plain to see.

Diane McClellan proved to be my saving grace at NAN. Although I wasn't familiar with the details of all the active cases, I read enough files and talked to enough clients to pick up on the fact that, without making a big deal of it, she'd taken on responsibility for some of what the social worker would ordinarily have handled. By the end of the week, I realized I not only relied on Diane, I trusted her. In spite of how dowdy she made me feel.

At one point, I'd complimented her on a sweater—another cashmere, a wrap in deep burgundy. Diane seemed pleased that I noticed, and collegial enough to explain the reason she got so dressed up for work.

"When I am out with an older person, people make assumptions. I am young and I am black, so they think I must be the home attendant. All kinds of people do it—the relatives, the neighbors, the security guards. I use my clothing to help them have the right idea. I like it here in the Estates because I've been here long enough so most of the residents recognize me. The ones who don't know me, usually they are smart enough to notice what I wear."

Then she flashed me a smile. "Too, I like how cashmere feels on my skin. Also silk. Clothes are my indulgence."

I would've asked where she shopped, but I was afraid the answer would be Bendel's; Diane didn't seem like a bargain hunter. For recreational shoppers like my friend Janis, half the point of a purchase is to see how much below the original price an item is marked down. Her motto is NBR: Never Buy Retail. Diane, I got the impression, would make her ability to pay full price a point of pride.

By Thursday, I was ready to get down on my knees and thank the women who came in each afternoon to answer the door and the phone. It wasn't only Olive, "sorry to bother you" every half hour; the volunteers dealt with video reservations, sent out invitations to the monthly birthday party, answered questions about senior MetroCards, did dozens of the more mundane tasks that kept NAN running. They also spent a fair amount of time talking to me, providing insights into the tightly knit workings of the Estates community. Underneath the chat, however, I felt a current of goings-on that were only hinted at. I was not accepted yet, for all they tried to make me feel welcome.

Addie Collins, the video volunteer who also did a weekday stint as an office volunteer, put my feelings about life at NAN in a nutshell: "One damn thing after another."

I was just as glad Mr. Neville never made it back with the list of names he'd wanted me to research.

10

MADE it to Friday before I hit up a stranger for a smoke with my morning coffee. As it turned out, I needed every milligram of nicotine and caffeine I ingested to make it through the day.

I was finally going to meet NAN's treasurer, the elusive Trudi Voss. I knew she was the only NAN board member under the age of sixty-five, although not by much, and she'd been with the agency since its inception. From Vivian's description—CPA, never married, devoted to her job—I was expecting someone a bit on the dowdy side, efficient and zaftig.

The only thing I had right was the efficient. I'd barely closed the door at two minutes to nine when Trudi let herself into the office. She looked to be in her late fifties, and apparently had a well-used gym membership. Her outfit, a charcoal suit with a skirt that came to a demure inch above the knee, its lapel-less jacket only a few inches shorter, put Trudi right up there with Diane in the fashion department.

Her hair was regularly and professionally cut and colored, a discreet henna red set off by thin-framed black glasses with a streak of hot red above each lens. I was definitely impressed.

Anxious not to get off on the wrong foot, I apologized for not being able to manage an evening meeting, as I knew she preferred. I started to explain that I had a young child, but that was as far as I got.

"I understand the difficulties of parenting, Anita, there's no need to explain this to me. Your hours are from nine to five, and I have arranged my schedule to accommodate you." The words were gracious, but her tone was all business.

"I was just trying to say how much I appreciate you taking time off from work. I know that this is a volunteer job for you, and—"

"Yes." Trudi brushed my soft soap aside. "I don't need to know what child-care arrangements my male colleagues make, and I'm not interested in yours, either."

"Fine," I said. Two can play at blunt. "What did you want to go over, then?"

Mollified, Trudi opened the ledger and proceeded to instruct me on the mail she expected to have put aside, unopened, for her. Bills, naturally, and bank statements. There might also be the occasional contribution, which I was not supposed to open either, although how I'd know it contained a check unless I did wasn't clear to me.

"Also, anything that comes from a law firm, please let me know immediately. We are expecting a major bequest," Trudi continued. "Vivian has set the goal to establish an endowment fund that will provide a secure future for NAN. Right now we depend primarily on the fund-raising skills of our executive director. It's much more important for our social worker to do social work. The board is actively pursuing testamentary bequests, and there is a brochure to be included with the direct-mail campaign when the letters go out next week."

Whatever was happening along fund-raising lines was not my first priority. Vivian, I was sure, would let me know what was expected when the time came. I nodded along, my usual response.

Next to Vivian and Diane, Trudi was the most important person I'd be working with at NAN. I wasn't as intimidated by her prickliness as I might have been; Trudi's sophisticated outfit notwithstanding, she reminded me of my grandmother—the trace of German accent, soft on the gutturals, and the way she had to control every detail of what she was responsible for. After I was done not opening bills, contributions, and letters from lawyers, the only thing left for me to read would be addressed to Occupant.

"Vivian discussed the mailing with you?" Trudi took nothing for granted.

"Yes, but she didn't go into the specifics." Either I was covering for Vivian, or I'd genuinely forgotten.

Trudi saw through me. I got an explanation. "Susan already wrote the letter and had five thousand copies printed. Also the envelopes, which should be stacked in the bathtub."

At least I could be genuinely affirmative about the envelopes. The printer had delivered them the day before, and Addie let me in on NAN's unofficial extra closet space. No one took baths in the office, and with the shortage of storage space endemic to New York, why not put overflow office supplies in the tub? Behind a flowered curtain, of course.

"Good. The board has decided to delay mailing the letters for a week. They were concerned that it would be—awkward—to appeal for money so closely on the heels of Susan's death." Trudi's tone said she didn't think it would be improper at all, and she might go so far as to resent the glitch in her plans.

Just like my grandmother; whether she came right out and said it or not, you always knew exactly what her opinion was. I could almost see myself being fond of Trudi.

Vivian chose that moment to join us.

"Have you gone over the mail-out?" Perfect timing. "I'm drafting a personal note to go along with the original solicitation. We can't afford to discard all those copies, but we do owe our donors an explanation as to why we're sending out a letter over Susan's signature."

I nodded again. I was beginning to feel like a bobbing-head doll, nodding and agreeing with whatever went on around me.

Trudi sat back and closed the checkbook. "I'll keep this at home for now. We won't be adding Anita as a signatory to the account, so there's no point leaving it here. Vivian, would you please sign ten checks for me? I will pay the end-of-the-month bills over the weekend."

"Yes, of course. Let me get my pen."

Trudi explained it to me. "The checks require two signatures. Vivian signs several checks ahead, so the executive director or I can use them as necessary for operating expenses. Come, I will show you where we keep the financial records. You won't need to do anything with them, but you should know where things are kept. The mail can be left in the same drawer."

Trudi went through the connecting door to the smaller office and unlocked the file cabinet on the right.

"The records are here." She tapped the second drawer of the right-hand file cabinet, clearly labeled "Finances," then pulled out the drawer above it. "The mail I've asked you to leave for me should go in this folder. Invoices, donations, bank statements, correspondence from an attorney's office, yes? I'll stop by one or two evenings a week to collect it. I have my own keys."

I didn't mean to be rude, but I had to ask. "Do you also have a key for the cabinet with the client files?"

"No." I couldn't tell if she was offended or amused. "There are two different keys, but both locks can be opened by either key."

Which meant Trudi had access to confidential information on people who might be her friends and neighbors. So did Vivian, for that matter. It wasn't exactly the most professional arrangement.

As if she'd read my thoughts, Trudi said, "Yes, I am aware that protection of our clients' confidentiality is the most important service NAN offers, and that the case files contain privileged information. Don't worry, Anita, I leave other people's business to them, and to you."

She brushed her hands along her skirt, smoothing imaginary wrinkles. Surely anyone as precise as Trudi would keep her word. After all, discretion was practically a requirement of her job; accountants learn the most intimate things about their clients' personal finances, and a CPA with a big mouth wouldn't last long.

"I understand you found Susan's body." It wasn't a question.

"Yes." I wasn't surprised that she brought it up. Curiosity is a natural response to death, especially one as unusual and unexpected as Susan's had been.

"Did you know her very well?" I thought I'd try a little curiosity of my own. Susan and Trudi had worked together, and might well have been friends outside the parameters of NAN.

But Trudi evidently had a rule about not mixing work and pleasure.

"No. I don't believe in that sort of thing. One's private life and one's professional life are two distinct spheres. Susan and I shared nothing apart from an interest in the well-being of NAN, which is why I find it so distasteful that she chose this office for the site of her 'self-deliverance.'" She gave the phrase a scornful emphasis.

"You don't believe in suicide as a valid way of coping with a terminal illness?"

"A terminal illness, yes. My mother suffered a series of strokes in her last year. She was a member of the Hemlock Society. Naturally I also read *Final Exit*. My mother wanted to be in control of her death." Trudi's tone softened. "We were fortunate that her last stroke took her completely. She did not need to make use of her plan."

Trudi stroked the back of her neck with the forefinger of

her right hand, a gesture that seemed to soothe her, although it rubbed the close-cropped hair above her collar in the wrong direction. "Susan Wu ended her life in a manner that pained many of NAN's people. I am sorry for her, and also I am angry."

A natural enough emotion, given the circumstances. I gave Trudi credit for admitting it. Direct, like my grandmother, and without artifice. Yes, Trudi would do.

A call from the head of the maintenance staff put an abrupt end to our meeting. He just wanted to let me know, he said, that "those people" were dumping bags of human excrement down the compactor chute again. His men were complaining, and he was concerned that the feces might carry contagious diseases.

As soon as I hung up, Vivian said, "That will be about the Stringers, I suppose."

I gave a noncommittal shrug. Vivian might have been my boss, but she wasn't a social worker, and client matters *were* confidential.

Trudi pursed her lips. "I don't understand why NAN doesn't do something about those two. How people can live like that!"

Exactly my grandmother's sentiments: zero tolerance for those who didn't manage to make their beds, sweep their floors, and wash their dishes on a daily basis.

Trudi and Vivian also reinforced the idea I was getting of how hard it was to keep a person from knowing anything about anyone else in the Estates. Just as Mr. Neville had warned me, the place was as bad as a small town.

After I'd met the Stringers, however, I had to agree with Trudi. There are times when drastic intervention is warranted. The squalor of their circumstances was as willful as Ms. Norris's had been, and something should have been done. I just wish I hadn't put off doing it until Monday.

11

B**UT** on Saturday morning, the smell of the Stringers' apartment was as forgotten as the dream I'd been having when the door buzzer from downstairs made its rude noise, demanding and abrupt as an alarm clock. I'd fallen back to sleep in the quiet after Benno and Clea left for her tap and ballet classes at Alvin Ailey. The late-morning sunlight spread warmth like an extra blanket.

I glared at the clock. Almost eleven. In this city, people never drop in on you without calling first. I wasn't expecting any packages. I would've thought it was someone with a fat finger hitting my button by accident if the sound hadn't been so long and insistent.

"Yeah, yeah," I muttered. I rolled out of bed and went to the intercom without pulling on my nightgown. Why bother for a wrong number?

Unfortunately, it wasn't.

"Wake it and shake it, Social Worker. NYPD calling." Detective Michael Dougherty, who the hell else?

On a Saturday morning? He wouldn't have said NYPD if

this were a social visit. I buzzed him in, went to put some clothes on and give my hair a quick brush.

"Advertising?" Michael greeted me.

I looked down at my chest. The navy T-shirt I'd pulled from the top of the pile said COLUMBIA SOCIAL WORK in big white letters.

"Bragging," I told him.

"Yeah, well, seems to me your profession don't have too much to be proud of this morning." Michael was his usually snappy self, in a black-and-gray tweed jacket that went well with the gray flecks making a distinguished appearance in his sideburns.

"You came over to insult me?" I stepped back so he could enter the apartment.

"Got any coffee in this joint?" Michael followed me into the kitchen.

I filled the kettle, set a filter in the cone, and measured out four scoops of French roast, the real thing, ground yesterday at Mama Joy's deli.

"How's Anne?" I asked. I'd introduced Michael to his significant other—Anne Reisen, the administrative assistant at my former job. They were living together, had been for some time, but Anne steadfastly held out against marriage. She was a good ten years older than Michael, burned by an early marriage and divorce. In spite of Michael's denials, she was convinced he'd wake up one morning with an urgent desire for the children she couldn't give him and had no desire to adopt. She wanted him to be free to seek a "breeder," as she so delicately put it, without the legal ties of wedlock to hold him back.

"Great," Michael said. "We just got back from three weeks in Paris. Man, they say there's nothing like April over there, but I'm telling you, end of September was spectacular."

After Senior Services closed, Anne had done what every laid-off person would like to: gone on vacation.

"I was just thinking about her." I poured the first shot of

water through the coffee and unhooked two mugs from the rack.

"Yeah, you oughta call sometime."

I set my grandmother's flowered china sugar bowl on the counter and added milk to the matching creamer. "Want a bagel?"

"No, no thanks. Just the coffee." He took two spoons of sugar and a generous shot of milk. "I'm here on business, Anita."

"Did the toxicology results come in already? Was there something unexpected?" I assumed it was about Susan. "And how'd you catch the case?"

"Toxicology report?" He looked at his watch. "We just found the bodies an hour ago."

"Bodies?" I scalded my tongue on the coffee.

"A couple of your clients. Ralph and Ora Stringer. Remember them?"

"I saw them yesterday, they were fine." In fact, I could still see them.

No amount of preparation or professional training could have prevented the embarrassment I'd felt when I walked into the Stringers' bedroom. Mrs. Stringer sat in the middle of the bed, the blankets thrown back. She wore a transparent, pale pink garment that came nowhere near to being closed across the huge breasts that hung down over her stomach, or to covering the wide white legs extended in front of her.

I backed out of the bedroom. "I'm so sorry. I'll wait until you're dressed."

"You're the new one?" Her voice was almost as deep as her husband's. "Come on in here where I can see you."

She'd made no effort to cover herself. I started to back out of the room again, stammering excuses.

"Help me with these blankets, would you? That damn girl.

Goes off to the store whenever she pleases, not so much as a by-your-leave."

I pulled the sheet across her lap. I tried not to look at her directly, but I couldn't miss the branching blue veins visible through the pale skin of breasts that defined the word *pendulous*. I believe in meeting my clients' eyes, no matter what, but it was difficult—although Ora Stringer herself seemed totally unconcerned with her nakedness.

"What happened?" I asked Michael. I couldn't imagine.

"Yeah, that's what we'd like to know. Seems the aide came to work this morning, found him in a chair in the living room, her propped up in the bed, both with bags over their heads."

The toaster oven dinged, and I jumped.

"You know anything about that, Anita?"

"Like what? I made a home visit yesterday afternoon, with the nurse. Neither of them told me they were planning a double suicide later that night."

"How'd you know they did it last night, not this morning?"

"I didn't. I just assumed—I don't understand what you're doing here, if it's clearly suicide?"

Michael sighed. "Yeah, suicide, or, excuse me, 'self-deliverance,' according to that damn book. Thing is, after that woman last week, and you know Detective Neville is head of security over there in the Estates now? They found that *Final Exit* next to the Stringer woman's bed. Neville doesn't like coincidences, and tell the truth, I think he's bored."

So Mr. Neville had mentioned his suspicions to Michael, too.

"So as a courtesy to him," Michael went on, "and you being my favorite social worker, not to mention maybe the last person to see the Stringers alive, I thought I'd come drink some of your excellent coffee and discuss how you've been expanding your horizons in terms of end-of-life issues."

Tactful as usual. I didn't take the bait.

"You should talk to the nurse, Diane McClellan. She's known them longer than I have, maybe she'd know if they ever talked about suicide. The conditions they were living in, I mean, they didn't seem too bothered about their hygiene, but it was really—" For once, words failed me.

"The nurse." He took a pad out of an inside jacket pocket and flipped it open. "Diane McClellan's next on my list of visits."

His pocket made a cellular chirp. With the same gesture, Michael flipped open a phone smaller than the notepad. After a series of grunts, he took his coffee to the nominally more private living room. From the sound of it, he was reissuing instructions that hadn't been followed correctly the first time. I was glad it wasn't me on the other end of the call.

I dunked a piece of bagel in my coffee and replayed the home visit Diane and I had made to the Stringers.

Susan's terse prose in the case file hadn't warned me adequately about conditions in the apartment. The two salient facts that had popped out of the progress reports were, first, that lack of resources was not an issue; the Stringers could afford as much help as they wanted. Second, they both had difficulty with ambulation.

No mention whatsoever of the fact that their shit habitually wound up in the compacter chute.

In the five minutes it took Mr. Stringer to steer his walker audibly across the living room and come to the door, Diane filled me in.

"I expect the aide has quit again." Diane shook her head. "She does it every few weeks. Susan always managed to talk her into coming back. Both of them have emphysema, and both of them smoke. It doesn't make a pleasant work environment. I always visit right before I go home, otherwise I smell like cigarettes for the whole of the day."

I'd given my shoulder a surreptitious sniff, hoping my morning indulgence wasn't obvious.

"Mr. Stringer does use a walker, but you can tell it takes him quite a while to get anywhere," Diane continued. "Most of the time, he sits in the living room with the television. When he needs to move his bowels, it takes him so long to get to the bathroom, he doesn't always make it. I provided a commode for him. When the aide is there, she does empty it. When she's not around, he just keeps on until it's all filled up."

"Why does the aide keep quitting?"

"You might as well ask, Why does she come back?" Diane arched an eyebrow, the first time I'd seen her anything like snide about a client. "After the commode is full, Mr. Stringer moves on to the kitchen."

"The kitchen?" My imagination didn't want to go there.

"They have a metal garbage can, almost the same height as a toilet. The lid flips up, just like a toilet seat, and so he uses that. The aide is supposed to empty all of the feces into the toilet. But the garbage can, you know, she just ties up the bag and puts it down the compactor chute. I've talked to her about it, but—"

A gray man with a stubbly face and uncombed hair opened the door. The cigarette smell from the apartment was strong enough to make me swear off forever.

"She's in the bedroom," he rasped.

"I'm here to see you, Mr. Stringer." Diane's voice was gentle and courteous as she took his elbow and turned him back toward the living room. "Anita is here for Mrs. Stringer. Why don't you tell me how you've been feeling?"

The intake of Mr. Stringer's breath came as a series of audible gasps. Diane nodded me down the hall. "Tell her that Macy's will deliver the new mattress and sheets tomorrow afternoon. Someone from maintenance will come and lift the carpet at the same time."

From the file, I knew Ora Stringer's lack of mobility was due to a strained lower back, which also made it difficult for her to shift herself from bed to commode. This had led to several "accidents" in the bed. Diane had provided a box of Depends adult diapers, courtesy of NAN, and helped Ora order a new mattress.

Once I got over my embarrassment at Ora's nakedness, I remembered that I was there on business.

"Is the aide here with you today?" I asked.

"Yeah, yeah. She quit Monday. I called her last night and offered her more money. That's what that what's-her-name who died told me to do. I don't like it, but there you are. She came back today. Gotta have her till I get back on my feet."

She huffed back against the pillows. I stepped away from the bed and glanced around the room, assessing her situation. As I moved, the rug under my feet squished, releasing the smell of ammonia. I took a closer look and realized that the sheets along the entire side of the bed where I'd stood were stained a pale, wet yellow. I'd attributed the pervasive smell of piss in the room to the commode by the window, but another step told me why the rug needed to be removed: It was soaked with urine.

Thanks to the weather, I was wearing waterproof boots. Lucky me.

I passed on Diane's message about the new bed.

Ora's response was a grunt, and "Pass me my cigarettes, would you? And the ashtray, that's a good girl."

I looked around for someplace to dump the soup bowl she was referring to, which was close to capacity with Benson & Hedges menthol butts.

"I'll just empty this for you." I hesitated outside the kitchen, afraid of what I might find in the garbage can. Then it occurred to me that the call from maintenance meant the bag of feces had already been dumped. I emptied the ashes into a clean can.

"Is Mrs. Stringer in her usual state of undress?" Diane asked from the door to the living room.

"Thanks for warning me." I smiled wryly. "She says the aide went to the store."

"Yes, Mr. Stringer also said Marietta came back to work today." Diane followed me to the hall. "I'll just check Mrs. Stringer's pressure."

She took two plastic bags out of her canvas carryall, slipped them over her suede pumps, and secured them around her ankles with rubber bands. Obviously Diane knew what she was getting into. I had a flash of resentment—she could've warned me about the urine-soaked rug! I let it go. Maybe Diane hadn't said anything because she wanted to test my reaction. I didn't care for that thought either.

In the absence of the soup bowl, Ora had added her ashes to the carpet. As Diane got out the blood pressure cuff, Ora flipped her cigarette to the floor, where it sputtered out. Well, no risk of burning the place down, I thought, as I put the ashtray on the end table where she could reach it.

After we left the apartment, I waited until we were in an empty elevator before I said anything. "So what's the next step?"

My lack of judgment about the conditions the Stringers had created for themselves paid off in the increased respect for my competence I could see in Diane's eyes. If it had been a test, I'd passed.

"I spoke to Mr. Stringer about a portable oxygen tank. I can't do it unless he stops smoking, and that he refuses to consider." Diane shook her head. "Susan's plan was to work with the management office on an eviction. They are creating an unsanitary condition."

Not the tack I would've expected NAN to take.

"I know," Diane responded to my unvoiced objection. "We are responsible to help them stay in their own home. It would only be a threat, something Susan could use like a stick and force the Stringers to accept more assistance from NAN. Sometimes you have to work with people from two directions."

It had sounded like a workable plan to me, so we'd left it at that until I could follow through on Monday.

As I went over it in my memory, I couldn't find anything that might have indicated the Stringers didn't plan to be around past that evening. Nor did I have any recollection of a copy of *Final Exit* anywhere in the bedroom. What had I missed?

Exactly what Michael wanted to know. "Okay, Social Worker, tell me again, nothing got your antennas up here? You're not going to tell me these people were murdered?" He pocketed the cell phone and sat himself down at the table again.

The crack about murder was a reference to when we'd first met, and I'd been right about two elderly women not dying of natural causes.

"Not the Stringers, although I'm a little surprised they managed to pull off a suicide. They just didn't seem—" I shrugged. Yes, their being dead bothered me, but at the same time, if that was what they'd chosen—well, it did solve an intractable problem. I know, it sounds cold-blooded. The truth is, some clients affect you more than others. Not that I wouldn't have done all I could for them.

"So how well did you know this Susan Wu? No problems with her scenario?"

Talk about impervious. Cops have it all over social workers when it comes to a casual attitude to death.

"Susan's husband is a friend of Benno's, but I didn't know her particularly well. Katsu was pretty upset about her death, and he feels responsible."

"Yeah, well, the spouses usually do. He got a special reason to feel guilty?"

No way I was going to share anything more specific about Katsu's emotional state with Michael. "I'm going to the funeral tomorrow, maybe you'd like me to ask him?" Two can play at sarcasm.

"Hey, Social Worker, no need to stir things up, now. They did a blood test, I told Neville I'd keep an eye out for the toxicology report. Should be in sometime next week. If any flags come up, you'll be the second to know. Thanks for the coffee."

I walked him to the elevator. "Has Anne found a job yet?"

Michael coughed. "Ask me if she's been looking!"

"Okay, has she?"

"Not so's you'd notice. I keep telling her she oughta go back to school, get herself a social work degree so she could get paid what she's worth. That, or manage an office for one of those Wall Street types and make twice what I do. I've always wanted to be a kept man."

Michael was right about Anne Reisen being worth her weight in a decent salary. What had made Senior Services function with any degree of efficiency was Anne. She not only answered phones, she also dealt with a good percentage of the problems that presented themselves on the other end of the line. Okay, so she occasionally stepped into what should have been the preserve of an MSW, but the assistance she'd provided was usually right on target.

Before Michael had made his appearance, I'd actually been formulating a plan to convince Vivian to hire Anne as a temporary solution to my workload. Anne wasn't a social worker, but she'd be able to handle some of the secretarial demands on my time and free me up to take care of clients.

An ad for a new executive director at NAN was scheduled to run in this Sunday's *Times*. The search committee, chaired by Vivian, would read through résumés and conduct interviews. I knew, however, that Vivian would rely on me to take care of miscellaneous organizational chores, like copying résumés for the committee. I'd already gotten a good sense of how much clerical work had devolved onto Susan's shoulders.

Working by myself, there was no way I'd be able to meet client needs and provide the board of directors with secretarial services unless I had help.

The elevator came. Michael opened the door. "Seriously,

Anita, you should call her. Anne could use someone to talk some sense into her."

"I will." I watched his face through the mesh covering of the round window in the elevator door until it slid down the shaft.

12

SPENT the afternoon in the backyard with Barbara, juggling my roles. The thing about social work is, it's not a job you turn off when you're not actually at the office. Underneath friend, spouse, parent, member of the board, the social work side of the brain just has to contribute its two cents' worth.

It was one of those late-autumn days when the weather provides a brief respite before winter. Barbara had ordered a mix of spring bulbs, exotic-colored tulips, miniature irises, and daffodils, but she was in too much pain to plant them.

The earth was damp. Even through the cotton gloves I was wearing, it felt heavy and cold. I plied the trowel, grateful for the square of rug sample I knelt on. As I sprinkled a pinch of bone meal in each hole, I tried not to wonder whether Barbara would still be alive in April to see the flowers come up and bloom.

Halfway through the bulbs, my back made a persuasive argument that it was time for a break. In spite of the sun, the air in the shade behind the building was full of October chill.

Barbara, stretched out in the chaise, was wrapped in a quilt. I peeled off the gloves and stood up.

"Anita—"

I made a shushing gesture with my right hand before she could thank me. I knew Barbara didn't want to feel beholden to me any more than I wanted her to feel that way.

"This is what I miss most living in New York, a garden to dig in. When I was a kid, my mother made me help her in the yard. I hated it then, but now it's—comforting, actually." Although the last thing I felt was comfortable. My knees creaked, my lower back felt like I'd never be able to stand straight again, and the way I was rubbing my fingers reminded me of my grandmother trying to ease the stiffness of arthritis in her hands. Forties isn't old, but there are definitely times when it tries out for the part.

"Except I have to tell you, this digging is a young person's job."

"You did enough, Anita. I'll get Tabitha to finish up tomorrow."

I wiped the dirt off my jeans and sat across the table from Barbara.

"I would've had the strength to do it myself except I spent the morning cleaning closets. Stuff in there hasn't been used in ages. The girls' prom dresses! Like I have room for all that."

It had to be six or seven years since the last of Barbara's three daughters had attended a prom. New York apartments: Long-term storage is an unknown concept, but the Super has access to all sorts of basement nooks.

"Lewis might be spending more of his time over here. I thought I'd better give him some room to practice, or that trumpet'll send me to an early grave."

We both listened to that casual remark as the clunk of deeper meaning hit.

"What a life. Can't drink, can't make jokes . . ." Barbara looked up to where a plane, dragging sound along behind it, made a white trail in the blue over our heads.

I watched with her until it passed out of sight. Far be it from me to be anything less than optimistic about Barbara's chances of survival. Denial is, in my opinion, what gets us through the day. If we all openly admitted all of our short-comings, flaws, and sins—well, not a one of us would have the confidence to step out the door. How do you think child abusers face themselves in the mirror while they shave every morning? Denial.

"I told Lewis, just because I'm sick, I'm not giving up my independence. I like a little company, that's all." She tried to put a laugh into the words, but they came out fierce.

Good, the will to fight was good. And if it was fueled by denial, well, defense mechanisms have their uses for good as well as evil.

"So you want a beer before you get back to work?" She offered out of politeness and habit, as a way to change the subject. I'm a seasonal beer drinker, and summer is it. Barbara knew that, as well as I knew she wound up her own days, winter, spring, summer, and fall, with a pair of Heinekens.

I shook my head, no. "Can I get you one?"

"You know, I lost my taste for it. Haven't had a beer in three months, and I don't even miss it." She located a pack of Winstons in the quilt and held it out to me. "Haven't lost the taste for these, though."

"I better finish the bulbs first." I took my stiff legs back to kneeling. By the time I had everything in, the sun had slid almost to the river, leaving us in cold shadow.

It was late enough that Benno and Clea were probably back, and I knew I should head upstairs. Barbara seemed to be asleep, the quilt tucked up around her chin. I'd tried to get her to go inside earlier, but she resisted. Pride; maybe she wasn't up to doing the work, but damned if she'd lie in bed while I did it.

I picked up the pack of Winstons where they'd fallen on the ground and lit one. At the scrape of the lighter, Barbara opened her eyes.

"Done already?" She held out a hand for the cigarettes. I gave her the one I'd just lit, and took another out for myself.

"You in pain, Barb?"

"About frozen is all."

"No, seriously."

"Not right now. Mornings are the worst. I lie there and think how am I going to move so it doesn't hurt. Then I have to go so bad, it doesn't matter. I swear, one of these days I'm going to wet the bed."

Just like Ora Stringer, I thought, the urine smell rising in my nostrils again. Before I could stop myself, I was back on the job.

"You want me to see about a commode? A hospital bed?"

Barbara glared at me.

"Sorry," I said.

But she didn't jump down my throat. "You want to do something, Anita, you could come to the doctor with me again. You're right, I should make an appointment, follow up on the chemo. It's not doing anything, I'll stop—go on that hospice care Dr. Andras was talking about."

"No problem." I moved the ashtray closer so she could stub out the cigarette. "Just tell me when, I'll be there."

Barbara allowed herself to take the hand I offered to pull her up from the chair, and I pretended not to notice the grimace as she rose.

Sunday afternoon, Benno and I brought Clea down to visit with Malik, Barbara's grandson, while we went to Susan Wu's funeral. Barbara looked rested; the lines that had been etching themselves around her mouth had relaxed, and she was able to stand straight instead of hunched over the pain in her right side.

"I upped my medication last night," Barbara told me. "I don't know what I was waiting for. Stuff doesn't get me high, but I don't like the idea of being on something addictive. I guess I just had to let the pain get bad enough."

Diane had given me a crash course in the oxycodone family of drugs, the newest thing in pain relief. For those with serious cancers, the time-release feature was a major advance. Of course, you build up a tolerance, and the dose has to be increased to remain effective. Not medications that should be prescribed for someone who might one day be fortunate enough to be weaned off them.

"Nothing like a good drug," I told her.

"My wife, child of the sixties," Benno grinned. "Never met a drug she didn't like."

Barbara smiled back at him. "At least I had someplace to go when the chemo took my appetite."

Benno squinted at me. "You did?"

I shrugged. "Yeah, I had an old stash of weed tucked away."

"Right," Benno said. "In case of medical emergency, I'm sure."

My husband, king of sarcasm. I knew he didn't approve; that's why I hadn't mentioned it.

I brooded over Barbara as we headed down to the park, a heavy sadness growing in me as the cancer grew in her. Hospice. The first step down a road with no way back.

October, the month when death begins to be all around us. We walked south through Riverside Park, toward the Buddhist church on 105th. The path had not yet been cleared of fallen leaves by the mayor's workfare crews, and we scuffled through them. I made a show of kicking the crumpled brown debris up in the air until Benno poked me with his elbow and told me to act my age.

I would've stuck my tongue out at him, except I realized his touchiness had more to do with where we were going than with my behavior. My childishness had the same cause.

It's not an easy thing, attending the funeral of a contemporary. Behind genuine grief at the loss of a friend lay the self-interest at the root of all emotion: *It could have been me. It could have been my spouse. I'm not ready for this yet.*

I stifled the urge to kick leaves, tucked my arm through Benno's, and slid my hand into his jacket pocket to curl inside his. "Do you think wearing a leather jacket to a Buddhist funeral is inappropriate?" I asked.

"Where do you come up with this stuff, Anita? I'm not in the mood for your cookbook Buddhism right now."

I pulled my hand away, offended. "I've actually studied more than a little Buddhism, you know. The monks don't even wear leather sandals or shoes." Before Benno could point out that he wasn't a monk, I added, "Never mind, no one will say anything. The main thing about the religion is kindness."

"Yeah, I know. Please don't tell me the story of the Buddhist monks who visited a Boston home and ate meat because it was a lesser evil than refusing the hospitality of their hosts. It's too late now, anyway, and besides, if you thought it would be a problem, why didn't you say something before we left the house?"

Marriage. Sometimes you pick a little fight without intending to, just to let off tension from other things. We crossed the street and paused in front of the temple to contemplate the statue of Shinran Shonin, founder of this particular school of Buddhism. I put my arm through Benno's again, and this time he put his hand over mine and squeezed. Easily started, easily stopped. We were as one again.

You live in a neighborhood for years, and there are places you never go. I was more familiar with the temple's outside from the framed tile representation of it in the Eighty-sixth Street subway station than I was from passing the real thing. I had to say, it looked better in the glossy glaze than in reality.

The peach and green tones of the tile lent the temple an air of reverence lacking in the real thing. Apart from the huge bronze statue of the man with the stern face under a wide round straw hat, which once stood in front of a temple in Hiroshima, the New York Buddhist Church's temple isn't much to look at. Built in the 1950s, it has all the graceless charm of modern architecture—straight gray walls, grubby with the passage of years.

Inside wasn't much more inspiring. Several older Japanese women in dark jackets over light silk blouses sat behind a table with a starched white cloth, accepting monetary memoriums and presiding over an open book where mourners signed their names. My knowledge of Buddhist customs came in handy here; I'd prepared an envelope to place in the basket. We bowed to the women, who lowered their heads in response. One of them handed Benno a program for the service.

We took seats midway to the front. I could see the back of Katsu's head, up in the first row, next to a blond woman who rested her head on the shoulder of an Asian man. Susan's parents, probably.

This was my first time inside the temple. The *hondo* itself was of a piece with the outside, unchanged since the 1950s; battered beige linoleum, metal chairs with padded green Naugahyde seats and backs, fluorescent lights mounted flat on the twenty-foot ceiling, dark wood paneling halfway up the walls. The altar, the soul of the room, was a shiny contrast to the shabby *hondo*.

I felt the calm of the space settle in my mind. A large pedestal, black and red lacquer, supported a pagoda roof and a central niche where a slender gold Amida Buddha stood. Long gold filigree ornaments dangled alongside the altar. It was all incredibly ornate, a richness of color and shape conducive to religious awe. A low table held vases of creamy chrysanthemums, pale roses, fat white snapdragons. The only plain things in the altar area were two large paintings on either side wall, old men in gray robes with beaded prayer bracelets around their wrists.

From somewhere behind us, a gong sounded, several quick, reverberating tones that filled the space with sound. The rustling of people in the *hondo* stopped. I closed my eyes to feel the vibrations. The next notes came at a slower pace, allowing time for the ringing brass echoes to resonate around the room.

Shutting off sight brought the charred scent of incense to my attention. I opened my eyes to see where it was coming from. Thin ribbons of smoke rose from an open brazier-type vessel set on a small pedestal in front of the altar area. Behind the incense burner, on a lower table overshadowed by all the ornamentation surrounding the Buddha, were two framed photographs of Susan, one a recent, laughing, color snapshot, the other a formal graduation picture. A second table held a bowl of tangerines and a bunch of scarlet gladioli.

As the slow beats faded into silence, they were replaced by a series of quicker strokes. The reverend walked slowly down the center aisle. On his shaved head, the pattern of his hairline gave the impression of a blue-black tattoo.

I let the tones of brass struck by wood echo in my thoughts until Benno handed me an open prayer book. We chanted along with the congregation, simple, incomprehensible syllables that seemed to originate low in the abdomen rather than from the lungs. I felt as though an unshed teardrop was finding release with each exhalation.

The reverend presented Susan's Buddhist name, followed by more chanting. As sound filled the room, people rose to offer incense and bow their gratitude and respect, not for Amida Buddha, but for the concept of compassion that he represents. *Gassho*, the word for the bow, came back to me, followed by *oshoko*, the offering of incense.

A young man moved up the aisle, signaling people when to get in line to *oshoko*, row by row. As he approached, Benno whispered to me that he was Katsu's youngest brother. We stood in our turn, and I watched how the others behaved: hands together and bow, take a pinch of loose incense and sprinkle it on the brazier, hands together for another bow, three steps backward, bow again.

When I got closer to the front, I noticed that next to Susan's photographs there were packets of food, Baggies of rice, dried fruits, nuts, and cookies—chocolate chip, which even I knew was her favorite. That the dead should not be hungry.

Katsu was achingly handsome, in a suit the same inky black as his hair. His face, set off by a white shirt, seemed almost radiant with grief as he nodded briefly in response to those who approached him. Attribute it to the whole scene, but I was feeling acutely sensitive to vibrations, and what I felt emanating from under Katsu's composure was not only immense sorrow but also a smoldering anger.

The man I assumed to be Mr. Wu had a vacant, emotionless expression as he acknowledged the bows of the mourners. Mrs. Wu, on the other hand, made no effort to mask how she felt. She stood behind her husband, well away from Katsu and the procession of people who would have reached out to her.

I turned to see my Italian husband, not content with the remoteness of a mere bow, grasp Katsu's arms with both his hands as he ducked his head in a quick nod. Katsu gripped back and met Benno's eyes for a fraction of a second. In the whiteness of Katsu's knuckles, I read confirmation of how much he was holding in.

I was surprised to see Mr. Neville in line behind us, waiting to make his *oshoko;* I hadn't realized he'd known Susan well enough to attend this service. His presence derailed my thoughts back to the Stringers, wondering what he'd have to say about the manner of their deaths, and I didn't catch much of what the reverend, Nakazono according to the program, had to say about the transient, illusory nature of life. Besides, Rev. Nakazono was young, with a heavy accent and a nervous tendency to giggle that made it hard for me to focus. I let the words wash past me and turned my attention to the other mourners. Vivian Brownell was there, sitting by herself; in the row behind her were two of the office volunteers, Addie Collins and Muriel Dodge. They weren't a pair I'd've thought were friends, but funerals do have a way of bringing people together. Although I scanned the *hondo* twice, Diane McClellan didn't seem to be present. Nor was Trudi Voss.

Then it was over, with a final boom from the large, stationary gong on the altar, chased by a tinkling music, like wind chimes with direction, that seemed to come from a state-of-the-art sound system on the side wall of the altar.

In spite of the friendly, gray-haired woman who urged us, "It's cold outside, why don't you stay for tea?" we headed for home. Benno, I knew, was more upset than he was comfortable admitting. This wasn't the time to impose the burden of having to be polite to strangers that would accompany introductions to the people from NAN.

After the dim, somber air in the *hondo*, the sun seemed too bright, the sky too blue. In wordless agreement, we crossed Riverside Drive back to the park. A crow cawed like a maniac from a tree on the lower level. We walked over to the stone wall and looked down into the park itself; there didn't seem to be any cause for the bird's alarm. I scanned the branches of the neighboring trees until I located the distinctive, hunch-shouldered silhouette of danger.

I nudged Benno to get his attention. "Hawk."

Just then the bird, as if it had had enough of the squawking crow, took off. My spirits rose with it, both comforted and elated by the soaring shape of the redtail as it spun circles in a cloudless sky, a familiar sight from my California childhood come to life over the Hudson. There was no wind, and the bird gave several slow wing flaps at the far point of every loop to catch the updraft that would carry it around.

"You know what the Buddhist said to the hot dog vendor?" Benno broke my reverie.

I knew it was going to be bad. "What?"

"Make me one with everything."

But sometimes bad is good. The image of Rev. Nakazono eating a hot dog, bowed forward from the waist so that big glops of sauerkraut, onions, and mustard wouldn't land on his purple silk robe, got me laughing so hard I had to sit down.

Tears and laughter. Between those two poles, life goes on. Benno sat next to me on the bench. I could smell the incense smoke caught in his hair. After the chanting, the grace of the redtail . . . all the busy week, even the sadness of Susan's death, seemed small and unimportant. I felt ready to get on with my new job, to let the past slip out the door and allow us at NAN to get on with the present.

I figured that would be it for death; Susan and then the two Stringers made three.

The hawk vanished into the blue. We headed home to work on a more earthly transformation: turning Clea into a four-armed, one-eyed green alien for Halloween.

I should've known it was wishful thinking, that Ralph and Ora counted as one, and there would be more to come.

13

WHEN I left the house to start my second week of work, I pulled my grandmother's "dignity" along behind me.

"Mama, do you *have* to bring that thing?"

For the life of me I couldn't see why a shopping cart was anything for Clea to whine about.

"You look like an old lady!" She refused to hold my hand.

"What, I should wear a pink hat with a pompom?" I nodded at the woman who'd just overtaken us.

"Mama!" Clea shushed me disapprovingly, but she couldn't help smiling. The woman had to have been my age at least, old enough to know better than to wear such ridiculous headgear.

I kept my voice patient while I explained that I had to stop at the copy place to pick up a job for work, and it was too much for me to carry without wheeled assistance. By then we were at the school, and a good thing, too. I let Clea go in without the humiliation of a kiss from a mother with an old person's accessory. In my opinion, she was still a little young for the critical-child routine, where everything one's parents do is excruciatingly embarrassing, but this definitely looked like an early warning symptom.

I sighed myself up the steep slope of 115th to Village Copier. The soft-spoken Israeli man who worked the counter congratulated me on my promotion from résumé-copying patron to employee of an organization with a charge account as he fit four boxes into the dignity. Now that it was full, I pushed the red cart in front of me, grandmother-style.

When you see an elderly woman behind an empty shopping cart, it doesn't always mean she's on her way to the store. My grandmother preferred to use her cart instead of a cane because she thought it made her look more competent, more dignified—hence the nickname. I could hear the sound of her voice as clearly as yesterday. "Anita, would you get my dignity out of the closet? I'm off to meet Ethel for lunch."

New York City is an excellent place to be old, I reflected, as I practiced pushing the loaded cart. Almost everything—groceries, drugstore, hardware, stationery, library, movies, restaurants—is within walking distance, whether you use a cane or a cart for support. Buses are half-fare, and they kneel to make it easier for arthritic knees to climb aboard.

If you can't get out, almost every store delivers; every building foyer is littered with takeout menus for everything from Chinese to Indian. With apartment neighbors so close, it's easy to find someone to pick up what can't be delivered. When the weather's bad, I do this for my own elderly neighbors, the Wilcox sisters. Building Supers are on hand to change a lightbulb or plunge a toilet. Not to mention the variety of social service agencies that provide friendly visitors and even discussion groups run over the phone in conference calls.

And of course, ready access to the two prongs of my personal retirement plan—Meals-on-Wheels and books on tape. I'll take New York over Florida any day. You don't need a car, and you're not isolated with only your own age cohort around you. When she sees Clea in the halls, I swear Catherine Wilcox drops ten years.

"You just missed Mr. Neville, Anita. He left this for you." Vivian Brownell handed me a sealed envelope.

No, Neville hadn't forgotten about those other deaths, had he? Just what I needed, one more item to add to the week's to-do list. A multipart item at that.

Vivian hovered, clearly interested in what Mr. Neville had to say to me, but when I left the letter, unopened, on my desk, she wheeled the shopping cart of boxes into the living room and started setting up card tables for the volunteers due in later to get the letters out.

With Vivian out of the room, I slit the envelope and took out a single sheet of lined yellow paper. Fourteen names— he'd added Susan and the Stringers to his original eleven— followed by probable cause of death. There were two other columns on the list: date of death and date of discovery. In six cases, the bodies had not been discovered until at least twenty-four hours after death had occurred. Interesting, but again, could be coincidence. When you live alone, elderly, isolated . . . in my years of experience with that setup, though, I'd had less than a handful of clients whose deaths had gone undiscovered for more than an hour or so.

With an ex-cop's thoroughness, Neville had also noted the day of the week on which each person had died, and, in the instances when the body had not been discovered right away, the day it had been found. That made another coincidence: all the suicides, including Susan and the Stringers, had died and/or been found on a Friday, Saturday, or Sunday.

The numbers weren't that high, even for a population of over two thousand, but it was definitely odd enough to be worth a closer look. I threw the envelope in the trash. The list of names, however, I stored in the security of my purse until I had time to delve into the closed cases file.

I was supposed to print out mailing labels from NAN's database of names and addresses, but after an hour of struggling with Mail Merge, I had to admit it was beyond my computer capabilities. In the wake of my failure, it didn't take long to convince Vivian that hiring a temporary administrative assistant was a good idea. Just the possibility of having Anne Reisen on hand took a weight off my shoulders.

After Vivian left, I went through the Stringers' copious case file from the beginning. Sure enough, among the early entries were several references to Ora's despair about her situation. Not that it was unusual for an elderly person with diminishing capacities to feel that death might be better than such a life, but for the most part, it's only talk. And in Ora's case, either she'd stopped feeling that way, or Susan had stopped recording that particular kind of comment. Only in hindsight was it obvious that something should have been done.

Exactly Diane's opinion when she stopped by, full of self-reproach for not having recognized how depressed Ora was.

"I told Susan they both should see a psychiatrist. Medication would really have helped them, but some people can be so resistant to taking care of their mental health. I should have pushed them just a little more!"

I let her talk it out; listening is all you can do for a person who's lost a patient she thinks she might've been able to save. If only Susan had been able to locate a relative, if only she'd gone to management before she died, if only Diane had spoken with the aide . . .

"It was really an untenable situation." Diane talked herself around to the point where she could stop feeling responsible for the Stringers' suicides. "Both of them deteriorating like that, and unable to help themselves. I'm sure they knew it would only get worse. In spite of the way they lived, they were intelligent people. Ralph was very sensitive, very proud. They just refused to consider any alternatives."

"They certainly had adequate resources to move to an assisted living facility," I said. With enough money, anything is possible. Even hiring people to dismantle an apartment, pack up forty years of accumulated possessions, and set them up in a new place.

"They were not at all interested in leaving the Estates. Well, I don't suppose the Stringers were suited to institutional living, do you?"

"Not unless there was a liquor store nearby that delivered."

That actually got a laugh from Diane. Uh-huh, I thought, so there is a sardonic side to your personality.

Addie Collins came early to direct the volunteer envelope stuffers, leaving me free to edit Vivian's copy for the NAN newsletter. My attention wasn't totally on what I was doing, however, and the scraps of conversation from the living room distracted me. I got up to close the door, but the topic of their gossip caught my interest.

"I suppose Trudi Voss is happy now." The tart voice belonged to a woman I didn't know.

"Yes, this should bring in a good response," Addie agreed. "Vivian certainly knows how to write a letter!"

"That wasn't what I meant."

"Didn't you hear about Ralph and Ora Stringer?" That was Muriel. "They took the final exit Friday night."

Evidently Addie hadn't; a chorus filled her in on the details. I know, I should've gotten on with my own work. Then the first voice picked up again.

"They lived right next door to Trudi. She was always complaining about Ora. She had her windows open all summer, and the cigarette smoke went right in Trudi's bedroom."

"Never bothered her mother." Addie's voice, gruff.

"Trudi doesn't believe in air-conditioning," Muriel explained. "Or so she claims. I think she just doesn't like the extra fee they put on the maintenance for it. Can you imagine?

Fancy job like she has, and she won't part with ten dollars a month!"

"Don't you know where Trudi's money goes?" The unidentified voice dropped almost to a whisper.

I found myself straining to catch the next sentence above the soft, papery sounds of folding and sliding.

". . . and that's why Susan wouldn't hear of a bus trip. Quite right, too, if you ask me." The voice rose back to normal. "Old women jerking on those slot machines like robots. All you ever get from slots is bursitis of the shoulder!"

"And how would you know that, Doris?" Addie teased.

In the pause, I could almost see Doris blushing. She covered by asking for more envelopes.

"I think a trip to Foxwoods is a good idea." This voice was easy to identify: Mary Tanaka, a retired librarian who came in once a week to organize NAN's active lending library of paperback mysteries. I'd only met her once, but it was enough to remember that her normal volume was almost a whisper.

"It's good to get away for a day or so. Foxwoods is not so far that you need to stay overnight. What's the harm in gambling? Some people find it entertaining, and you don't have to play the slots, Doris. I understand the Indians have a wonderful museum there, and several restaurants. I think Susan was wrong not to arrange a trip, if that's what people wanted."

Silence settled around Mrs. Tanaka's comments.

"Mary's right. We should be able to choose where we go, instead of leaving it up to the director," Addie spoke up in her defense. "I'm not saying I'd ever visit a casino, but if other people want to, why shouldn't they?"

"Exactly." Muriel again. "If you ask me, those Indians have every right to fleece us, after what we did to them. I'm all for them getting a bit of their own back, a dollar at a time if that's how it works. Especially if the money comes from people foolish enough to throw it away in casinos!"

"I must say, Muriel, you do have a way of putting things." The gossipy Doris sounded almost shocked.

Curiosity got the better of me, and I walked out to put a face on her personality.

Doris turned out to be a pleasant-faced woman in a red turtleneck and a plaid wool vest. Not the kind of person you'd think had a malicious bone in her body, except it's always the ones that look like Grandma who turn out to have the sharpest teeth.

14

HALLOWEEN Tuesday, I left NAN early to collect Clea after school. She and Tamika had plans.

In a city of high-rises, there's no going house to house ringing doorbells, so New York puts its own spin on trick or treat. According to protocol, apartment residents decorate their doors to indicate their willingness to hand out candy to their neighbors' children. The only thing urban trick-or-treating has in common with suburban is that it's done by a pack of kids.

Since Clea's the only child in our building, we rely on invitations from her friends. This year she'd be joining Tamika, who lived, conveniently, in the Estates.

And yes, I had an ulterior motive for doing escort duty: some of the doors they knocked on would belong to older people, NAN clients and volunteers. Meeting my daughter would boost my profile in the complex and, I hoped, make me seem more accessible, friendly, trustworthy.

Clea was a knockout, I have to say. Her four arms were constructed from two pairs of green tights, one of them her real arms, the other stuffed with rags and a pair of gloves for hands. Benno had attached two dish-scrubber antennae to her bike helmet and spray-painted the whole thing green. It was a costume worthy of that other typical New York Halloween observance, the parade in the Village.

Tamika, swathed in metallic silver fabric, made a delicious Hershey's Kiss. Held together at neck and knees by elastic drawstrings, the costume had a Hula-Hoop inside it to form the wide bottom and a handful of crumpled newspapers to add volume. Tamika's skin, a perfect chocolate color, required no makeup; a strip of paper with "Hershey's" printed on it in blue ink attached to her ponytail provided the final touch.

On the walk to the Estates, we made time for another New York tradition—trick-or-treating the neighborhood businesses. Merchants set out bowls of candy for whoever stopped by—in costume, that is. Columbia Hardware gave out lollipops. At Häagen-Dazs it was wooden nickels good for a free topping; Papyrus Books had mini chocolate bars. The girls darted into each store while I waited on the sidewalk.

The pair of them, not that I'm biased, were adorable.

As she watched the girls come down the hall toward her apartment, Tamika's mother's smile was as wide as mine. She'd ordered a pizza, and we made the girls eat a slice each while they waited for a few more kids from upstairs.

"At least they'll have some real food in their bellies before the candy goes in," Carla said.

Clea and Tamika had bonded instantly, the way girls still do at that age, and the more I talked to Carla, the more I thought we big girls would be friends as well.

A supervisor in the outpatient department at St. Luke's and a single mother, Carla had an "okay, this is what's happening, now what can we do?" attitude that jibed with mine. Plus I liked it that she was almost as short as me, and her wardrobe, even of work outfits, tended toward the comfortable, as mine did—long on corduroy slacks and tunics rather than skirts and stockings and tucked-in blouses. Her hair, waist-length dreads threaded with a trace of gray, was gorgeous; Carla could have carried off any look she chose.

"Anita, could you come in here a minute?" Carla called from the kitchen.

She turned on the water and let it run. "I don't want the girls to hear, but I thought, now you're working over there at NAN—well, we've had more than a few deaths recently in the Estates, mostly of elderly people, and you know how rumors start. What I've been hearing makes it sound like NAN's on a mission to convince people to kill themselves when they get too old or sick."

So Mr. Neville wasn't the only one who'd taken note of how many people had died lately. For Carla's sake, I made light of it. "What, like toothless Eskimos crawling off into the snow to die?"

"I know it sounds ridiculous, I'm just passing on what I heard." Carla let the sink fill with water. "Might as well do up these dishes while I'm at it. I don't pay much attention to what goes on at NAN, you know, it's not my age group, but I got the impression that they offered some kind of discussion group about death last spring. Apparently it got so controversial they put a stop to it."

"Death? Discussion group? I wasn't here last spring, I have no idea what that could be." The book group? Someone misinterpreted the Black Death part of the title?

"The variation I got from a pair of aides—no, I don't have any idea who they work for—it was down in the laundry room. I wasn't really listening, until I heard 'voodoo' and 'NAN' in the same sentence. Seems that several of our more troublesome elderly folks died over the summer, and these aides were speculating that the nurse put a curse on them."

"Good grief. Where do people come up with that kind of stuff?" It was beyond absurd. But— "Anyway, Diane McClellan's from Jamaica, not Haiti."

Carla shrugged. "Jamaica, Haiti—you know how people are. Anyway, I caught something about the nurse from Lucille Dolan, too. In her eighties if she's a day, lives out of the Dumpster behind Met Foods, but I hear she's a millionaire. The woman with her, don't ask me because I don't know who she was, complained that the nurse took all her old medications away. Lucille said the same thing happened to her—the nurse made her bring all her prescription bottles to the office in a paper bag, and then she kept most of it."

"Standard practice," I said. "They call it 'brown-bagging.' Any nurse worth her salt would do it. You'd be amazed what people hold on to. They use old prescriptions to self-medicate, they 'lend' pills to other people. The only real way to stop that behavior is to take the drugs away."

"Take whose drugs away, Mama?" Clea carried her paper plate into the kitchen. I scooped up the two inches of crust before it hit the garbage pail.

"You're throwing this perfectly edible food away?"

"You can finish it if you want." Clea vanished, along with her question.

Nothing like maternal nagging to change the subject. I dumped the pizza in the trash.

"Ready to go?" Carla asked. "We can talk while we walk."

Standard procedure for apartment trick-or-treating begins with a photo op in the lobby. Then the elevator to the top floor and walk down, stopping to canvass each floor on the way. While the kids crowded down the long hallways, Carla and I stood in the open area in the middle and continued our conversation.

"At the Camera Club meeting, a group of high school kids were going on about NAN being a front for a euthanasia cult in the Estates, you know, helping terminally ill people die. They heard that the nurse had pills for anyone who wanted them, and—I'm sorry, Anita, I'm not making this up—Susan killed herself to show everyone how easy it was."

"You've got to be kidding!" I couldn't imagine there was even a grain of truth concealed in the oyster of *that* rumor.

"Teenagers." Carla shrugged. "These kids have lived in the Estates all their lives, and at least one has grandparents here. They hear the grown-ups talk, and—oh yeah, Vivian Brownell's name came up, too. Isn't she the president of the board over there?"

I nodded. Euthanasia? Cult? Vivian? What the hell was going on?

"Do you think there's any truth in what they were saying, Carla?" I was appalled.

"I don't know, Anita, that's why I'm telling you about it. The kids—I'm sure they're exaggerating, probably a combination of what they overhear from their parents and too much television."

We followed the kids down to the eighteenth floor.

"Can you believe, Tamika gives me an argument because I think she's too young to watch *Buffy the Vampire Slayer*? Have you ever seen it? Demons are the least kind of creature she's fighting. Makes Linda Blair seem quaint."

That's what I mean about Carla; same exact battle we went through with Clea.

"You think they came up with this idea from something they saw on *Buffy*?" Television made me do it?

"It does seem like there've been more people dying than usual." Not a direct answer. Whatever was going on, Carla took it seriously. I sobered up and listened.

"When the Estates went private, there were some who wanted to force senior citizens living alone in three-bedroom units to move to smaller ones. Some old guy got up at one of the meetings, told the pro-privatization contingent they might just as well euthanize everyone over seventy-five and be done with it!"

Community meetings; there's always a drama queen.

"Feelings were very high at the time," Carla continued. "If

people had started dying off then, I could've understood this kind of talk. But that's over a year ago now, and everyone's adjusted to the change. I think this business about a death cult is just kids trying to stir up excitement."

Our children hustled down another flight of stairs. When we followed them to seventeen, they were banging on a door whose occupant was taking a long time to answer. It seemed to be the only one on that floor with a decoration—a glow-in-the-dark skeleton dangling from the knob.

Carla and I ambled down the hall to see what was up.

"Lucille Dolan." Carla read the name on the door plate. "Huh. I wouldn't pick her as one to be offering candy. Come on, kids, let's move on. She's not answering, and we've got plenty of other apartments to visit."

"But Mom, the skeleton!" Tamika protested. "It means she's there."

"Mrs. Dolan never goes anywhere," a girl in a witch costume piped up. She banged on the door and made the cardboard bones dance.

"Well, there's a first time for everything." Carla frowned at the papers on the mat in front of Lucille Dolan's apartment. "Hasn't taken in any of these announcements, either."

The kids lost interest and made for the stairs, with Carla shepherding them along. I bent down and looked at the papers. The Estates newsletter, a notice about Halloween safety precautions, and an advertising circular from Met Foods, all delivered in the past two days. In the now-quiet hall, I knocked again and put my ear to the crack to listen for movement.

What I noticed instead was a smell. Sweetish, rotten. Not a odor you forget if you've ever encountered it.

By the time I caught up, our group was on fifteen.

"Carla, I think there's something wrong at Mrs. Dolan's. I'm going out to talk to the security guards, okay?"

Without asking any questions, Carla nodded. "Sure. Clea can wait for you in my apartment if you're not done by the time we are."

At that hour, the main security office was closed, and Mr. Neville presumably at home. I headed for the twenty-four-hour guard booth by the Amsterdam Avenue entrance to the Estates, where someone was always monitoring the video images from the lobby cameras. I explained the situation, twice. An elderly tenant not responding, the smell of decomposition.

The guard tried to stonewall me into waiting until the next morning before calling in the cops to break Lucille Dolan's door open. I insisted right back that he call Mr. Neville, as well as 911. A major advantage of age, I've found, is that you no longer worry so much about making a fool of yourself. In situations like this, calling in the cavalry and not needing them is a best-case scenario.

15

Lucille Dolan was, indeed, dead.

I hadn't hung around for the breaking and entering, but Mr. Neville repaid the favor of my calling him at home by waking me at twelve-thirty that night to tell me about it. After I hung up the phone, I lay in bed remembering a comment Michael had once made: Old people die.

I'd thought it cold-blooded at the time. Now I found it comforting. According to Mr. Neville, Lucille Dolan had been dead since sometime Saturday. In her bed, apparently of natural causes, although considering the circumstances and with no relative to object, there would be an autopsy. I'd never met the woman; she was eighty-three; I had no reason for self-reproach.

Old people do, in fact, die, and Monument Estates had more than the average number of old people. In socialspeak, it's become a NORC—a Naturally Occurring Retirement Community. Of the thousand-odd apartments, more than half were occupied by people sixty-five or older. The complex hadn't been built as a retirement community, but the original tenants had stayed on, "aging in place," until they were a majority of the population.

The Estates also, apparently, had more than the average death rate. I bumped Mr. Neville's list of names up on my agenda for the week.

As far as Lucille Dolan went, well, I'd look up her file in the morning, see what assistance, if any, NAN had been providing. I curled around Benno, tucked my arm over his waist, and fell asleep.

Wednesday, I got my customary Bread Shop coffee to go. It was Anne Reisen's first day, and I wanted to be there when she arrived. Vivian, for a change, hadn't beat me in, so I had to deal with the alarm lock. It wasn't complicated; a quarter-turn of a round key. You'd think Addie Collins would've been able to remember whether she'd had to turn it off on Saturday.

Mr. Neville was knocking at NAN's door before I even got my coat hung up. Probably had the guard posted at the 123rd Street entrance booth radio him as soon as I set foot in the Estates. What he was after was information on Lucille Dolan's next of kin.

NAN did have a case file on her, and Carla's information was correct—Lucille had been a millionaire, a teacher who'd invested modestly in blue-chip stocks in the 1960s. Over time, the market had done the rest. Judging from the copies of letters crammed into Lucille's file, she had a gaggle of nieces and nephews in California, and she'd evidently promised to pay college tuition for any of them who were interested in higher education. There was no information on any of their parents, presumably Lucille's siblings.

Complaints about Lucille's habit of Dumpster diving were sprinkled throughout the file. Met Foods had written several letters; a few people had reported Lucille as a person in need of NAN's services, although some were more concerned that she was behaving "like a bag lady" and "bringing down the tone of the Estates." Those letters, of course, were anonymous. When confronted, Lucille's defense was that she was rescuing dented cans and perfectly good fruits and vegetables.

According to the Progress Notes, Susan had apparently been advising Lucille to make her personal scholarship checks out to educational institutions rather than directly to the eager young people who importuned her to fund massage programs and holistic healing degrees. One niece, however, was working on a master's in education at UCLA, and she was the person Neville and I chose to be the recipient of the bad news.

It was a depressing case file. None of her opportunistic relatives had ever made the effort to actually visit Lucille in person. Here she was, putting a dozen people through college, and living an extremely frugal life. To have so much money, and spend it on ingrates.

Anne Reisen's appearance at the door thrilled me the way delivery of a dozen long-stemmed red roses would have. We started with a hug and a burst of "I'm so glads" and "you look so greats," before we backed off, laughing.

"Whoa, Anne, you've made a major style change."

She'd traded in her flowing skirts and tunics for a pair of belted black silk trousers and a tailored cream blouse, colors more muted than I'd ever seen her in. "Paris?" I asked.

"And Michael." Anne blushed. "I've been going to this martial arts class with him, and without even trying, I've lost ten pounds. I figured I might as well show off my figure while I've still got it."

Anne's in her early fifties, and she's never shown any signs of sagging. Her hair was still long, but she had it twisted up at the back of her head in an elegant chignon held in place with a pair of lacquered sticks topped with jet beads.

The second office, with the flea market two weeks away, was already filling up again with donations, but I'd cleared the desk for Anne. She adjusted the swivel chair to the height she liked, locked her purse in the bottom drawer, and sat with her hands folded on the desk.

"So, boss, what's up?"

It was a huge relief, just to laugh. I moved an empty fish tank off a chair and ran through some general background information on NAN and the Estates. Anne's main responsibility would be administrative work for the board, leaving me free to handle clients and volunteers, so I was basically filling time until Vivian showed up.

By 9:20, I was worried. It wasn't at all like Vivian to be late. I'd just decided to call her when she walked in the door, completely serene, with neither explanation nor apology.

"Ms. Reisen, very glad to meet you." Vivian offered Anne her hand. The pair of them stood eye-to-eye, making me the height-impaired member of the staff.

They appeared to approve of each other. Vivian unlocked the right-hand file cabinet and took out a stack of manila envelopes: résumés and application letters for the executive director's job. I left them slitting envelopes open and went to debrief the answering machine.

I expected the rest of my week would be a piece of cake, comparatively speaking. I was wrong, as usual.

Since Vivian was in the office and I couldn't open the closed-cases drawer without catching her attention, I put Mr. Neville's list aside and went for the newsletter files instead. Whatever NAN offered, the newsletter was how it spread the word. The folder of back issues was conveniently located in Susan's desk.

I didn't think any such animal as a euthanasia cult existed, certainly not one operating under the aegis of NAN, but I do tend to credit the theory that at the core of every exaggeration lies a seed of truth.

Nothing special in January or February; in March, however, an elder-law attorney gave a presentation on "Estate

Planning and Other End-of-Life Issues." Nicely ambiguous, but kind of a stretch from there to euthanasia. What a word. Every time I hear it, I see a placard from the anti-Vietnam protests: Youth in Asia = Death.

April's newsletter announced that "due to expressions of interest in topics raised during the previous month's special talk," a new group would be forming. Pretty turgid prose, for a newsletter. I wondered if it had been Susan or Vivian who'd written it. Whichever, the name of the new group showed a flair for the apt word: Issues of Later Life. Kind of an unfortunate acronym, though—ILL.

Attendees would read books "related to the aging process," such as Betty Friedan's *Second Half* and *A Journal at Seventy* by May Sarton. On the more practical side, the group would provide assistance in filling out living wills and health care proxies. No mention of who exactly would be running things. Susan, I hoped, at least in terms of professional guidance for the forms; no one should sign those documents without fully understanding their implications.

In May, I noticed, ILL was not included in the regular schedule of activities that ran every month. It wasn't mentioned in June, July, or August, either.

Okay, now I had a bit of reality that could have grown out of proportion: a group to discuss death-related issues, which seemed to have vanished almost as soon as it started. Canceled because it was too controversial, Carla had said. So how far off the ground had it gotten? NAN was meticulous about sign-in sheets; funders require documentation of how many people participate in the activities. There was a file drawer labeled "Programs," where schedules, sign-in sheets, and flyers for NAN's various recreational activities were kept. That was the next place I looked.

"Birthday Parties," "Blood Pressure," "Book Discussion," "Knitting," "Sing-Along," "Tuesday Lunch." All nice and orderly, but nothing under *I* or *L*.

At the very back of the drawer, I found a second alphabet.

Thin folders labeled "Card Games," "Current Events," "Haiku"—and there it was, a tab marked "ILL." Issues of Later Life, Inter-Library Loan. Sick, was more like it.

Most of what the file contained was forms—health care proxies, living wills—and a good supply of pamphlets from the Hemlock Society, which I suppose someone rabidly opposed to their philosophy might consider a death cult. But still—it was completely logical that the group would have been interested in information from an organization devoted to that particular issue of later life.

Having a health care proxy at any age is a good idea. No one likes to think about this stuff, but it's best to make arrangements *before* you're confronted with a crisis. I take a prophylactic view of preparedness, myself—if you're braced for it, then the thing you fear won't happen.

The Y2K scare was a bust, but I still have five gallons of bottled water in my closet.

From "Deciding to Die: What You Should Consider" to a reprint on pain management, the society's literature focused on considering all the alternatives before choosing self-deliverance.

Until I got to "The *Final Exit* Technique": self-deliverance from an end-stage terminal illness by means of a plastic bag, complete with a materials list, directions for making a trial run ahead of time so you'd know what to expect from the experience, and a detailed thirteen-step procedure—including photographs from a practice workshop.

That was good, thirteen steps. One more than on the recovery road. Addiction, redemption, death.

A half-dozen colored flyers advertised various other Hemlock Society services. Patient Advocacy Program. Caring Friends Program. I hate euphemisms. What kind of friend "makes sure that the [person] has thoroughly considered all alternatives, does not die alone, and does not fail in the attempt"?

A caring one, of course. Beyond the call, you might say.

Another thing I hate is confronting my limitations. The professional part of social work education involves learning to set aside personal prejudices, suspend judgment, observe with an open yet skeptical mind. When it came to dying, I had my opinions, and any attempt I made to give unbiased counsel would be indelibly stained by them.

Stop it, Anita. How can you know what you'd feel, faced with the unthinkable? A terminal diagnosis, in extreme pain?

What Barbara was up against. The door of my mind thudded closed on that one.

I needed to talk to someone who'd attended the group, find out firsthand exactly how deeply they'd delved into this stuff, and why they'd stopped meeting.

I searched through the folder for a roster. Paperwork, certain as death. But there was no sign-in sheet, no list of ILL participants.

16

NITA, what the hell did you give Clea to read?" Benno never swore in front of Clea, never. He shook a copy of *Final Exit* in my face. "This is not appropriate for her!"

"Then it's a good thing you took it away." I kept my voice calm, but the frozen lump of Benno's marinara sauce I was heating up for supper got a vicious jab with the wooden spoon. We have our disagreements on child rearing, yes, but we try to handle them without raised voices, and out of Clea's earshot. Benno is the more conservative parent, having grown up in a traditional East Coast home, and he consistently comes down on the other side of permissiveness from me.

You have ideals and theories, and then you bump up against reality. I don't believe in censoring what Clea reads; I figure forbidding fruit makes it more of a temptation. In this instance, however, I agreed with my husband. Self-deliverance was subject matter that Clea was in no way ready to handle emotionally, yet at the same time it was just the kind of thing to grab her imagination and provoke more questions about death than I wanted to answer.

"Why can't I read it?" Clea plunked herself down at the counter to plead her own case. "It's educational!"

Benno gave her a warning glare. "This is a grown-up conversation. In your room."

"What's wrong with it? I think it's interesting. There was this man, and he attached a battery to a gun so when the sun came up it shot him right in the heart."

Sometimes I swear I can hear the approaching hoofbeats of the defiant horseman of adolescence in Clea's voice.

"You see what I mean?" This time Benno's dagger-eyes were pointed at me.

"Go on in your room, Bops, and let Dad and me talk. Supper will be ready in ten minutes." I measured a tablespoon of salt in the palm of my hand, poured it into the boiling pasta water, and added a pound of linguine. "I'm sure she's not reading the whole thing, Benno. It wouldn't make any sense to her. She's just picking up the factoids, you know that's what she does."

Clea is a sponge for information; whenever we need an example to illustrate a discussion, she's off to her room to look something up. Of course, her favorite source materials are Scholastic books with titles like *The Terrible Tudors* and *The Vicious Vikings*, but she's also intimately familiar with the part of the dictionary devoted to presidents and states, and a devotee of the *World Almanac*. When he's proud of her, Benno refers to Clea as the family librarian.

"Oh, so she should be able to look up the fatal dose for Valium? Which happens to be fifty pills at one hundred milligrams." Benno was flipping through *Final Exit*.

"Relax, Mary. We don't have any of those drugs in the house."

"What about her friends' parents? You don't know what kids get up to when they're unsupervised—"

"Dad!" Clea just couldn't stay out of it. "I didn't read any of that stuff, it's boring. All I learned was that you can't die from a needle full of air, even though they pretend in the movies that you can."

"Well, I'm greatly relieved to hear that."

Sarcasm spoken here.

"Who's ready for spaghetti?" I put a glass of wine in front of Benno, and that was it for the moment.

Final Exit. Why would anyone who wasn't already knocking on death's door want to read such a book?

I certainly didn't. Given the role it had played in recent events, however, I'd pulled my copy off the shelf a few days ago and left it on my end of the couch. Unfortunately, I hadn't gotten to it before Clea the curious did.

Studying up on ways to die voluntarily made me uncomfortable, to say the least. Part of my reluctance had to do with Barbara. I couldn't imagine her wanting assistance to step over the threshold. Magical thinking can be irresistibly powerful: If I didn't read about death, then Barbara wouldn't die.

Irrational, but it got me through dinner and into bed.

Denial, however, has its limits. As soon as I lay down, my conscience started acting up. If for no other reason, I should read the book to deepen my professional awareness of the issues facing my clients. Plus I felt I owed it to Susan, and the Stringers as well, to try to understand what they'd done.

I got out of a sleepless bed at midnight, poured myself a Metaxa, pulled the afghan over my knees, and settled in to read. When it comes right down to it, I believe it's better to know what you're up against, even if the knowledge brings grief. Whether or not Barbara would ever have any desire to ease her own way out, I should be prepared.

I started at the beginning, and found myself reading with Susan more on my mind than Barbara. A responsible treatment of the topic would have a section intended to talk people out of voluntarily ending their lives.

Which *Final Exit* did. The introduction devoted all of two paragraphs to those who misused it to commit suicide. Derek Humphrey washed his hands with blunt words: "Life is a personal responsibility. We must each decide for ourselves." Then he went on to console himself with a pat on the back for those he saved from messy, unreliable means of death such as guns and nooses, and encouraged the depressed to "first seek medical help and counseling."

I put my finger in the book to hold my place and stared at the blank television screen. Had Susan been seeing a therapist? Not that anyone at NAN would necessarily know, or that Katsu would have told Benno. A sip of Metaxa later, it occurred to me that cultural beliefs might have kept Susan from confiding in her husband, especially if she had doubts about adopting.

Then I came to the one-page "Caution" right before the first chapter.

> If you are thinking of ending your life because you are depressed, or cannot cope with the pressures of this difficult world, do not use this book. It is for dying individuals who need such information and will find it a great solace.
>
> I ask people with suicidal thoughts to share them with family or friends and if this does not help to call one of the hot lines or help lines listed in their local telephone book, and presented in Appendix D of this book.
>
> Please respect the true intentions of *Final Exit*: the right of a terminally ill person with unbearable suffering to know how to choose to die.

It seemed aimed so precisely at Susan that it was impossible to imagine, one, that she hadn't read it, and two, that as a social worker she wouldn't have heeded its warning.

I was patting around on the arm of the couch, bewildered, before I realized how hard old habits die: I was looking for my cigarettes. There's nothing like the simultaneously soothing and thought-inspiring effect of nicotine. Bumming is one thing; I've learned not to keep any in the house in case of emergency urges like this.

I put the itch for coffin nails out of my mind and went back to see what Mr. Humphrey had to say that might be of use to the living.

He put a good deal of emphasis on advocating for pain management. People who want out before their time often feel they can't go on because they're in pain. With the advances of modern medicine, there's really no reason to suffer other than that many physicians are reluctant to prescribe adequate amounts of addictive drugs.

Thank market forces and the big pharmaceuticals for the development of OxyContin.

Which, I noticed, was too new a drug to have made it onto the list of medications and fatal dosages that had so incensed Benno.

I paid attention also to Humphrey's advice for those who assist in a self-deliverance in any way, including being present as a witness. Best not to have a close relative, a loved one, or anyone who stood to benefit monetarily by your death, be present while you died; asking a close friend to be your companion is a better choice. The premise that no one should die alone is one of my core beliefs, so I had no problem with that. Humphrey put a practical spin on it: the companion is also there to help should anything go wrong.

Like you vomit up the pills before they take effect, or fall asleep before you've managed to swallow a fatal dose.

In any case, the beauty of the plastic bag method was that it could be self-administered, and it was practically fail-safe.

The author went on to advise that, regardless of whether or not the companion was actively involved in ensuring that death occurred, arrangements should be made for someone else to "discover" the body.

Right, a Caring Friends Volunteer.

What if there was one operating in the Estates?

Except some of the people on Mr. Neville's list hadn't been found until several days after they'd died, and surely a caring friend would have arranged for them to be discovered sooner than that.

Unless it was Susan, say, or Diane. A discreet Friday-afternoon visit on the way home; it could well be days before a reclusive resident would be missed, and by then death's little helper would be well out of the picture.

You've got a suspicious mind, Anita. Cut it out. What could be further from the code of ethics for a social worker or a nurse than assisting a person to die?

When it comes to terminal illness, ordinary rules go out the window. Some people get downright fanatical on the subject of a person's right to choose death.

Dr. Kevorkian springs to mind.

Physician-assisted suicide is one of those things it's easier to agree with in principle than in practice. As with abortion, I believe it should be legal. When it comes to my own personal feelings on the subject, though, I can no more see myself helping someone die than I can imagine terminating a pregnancy. Maybe it's because I've been unable to conceive a child myself; maybe it's some latent Catholicism embedded in my psyche, or a tendril of Buddhist belief in letting life be. It just seems to me that life should begin and end when it will, without human or technological intervention.

Don't even get me started on assisted means of reproduction, or the death penalty—I'm opposed to both. If you ask me, state-sanctioned killing is still murder. With fertility treatments, hey, if that's what floats your boat, it's your own business. Some of my best friends' children came from Petri dishes, and I wouldn't not have them in the world. Where someone else draws the line doesn't have to be where I do.

Do I think what Jack Kevorkian does for his terminally ill patients makes him a murderer? Easy to answer in the abstract, no, not if his victims come to him for a way out.

Victims, Anita. You referred to them as victims. There's your answer.

Okay, get back to the situation at hand. If Diane provided the pills for Ralph and Ora Stringer to swallow, what does that make her?

Some questions are best not asked at 2:00 A.M., when all answers are at their bleakest.

17

EIGHT-THIRTY in the morning, however, is a fine time to search for information. I skipped the Bread Shop and took Mr. Neville's list straight to the file cabinets. With Anne on the job and Vivian not due in until eleven, I had two hours for the files.

Eleven names. With Susan Wu, Ralph and Ora Stringer, and now Lucille Dolan, fifteen. I had no clear idea of what I was looking for in the files; Neville had only asked for my impressions. I decided to start with cases where the bodies hadn't been discovered immediately.

All six of them had been NAN clients. I pulled their files and went to put up a pot of nasty coffee, reminding myself as I had every morning that I needed a stop at Mama Joy's to pick up a bag of real French roast.

While the coffee was brewing, I opened the venetian blinds in all three rooms. The flood of morning sun made the overhead fluorescents redundant. It occurred to me that there were two concrete things I could look for: whether these people had had terminal diseases, and participation in

Issues of Later Life. The other thing to pay attention to was state of mind.

The November light seemed to have solved everyone's problems that morning. The phone didn't ring a single time. Olive gave herself no occasion to apologize for bothering us. Anne copied application letters and résumés. I poured myself a cup of coffee-scented hot water, closed my office doors, put my feet up on the desk, and read.

I took notes as I went. When I was done, I had four people with cancer; stomach, pancreas, and gallbladder, all of whom, coincidentally, had been treated by Dr. Andras, Barbara's physician. Dorothy Norris, whose apartment Diane and I had visited, had had lung cancer. A fifth had had Alzheimer's disease, still being cared for at home but beginning to exhibit the difficult symptoms of the middle stage, such as occasional instances of hostile behavior, wandering, inappropriate outbursts, incontinence.

The remaining person had exhibited signs of various non-specific dementias and forgetfulness—she kept trying to cook and leaving things on the stove until they burned, which set off the smoke alarm and frightened the neighbors, and she had a tendency to walk the grounds at night, complaining to the security guards that someone was trying to break into her apartment.

In all the cancer cases, Susan's notes made reference to expressions of despair. Around the time he'd received his diagnosis, the man with Alzheimer's had also spoken about taking his own life before things got too bad. It's one of the ironic mercies of Alzheimer's that as the disease progresses, awareness of its eventual consequences fades. Not surprisingly, so did mention of suicide.

Which made it all the more unusual that he'd managed to carry out the plastic bag routine. It took a fair amount of organization to assemble the necessary items—the bag, rubber bands, painter's mask—not to mention obtaining the right medications and taking an adequate dosage. On the other hand, the nature of the disease went a long way toward explaining why he hadn't left a suicide note.

According to her progress reports, Susan had encouraged the cancer patients to attend Issues of Later Life, and at least two of them had done so. I couldn't see a connection there yet, but I added the information to my page of notes.

At ten-thirty, I replaced the files and locked the file cabinet.

Anne was impatient to Mail Merge with the computer; Addie and Doris were due in at three to put labels on the stuffed envelopes.

18

FRIDAY afternoons were not turning out to be the best time of the week for me. I won't say she planned it this way, but Diane McClellan once again had me on a home visit to a client who seemed likely to be dead of self-deliverance before the weekend was over. At least this time I was going in prepared.

I'd read Harry Silverman's case file. Although Susan had visited him weekly over the past several months, her notes were oblique at best. "Counseling on end-of-life issues" was a typical entry, with an occasional additional comment such as "Discussed impending visit from grandchildren," followed a week later by, "Visit went better than anticipated."

Diane fleshed out the details while we walked over to the Silvermans' building, accompanied by the sound of leaf blowers as the grounds crew cleared the litter of downed leaves from the walkways and steps.

According to Diane, what Susan had actually been up to with Harry involved an ongoing discussion of self-deliverance. From what she knew of their meetings, Susan had been scrupulous in helping Harry to clarify his motives, as well as including his wife, Judy, in the decision making. She wanted me to meet the Silvermans not only for Harry's benefit but also for my own sake.

"You've only seen the way Susan and the Stringers took their own lives. It's time for you to meet someone who's doing it properly" was what she'd said.

Harry Silverman's wife—third wife, to be exact—opened the door for us and greeted Diane with a quick hug. I didn't see our competent nurse as the huggable type, but that didn't stop Judy.

From her appearance, my immediate assessment of Judy was that she was a woman I was going to take to. Tall, early sixties, a teal cotton turtleneck tucked into brown cords, and for aesthetics, an eclectic strand of beads—amber, silver, amethyst, freshwater pearls. She wore her long hair pulled straight back and held with a clip. Although there were no traces of gray, its natural brown didn't look color-enhanced.

Judy clasped my hand between both of hers and favored me with a long look. "I'm so glad you've come to visit my husband."

I opened my mouth, but she didn't pause for reciprocal pleasantries.

"Here, let me take your coats, we can just leave them on the couch. I have water on, it's peppermint tea for Diane, so tell me, Anita, what would you like? I have real coffee, and more kinds of tea than you can shake a stick at."

Crossing my fingers that it wasn't Maxwell House, I agreed to coffee, if it wasn't too much trouble.

Of course it wasn't. Judy approved of coffee in the afternoon, she would have some herself. Diane and I sat at the round table under the kitchen window while she measured and poured and delivered a status report on her husband's condition.

"Those hospice aides are so gentle with him, it's like a dream come true. And it's such a luxury, clean linens every day. The whole room smells fresh when they leave. I have to argue with the aide every time so she'll let me wash Harry's personal things."

"You're not supposed to do his laundry, Judy," Diane rebuked her.

"I know, I know, but I feel like such a parasite. I'm so grateful that they bathe Harry. I never thought he'd accept it, but that Roxanne, she has a way with him. I think he prefers her touch to mine." Judy poured water through the filter for, yes, French roast. "It won't be long, Diane. Applesauce and ginger ale are about all he'll take. God, I wish Susan hadn't gone first."

Diane moved her head twice, side to side, as if signaling to Judy that the topic of Susan's death was a no-no. I glanced at Judy in time to catch the slight dip of her head in acknowledgment of Diane's warning.

Gone first? It seemed an odd way of putting it, unless she knew something I didn't. "Did Susan—" I started.

"Milk and sugar?" Judy asked, cutting off my question. She set a hand-thrown pottery mug, shaped like a big-bellied goose with its neck bent to form the handle, in front of Diane.

"No, thanks. It smells wonderful." My mug was a slim cylinder with a metallic sheen to the glaze.

"Both the boys and their families are coming this weekend, and we had Vera yesterday." Judy wrinkled her nose and explained to me, "That's Harry's first wife, his sons' mother. We put her off as long as possible, but making peace is making peace, and Harry wanted to explain the terms of his will so she wouldn't make trouble later."

This was maybe more information than we needed to hear, but I took my cue from Diane and let Judy rattle off whatever was on her mind. When death is this close, the rules are different. And I had to say, she'd won my sympathies immediately, regardless of whatever she and Diane might be in cahoots about. Judy Silverman was an easy twenty years younger than her husband, and I thought her mix of hospitable manners from an older generation and the frankness of my cohort made a winsome combination.

"Harry basically split his estate three ways, a third to each of the boys and a third to me, with nothing that has more than sentimental value for Vera. After all, she's remarried, he hasn't supported her for years, and he decided he'd rather the boys have it. Besides, he could have left them with a fourth each, and me with half to myself. There's plenty to go around, either way. Harry just wanted to be sure Vera heard it from him."

As if all her neurotransmitters had overloaded at once, the animation went out of her face.

"I can't—" She turned her back to us, dumped the used coffee filter into the trash, put the box of tea back in a cabinet.

Diane stared out the kitchen window at the treetops, where the last yellowing leaves were departing in the wind. I got up and put a hand on Judy's shoulder. She wasn't crying; the look in her eyes said she was long past the crying stage. The eye of the hurricane, I thought, the deceptive calm before the onset of mourning, when tears would return.

I've visited more than one deathbed in the course of my work with the elderly, and it's not something I'll ever take in stride. The room Harry and Judy shared was almost all bed—hospital bed alongside marital double bed, with a nightstand between them and a commode by the closet.

The curtains were open, allowing afternoon light to pour over a green-striped afghan covering Harry's feet. A foil-wrapped pot of purple chrysanthemums dominated the windowsill, almost hiding the clutter of medical supplies—latex gloves, prescription bottles, alcohol swabs, a can of Ensure. On the bedside table, a portable CD player sent a Beethoven string quartet floating around the room.

There was also a copy of *Final Exit* tucked under a box of tissues.

Harry himself—his closeness to death was evident. Emaciated, skeletal, wasted; he was all of these, skin and prominent bones. In his case, the yellow skin coloration that comes with liver disease had a lemony cast that made his thick hair seem whiter in contrast. His eyebrows were spectacular, like a finger of unruly snow above each pale blue eye.

The smile he greeted us with was warm, but the vacant expression in his eyes said he was already moving away from the need for social graces. When Diane introduced me, however, his interest caught and held.

"So you're the new Susan?"

"Yes." I was amused by his way of putting it. "How are you feeling today?"

Harry huffed an ironic sigh. "Rocked by the hoofbeats of Morpheus, I ride to my eternal night."

"A quote?" I wondered out loud. "Not something I recognize—your own?"

This earned me a closer examination. "No to both." Harry drew in a long, shallow breath, sighing his words on the exhale. "A description of my current state. A consummation devoutly to be desired."

That one I knew. "Hamlet." Easy as shooting fish in a barrel.

"Very good." Harry watched Diane take out a stethoscope and blood pressure cuff. "She'll do."

"Yes, I thought you two would get along," Diane answered.

"Your blouse is the exact shade of my flowers."

A pleased look briefly disrupted Diane's neutral, professional expression. She put a finger to her lips to shush him. "Take a deep breath."

Harry and I waited in silence while she went through the blood pressure routine. I wondered if Diane chose her vivid colors deliberately to cheer up her patients.

"Tell me, Doctor, will I live?"

I liked Harry as much as his wife. Some clients do that to you, seduce you out of your professional distance right off the bat.

"Yes. How long is up to you."

"She doesn't beat around the bush, this one."

Our presence seemed to have lifted Harry more fully into the present world.

"It sounds like you appreciate that quality," I said.

Harry raised a sardonic eyebrow. "Yes, Diane is my self-appointed guardian angel, determined not to let me shuffle off before I've wrung the last ounce of sweetness from the fruit of my years."

I made a face at him. As metaphor, it was a little hokey.

"Yes, you'll do. In deference to my advanced stage of decay, Susan kept a lid on her sense of humor. Diane here, she's more concerned with my body than my soul."

It was said affectionately, and Diane didn't take offense. Harry's next remark, however, provoked a frown on her smooth brow.

"The game's afoot, Watson. I've found someone to administer the coup de grâce." He closed his eyes for a moment, then went on. "No, I'm not going to tell you who it is. Not Judy, that's all you need to know. You'll be relieved to hear that we have no appointed hour. So let's get on with it now, if we must. I'll strut my stuff for Susan's replacement here, and she can do the fretting."

Man after my own heart, mixing Sherlock Holmes with his Shakespeare. Not to mention getting straight to the point, and inadvertently answering the question I hadn't had time to ask Diane.

She'd been telling me that Harry had made a plan, but she didn't know anything about the details—like who would be with him to help, if necessary.

When I'd caught that warning look from Diane to Judy at the mention of Susan's name, I wondered if Susan was supposed to have been the "caring friend." If she thought her mission included empowering people to take control of their final moments, would Susan have gone that far? And Diane, what would she do to help a patient to have a good death?

So I was glad Harry broached the subject himself, and made it clear that Diane was to be kept out of the final loop.

His matter-of-fact approach made it easier than I'd thought possible to set aside my personal bias and listen. As I saw it, once the decision had been made, my responsibility was to be sure Harry was in his right mind, not feeling coerced, and that his wife agreed with his decision. It didn't take long for Harry to reassure me on all these points.

Before I left, though, I had to ask him about Susan. "When you talked, did you ever have any idea that she was considering the plastic bag method herself?"

Harry spoke with his eyes closed. "Never. She never gave the slightest hint. I've given much thought to that, and to whether I bear any responsibility for her suicide." He opened his eyes and looked directly at me. "I was shocked. Susan made a point that one shouldn't take one's own life out of despair or depression. She insisted that I speak to my doctor about an antidepressant, in fact. Neither he nor I thought adding yet another medication to my regime would be of benefit. Susan's death was a terrible thing. The last thing I expected was to outlive her."

19

O N Sunday afternoon, we made a family visit to Katsu. He'd invited us for tea, and to collect a box of Susan's social-work-related books he'd put aside for me, so we brought the dignity to carry the books home. I spared Clea the embarrassment of pulling it myself, and let her do the dragging. She had a thing about the way the folded cart rattled over the octagonal pavers of the promenade in Riverside Park. We let her make as much noise as she wanted. The sky was like the inside of a pearl, the yellow leaves shining luminous against low clouds. I loved this early-winter light, so unlike anything California has to offer.

Benno never went to anyone's house empty-handed, so we stopped on Ninety-sixth to buy a pot of narcissus bulbs for Katsu, four brown lumps with the merest sliver of green poking up from each one. In another month, they'd be tall wands topped by clusters of white flowers that smelled like cheap perfume. It was the right subtext, though—regeneration.

Clea skipped ahead to greet the Virgin Mary. The statue that stood in an alcove of the church on the corner was a neighborhood favorite, mostly because of her halo—a large blue cone with a gold rim that resembled a satellite dish. She was known locally as Our Lady of Good Reception.

"Daddy, come look! They took our lady's dish away!" Clea dragged Benno up the street. Sure enough, the halo was gone.

"Well, I guess Our Lady of Good Reception isn't getting any, huh?" Benno couldn't resist.

The joke was over Clea's head. I jabbed him with my elbow anyway.

Katsu's apartment was as wonderful as Benno had described, from eat-in kitchen to sunny south windows. We sat on pillows around a black-lacquered table in the living room. Katsu set out rectangular china plates that held mounds of *mochi*, made from sweet rice, and cookies decorated with a perfect starburst pattern of sliced almonds. For Clea, there was a marzipan mouse dipped in chocolate, with a delicate tail dripped across its back.

We made small talk about the changing season's weather and drank bitter, smoky tea from tiny porcelain cups, each one decorated with a different brush-stroke flower in the bottom, which delighted Clea. She nibbled her mouse down to crumbs and tried not to fidget or stare at the items laid out on a low table across the room. A pyramid of clementines, a bowl filled with grains of rice, and a small incense burner were arranged in front of a framed photo of Susan. I knew Clea was dying to get up and examine it more closely, but she was too well-mannered to ask.

Or shy, more likely. I couldn't resist studying the altar either; it was so unlike anything in our own home. The offerings included two rings on a small red pillow. On one, a diamond sparkled. The almond cookie tasted like ashes in my mouth.

Looking for something else to focus on, I noticed a row of carved animals, the same translucent celadon green as our plates, marching across the shelves of a bookcase along the opposite wall. I tapped Clea's arm to draw her attention away from the altar.

Katsu noticed, and nodded at the animals. "You would like to see?"

I realized he'd been aware of our fascination with the altar, and I blushed at the thought of how rude I'd been. Clea was a child, but I should have known better. At least Katsu had the manners to distract us.

Clea scampered up like she'd been released from a box. "Tigers!"

"And horses," Katsu said. "In Chinese zodiac, I am the horse. Susan was the tiger. Good combination."

Clea carried the figurines one by one to the windowsill, where she lined them up and spent the next half hour organizing a complex society of some sort. Nine is a lovely age; old enough to be conversational and interested in adult events, yet still capable of being absorbed by the inner world of childhood.

While Clea played, Katsu showed me into the second bedroom, which they'd used as a combination study and studio. Susan's computer setup was surrounded by now-empty floor-to-ceiling bookshelves. His folded massage table leaned against the wall directly in front of us.

To the right, half-hidden by the open door, stood a crib.

I stopped abruptly, three steps into the room, causing Katsu to bump into me. His profuse apologies gave me a moment to compose myself. The emotions hovering around the crib came at me like a wave, so heavy and sad, from such a beautiful thing. It was made of maple and cherry, the stiles and rails neither round nor square but gently softened at the edges. The dovetail joints had been used as decorative as well as structural elements, forming a design at each interlocking corner. It was stunning, the contrast of pale and dark woods, the oval rails.

I felt I should say something, at least acknowledge the crib's presence. Its mattress was covered with a pale yellow sheet. A quilted red blanket with a pattern of tumbling yellow stars lay folded at one end; a teddy bear waited with open arms at the other. The stiffness of Katsu's back, firmly turned to the crib, stopped me.

What that crib means to him is none of your business, Anita. I repeated that sentence to myself while Katsu explained that he wanted me to look through the books he'd put aside for NAN. None of my business, right, but social work instincts don't always lie down on command.

I'd done enough counseling of recently bereaved people to know that cleaning out the loved one's possessions immediately after the funeral is not automatically therapeutic, any more than hanging on to them for months and years is. I suggested that Katsu might want to wait a bit before he gave anything away, that it might be too soon for him to know clearly what he would regret not having kept.

Thanks to the polite reserve of Katsu's culture, I had no idea what he was really thinking or feeling while I spoke. He let me wind to a stop. To my relief, I hadn't brought the crib into my discourse. It had been on the tip of my tongue, but we didn't yet have a relationship with a solid enough foundation to be treading on such delicate areas.

Benno, listening from the doorway, started to speak. Katsu raised the fingers of one hand slightly to stop him.

"What you say is maybe true." He nodded. "But all things must go now."

Katsu hesitated. I knew there was more. He turned to Benno.

"I am sorry to tell you this, Benno-san. I return to Japan in one month."

Benno launched into how it was a good idea for Katsu to visit with his family, get away for a while, take some time.

Katsu made the silencing gesture again and shook his head, no.

The real meaning of what he'd said hit Benno and me at

the same time: Katsu wasn't going on a vacation, he was moving. For good. With the unity of married thought, we both looked at the crib at the same time.

Katsu nodded. "My big problem. I would like to give to a baby. Maybe you know someone, Anita, who will like to have this crib?"

"Oh, no, Katsu, you can't give it away! We could store it for you, then whenever you're ready—"

"Anita." I'd transgressed Benno's internal comfort level and gotten too personal.

It didn't seem to bother Katsu. He answered as plainly as I'd asked. "Thank you, but I don't think I will be having a baby. Crib should be used now. I can make another one."

"You have family in Japan, right?" A blatant change of subject from Benno.

"Family, yes." He didn't look happy about it. "My mother is alone. She will like me to live with her. Such a big apartment is too much expense for me, in New York."

It sounded like a plan. Still, I wanted to be sure that this was a considered decision rather than an emotional rejection of his current life caused by shock, grief, and altered financial circumstances. If Katsu didn't want to leave the city, there were alternatives. "Have you considered asking your mother to move to New York to live with you? Or finding a roommate to share expenses? Moving to a smaller place? Give yourself some time to consider all your options." Ugh, social work–speak.

"In Japan, I will live very cheap. I have still big payment to make for treatments to be pregnant."

Ignoring Benno's obvious opinion that I ought to shut up, I ventured another question. "The herbs were very expensive?"

Katsu studied his slippered feet. "Herbs, no problem. Also we tried in-vitro fertilization. Very expensive, and insurance does not pay for this."

Before I could probe any further, Benno put a stop to it. "Look, Katsu, maybe Anita's right, you shouldn't be making any big decisions right now, but if you've made up your mind, anything I can do to help, just let me know. I'll be happy to store the crib at the shop until you're ready for it. Whatever you want, I'm with you."

Benno gripped Katsu's forearm. Katsu raised his head, met Benno's eyes for a second, then bowed his head, a quick dip. There were tears in both men's eyes.

Benno stepped back and gestured at the boxes. "So what about these books?"

Men. Can't cry in each other's arms, which is what they both wanted to do.

"I'll get the shopping cart," I said, and left them alone for a minute.

What I really wanted was a look at Susan's computer. The phantom file was still the only tangible sign I'd seen that Susan had had something on her mind before her death. If Benno hadn't been there to squelch what he considered my overactive imagination, I would've come right out and told Katsu about the file.

As it was, I explained my curiosity to Katsu in terms of wanting to make sure Susan hadn't left anything work-related on her home computer. He let me boot it up and have a look. There it was, the same ghost-file name, A:Deaths, worked on from the external drive without being saved to the hard disc. There was a box of neatly labeled 3.5-inch discs next to the computer. I ran all ten through the A drive; none had a file named "Deaths"—or anything else that seemed remotely pertinent.

Before we left, Katsu insisted that Clea choose a figurine for herself. Without pausing to consider, she pounced on a galloping horse. Katsu slipped a small object from his hand to mine and curled my fingers around it. From the feel, it was a smooth, irregular stone that radiated warmth from being held.

"Anita, please to place this on your desk at NAN. Spirit of Susan will help you."

I didn't look at it until we were on the street. Nestled in

my palm was a tiger, carved from the darkest green jade I'd ever seen. The tiger lay on its belly, tail by its side, front paws outstretched. Not a very unusual pose, except for the head, which rather than resting on the forepaws was raised and cocked a bit to the side, as if the tiger were listening for the faintest sound, on the alert for the unexpected. I held it out for Clea and Benno to see.

"Mama, Katsu told me that's the oldest one, older than America, that's why he's losing his shape."

Whether it was the antiquity of the carving or the quality of the jade, I definitely felt a power emanating from the watchful tiger.

I read the thought even as Benno opened his mouth to tell me I couldn't keep something so valuable, and he read the counterargument I was about to make. He shut his trap without a word. No way either of us was going to be ungracious enough to go back up to that apartment and return Katsu's gift.

I rubbed the smooth top of the tiger's head, between his ears, with my thumb. I'm sure it was my imagination, aided by an exhalation of exhaust fumes from the M96 bus as it pulled out of the stop in front of Katsu's building, but I could have sworn I heard someone call my name. It was no more than a whisper, a hopeful sigh, but it sure sounded like Susan's voice.

20

ELECTION day was an ordeal. The Estates had its own official polling place, with voting machines set up in the Community Center. NAN offered assistance in getting to the polls to anyone who requested it, so Anne and I spent the day running a wheelchair taxi service.

Anne opted to collect the chair that was kept at Security so she could visit with Mr. Neville, Michael's former colleague. I headed for the nurse's office, where the NAN wheelchair lived. Since Tuesday was an off day for Diane, I used the copy of her key kept in a small, conveniently labeled manila envelope in Susan's top desk drawer.

I hadn't yet had a reason to visit the one-room professional suite allotted to the nurse, and it seemed creepy to be there without Diane. The entire place was slightly larger than my office. Her desk stood in front of the window, facing the door and two sturdy wooden-armed chairs. The folded wheelchair was parked in one corner, opposite a credenza that held a lamp with a cut-glass base and a frilly pink shade. Diane seemed to favor rose-themed tchotchkes, including a serenity prayer framed in red ceramic roses, a bowl of rose-petal potpourri, and a wreath of dried rosebuds on the closed closet door.

Call me incurably curious; no way was I walking out of there without checking out the closet. Mostly it was medical supplies—three shelves full of gauze pads, tape, alcohol swabs, rubber gloves, cotton balls, and a blood pressure cuff, along with a case of Ensure, a few boxes of Depends and in-continence pads, neatly rolled Ace bandages, a heating pad, and a neck brace. On the floor in one corner was a collection of canes, adjustable aluminum in both regular and the three-legged variety.

The higher two shelves held office supplies: three reams of paper, a box of hanging files, pens, stapler, various sizes of notepads, yellow stickies. A much better stockpile of the ba-sics than we had in the main NAN office. In fact, while I was here . . . Anne had been complaining that we were almost out of those pink pads for phone messages, and I could use some Wite-Out myself. I figured it wasn't stealing, since Diane's supply budget came from the same place as mine.

I pulled out the nice solid two-step stool, metal with ridged rubber treads, that was tucked under the lowest shelf. From the higher vantage point it provided, I got a glimpse of the topmost shelf. Some kind of sling thing, foam in a dark blue cover with a tangle of straps, and a small green file box, about the size of an index card. Locked. I shook it. Not paper; something that rolled, and a loose rattle like seeds in a gourd. Or pills in a bottle.

The lock was one of those things a movie heroine would open with a hairpin. I preferred to use my vast knowledge of human nature—less muss, less fuss. People don't usually add this type of little key to their rings; tiny keys get stashed in ob-vious places, like the paper-clip section of a desk drawer. I turned around to step down from the stool, and there it was, more conveniently located than I'd expected, thumbtacked to the wall just inside the door frame.

I contemplated the red plastic pushpin stuck through the key's hole, trying to figure out why someone would keep a key so near the lock it opened. The locked box was odd enough, but this was odder. Why not in the desk?

Because someone might find it there. Once you had the key, you could infer a lock, and go looking for it. Cool it, Anita, you're getting way too convoluted here, jumping to conclusions. Just open the box.

I unpinned the key and sat on the top step of the stool with the box in my lap. It held three opaque plastic bottles with eyedropper tops labeled OxyFast, and two brown plastic prescription drug bottles with childproof caps. Both were for OxyContin, 80mg. According to the labels, one of the prescriptions was for a Dorothy Norris.

So Diane had found what she'd come for after all, that day when I'd packed up the glassware from Ms. Norris's dusty apartment.

I recognized the name on the other brown container from Mr. Neville's list. If I remembered correctly, he was the person with pancreatic cancer, the one who'd used the plastic bag method and left a letter detailing what he'd done and why.

There were maybe a dozen small white tablets with a score down the center in each bottle.

OxyFast, OxyContin—friends of those in extreme pain. What got Barbara through the day, and night.

I could think of only one reason, a quasi-legitimate one at that, to keep a stash of this particular medication.

Although the Oxys were too new to be among the drugs detailed in *Final Exit*, the concept of amassing a supply of suicide drugs was clearly spelled out. AIDS patients who committed suicide had been known to will unused pills to other sufferers. I had no idea how many it would take to make a fatal dose, but Diane might.

Was she saving deceased clients' leftover OxyContin to be used by others, like Harry Silverman, who intended to make their final exits?

Euthanasia cult indeed.

I locked the box, replaced it on the shelf, re-tacked the key to the wall.

As I fitted the red pushpin into its hole, a less altruistic reason for Diane to have this stash of opiates occurred to me. She wouldn't be the first medical person with access to prescription painkillers who had a habit. How better to feed it than by gleaning pills from her elderly patients?

Or if she wasn't using herself, maybe she was selling the stuff? It wasn't unheard of for a nurse to deal, either, but no, I didn't really think so. Not Diane McClellan, not in my opinion.

The real question was, what was I going to do about it, now that I'd found her stash? Confront Diane? Uh-huh, and admit I'd searched her office thoroughly enough to have discovered her hiding place? And we were going to work together how well after I'd admitted my trespasses, let alone that I suspected her of being an addict?

Not for the first time, I devoutly regretted having poked my nose someplace it had no damn business.

Which didn't stop me from cruising the bathroom before I left. In the tub, hidden by a fabric shower curtain patterned with pink cabbage roses, was a jumble of bath chairs and benches. The contents of the medicine cabinet were reassuringly normal: a can of disinfectant spray, two bars of rose-scented soap, tampons, a Bobby Brown lipstick, several bottles of nail polish. Everything the well-groomed nurse might need to keep up appearances.

I put my purloined office supplies in the wheelchair and tried not to fret about the green box while I pushed elderly people to the polls and hoped they voted for the candidate who wasn't going to privatize their Social Security accounts.

When I got back to the office after my last wheelchair run, I walked in on Vivian and Anne facing off in the living room.

Vivian clutched the green file folder of set-aside mail to her chest. There were two spots of color high on her pale cheeks.

". . . been a trying time." Although Vivian kept her voice level, I could see it was an effort. "I'm still in shock about the loss of Susan Wu, and we've all had to adjust to working together."

Anne looked down at the carpet, for all the world like a toddler caught with her hand in the cookie jar, and said nothing.

I felt like a very welcome interruption. Vivian tried some small talk about the election with me, and left as soon as she could.

"Talk about a steel magnolia! I've never seen such a controlled, ladylike, violent display of anger." Anne shook her hands in the air like she was cooling burned fingers.

"What set her off?" I asked.

"I got carried away with the letter opener." Anne sounded a bit sheepish about it. "I'm not used to these distinctions, 'Put this here for me, put that there for Trudi, open this and don't open that.' I'm the administrative assistant, I open the mail. It's just a habit, slitting everything that's not marked personal. I mean, okay, I put the bills and bank statements aside, but honestly, Trudi's got so many categories, who can remember?"

Anne took a Snapple out of the fridge. "I wasn't sure I should mention it to you, Anita, because I did open it by accident, and—" She twisted the top off the bottle and flipped it into the sink. "Vivian actually ordered me not to say anything about it to anyone."

It seemed like it was going to be complicated, so I sat myself down while Anne debated whether to obey Vivian.

It didn't take long for her to decide. "Okay, you twisted my arm. Vivian getting her knickers in a twist was too weird, on top of the letter itself. Which maybe wasn't so unusual, I'm not too familiar with how they do things around here yet, but I don't understand why you shouldn't know."

I gave my watch an exaggerated look and made a scooping motion with my hand, encouraging her to get on with it. I still had Clea and supper to deal with.

"Yeah, yeah." Anne ran a hand over her hair. "Ralph and Ora Stringer? They're the ones Michael told me about, who did the plastic bag thing?"

I nodded.

"Well, that letter I inadvertently opened was from their lawyer, a notice in advance of probating the will. They left fifty thousand dollars to NAN."

"What?"

"You heard right, fifty thousand dollars. Nice gesture, huh? If anyone ever donated that kind of money to Senior Services, Emma would've been dancing on the desks. So why do you suppose Vivian pitched such a fit?"

Fifty thousand would have been a fourth of our operating budget at Senior Services, and might have kept the agency open. No way our former boss wouldn't have shared that kind of news with us immediately.

"Vivian practically turned white when she read the letter. I would've pretended I didn't know what it was about, but she didn't give me the chance. These well-bred women—she never raised her voice, but I felt like I was being flayed. Maybe she's got a point about confidential information and the separation of fund-raising and service provision, but the way she reacted was totally off the wall."

"Emma was fanatical about me not knowing who donated what, so it wouldn't affect how I treated the clients," I said.

"Yeah, but come on, Anita, you usually knew. I certainly did. I mean, I opened all the mail for Emma. Maybe you chose not to pay attention, but you could've found out whatever you wanted, no problem. In a small agency, nothing's secret if you go looking for it."

I shrugged. At Senior Services, I'd been happy to leave the financial stuff to Emma. I wasn't any more interested in NAN's finances, but having caught the tail end of Vivian's tirade, I had to agree with Anne that her behavior seemed out of proportion to the crime.

Steel magnolia, indeed.

"So do you know any more than I do about this endowment fund they're working on?" Anne asked.

"Not much." I got up to leave. It was after five already. "Just that Trudi's setting it up from home, so she can do the transactions on-line. It's supposed to be a reserve thing, where they can use the interest to carry programs if there's a gap in foundation funding. Vivian explained it to me when I first started, something she wanted to do for NAN as part of her legacy to the organization."

It had been just one more thing coming at me, and since it wasn't directly related to client needs, I hadn't paid much attention. "I think her goal was $500,000, and they were maybe halfway there? That's what that item in the Newsletter is all about, encouraging people to remember NAN in their wills. Sounds like it worked with the Stringers."

"I'll say." Anne put on her coat and followed me out the door. "I still don't get it, though. Why shouldn't I open all the mail? I'm not a kid—I know my job. An administrative assistant is a one-way door. Things pass through me, but only to you or Vivian. Nothing goes out to anyone else without permission."

We walked toward Broadway. It was already almost full dark, and cold. More than time to call the cleaner's and pick up the winter coats we'd put in storage over the summer.

"Maybe it's as simple as what she said, Anne—a stressful time, and Vivian's not used to having anyone open her mail to begin with."

"Maybe. But it's not her mail, it's NAN's. Didn't Susan open whatever came in?"

"I suppose. But you know, we're new, and Vivian is totally responsible for whatever we do. How does she know we won't go gossiping all over the Estates about how much money the Stringers donated? People might get the idea they didn't have to give, because NAN already had enough."

"Whatever." Anne shrugged. "I have a feeling I'm not going to last on this job. Much as I like working with you again, Anita, I won't be chewed out like that by anyone more than once."

She ducked her head to check out my expression. Dismayed, of course. I'd be lost without her.

"All right, make me feel guilty. No promises, but I'll stay at least until you're okay on your own." A subway train rattled and clacked out of the tunnel, heading for 125th Street. "Damn, that's my train!"

Anne ran for the station like she actually thought she was going to catch that particular train.

Me, I crossed over to the bus stop. It might be only ten blocks home, but it was uphill all the way.

21

ENNO and I stayed up late watching the election returns come in, but not late enough. Disgusted, we went to bed after Gore's concession phone call. It wasn't much consolation to wake up and find out he'd taken it back, or that, for the moment, no one had won.

We weren't the only ones distressed by the lack of a clear outcome. As a public service to our clients, Vivian insisted we have the large-screen TV on. I wasn't so sure providing more noninformation to a room full of agitated elderly people was such a productive thing to do; everyone's blood pressure was elevated on Wednesday.

A call from Judy Silverman got me out of the chaotic agency atmosphere to make a home visit.

"I'm just waiting for him to say the word," Judy greeted me at the door. "And when he does, it will be 'mayonnaise.'" A tremble of laughter shook her voice. "It's Harry all over. He wanted a word that would be unmistakable. You know, if he said, 'It's time,' or 'I'm ready,' it could mean time for his next pill, or he was ready for the urinal. So mayonnaise, that means he's ready to put Plan D into action."

Judy went for a tissue to dab her eyes, then explained. "Don't bother asking what the D is for. Harry's sense of humor can be awfully obvious."

By mutual, unspoken agreement, we skipped the coffee routine.

Although fluid retention had swollen his abdomen, Harry didn't look like he was ready to give birth to death quite yet. When I touched his hand, he opened his eyes, startlingly blue against the yellow of his skin.

"I hear you're making book over at NAN, what'll happen first—they figure out who's the next president or I kick the bucket."

Making book at NAN? The idea that anyone at NAN might be betting on the outcome of the election was startling enough, but that they might be laying odds on when Harry would die—it took me a long moment to realize he was ribbing me.

"Gotcha." Harry grinned, a big bad wolf, his teeth large and brilliantly white in contrast to his jaundiced face. "Nothing I like better than a woman at a loss for words."

I laughed with him. "Good thing I put my money on the outcome of the election being decided first!"

"I'm sorry I brought it up." He turned his head away on the pillow. "If that clown from Texas steals the election, I can honestly say there's a day I don't want to live to see."

"I know exactly what you mean."

That got me the full force of blue rage. "Don't ever say that. You've got your whole life ahead of you. What the hell difference does it make who's running the damn country? Take care of your family, that's what matters."

Harry closed his eyes. I counted the seconds between each inhalation until they steadied out at eight, and stayed that way. As easy as that, Harry slept.

It seemed to me he was well on his way to dying naturally,

the inevitable shutting down of bodily functions eased along by pain medication. Why not simply continue like that until death came?

As with so many things, it came down to being an issue of control. A cesarean instead of a vaginal birth—the result is the same, but with one, you have some say in the timing.

The next morning there was a message from Judy Silverman on the answering machine. Harry had died at seven o'clock the previous evening.

Life at NAN made a seamless transition from electoral disarray to flea market organization. We closed down to all but emergencies, and Anne and I joined the crew of volunteers who were sorting and pricing for the weekend sale. It was the best time I'd had in ages.

I have the soul of a collector, kept in check only by the size of my apartment and the disapproval of my husband. Out of deference to Benno and reality, I confine myself to small items, buttons that can be stored in cookie tins, two shoeboxes of beaded necklaces that someday I intend to restring in different combinations.

I was enchanted by what came in the door of NAN. From a rowing machine, six rhinestone-studded belts, and a straw cat carrier to a miniature ceramic Nativity set, silk scarves, and painted-fabric tablecloths from the 1940s, every bag that anyone dropped off, I poked into. Even before the sale, I'd put a few choice items aside. Three strands of black Swarovsky crystals; an African cloth doll with her baby swaddled on her back for Clea; a chain-link evening purse with a Deco-style clasp—treasures small enough to be tucked away without being scrutinized by Benno's critical eye.

The entire recreation room, in the basement of NAN's building, was occupied by tables devoted to linens, jewelry, glassware, pots, pans, and tchotchkes divided into collectible, cheap, and, courtesy of the Estates' sizable Chinese and Japanese population, Asian. One corner held a miscellany of small appliances—humidifiers, fans, an IBM Selectric, irons, radios, ink-jet printers—all of which had to be tested and labeled as working or not. It was almost enough to make me rethink my career choice. If I'd lived anywhere but New York, where space is at a premium, I would've considered going into the second-hand business.

My particular assignment was jewelry. I did the best I could, but by Friday morning I was bored by the wealth of outdated costume jewelry, most of which, to be brutally honest, was dead ugly and not worth the dollar a strand we were hoping to get for it.

I stretched my back and looked over the scene. The recreation room wasn't a pleasant space; the walls were an institutional mustard yellow, the ceiling a grid of pipes and fluorescent lights. A clothesline strung between support columns displayed a pair of African wall hangings; a dozen baskets dangled from strings tied around an overhead pipe.

"Quite a bunch of junk, isn't it?" Vivian, dressed for work in stretch pants and an oversize, man-tailored white shirt, managed to look chic as usual. "But you'd be surprised at how much money we take in."

I was glad to hear it, because there were an awful lot of people putting in an awful lot of long hours for this fund-raiser.

"Honestly, the things some people give us—" A woman held up one of those clear plastic, pocketed things to hang on a door to hold shoes. It was yellowed and stiff, almost every section ripped or cracked.

"Throw it away!" someone shouted.

"What do you think this is?" A metal stand of some sort, chrome diagonals as confusing as a Chinese puzzle.

It was easy to get distracted. When Muriel came in with a shopping cart of exotic kitchen equipment, I wandered over to check it out. Along with an assortment of cake pans, muffin tins, and several different styles of graters, the cart held a pasta maker and a bread machine, still in their original boxes.

I was debating the pasta machine for Benno. Not that he'd ever expressed any interest in spaghetti from scratch, but—

"That belonged to Judy Silverman," Muriel told me. "You know her husband died, day before yesterday?"

I nodded.

"She asked me to bring her stuff over when I came. Funeral's this morning. Are you interested in that gadget?"

I wasn't, not after I knew whom it had belonged to.

By then two other women had gathered around the cart and were assessing its contents. I left them to it and took myself back to the jewelry mines. It wasn't far enough away for me to avoid overhearing their conversation. About Harry Silverman, from the sound of it.

". . . was at the movies when he died." That was Doris, in a bright red cardigan and baggy jeans.

"You mean she left him alone?" From a small, solid woman, her gray hair pinned up with real, old-fashioned wire hairpins.

"Oh no, Judy always found someone to stay with him," Muriel said.

"Is it true, Muriel, that he followed the instructions"—Hairpins lowered her voice—"in *Final Exit*?"

I was extremely interested in the answer to that question, but Muriel ignored it.

"Well, I didn't hear anything about him being found with—"

A blender whirred to life in the appliance corner.

"—didn't take it off by himself, now did he?" Doris finished.

Muriel made no answer to that, either.

I'd been assuming Harry had died from an overdose of oxycodone, either from his own hoard or with the aid of Diane's pill stash, but if the women had it right, he'd also used the plastic bag method to hasten his death. Well, it made sense.

Final Exit warned that regular users of opiates built up a tolerance, and might need a backup plan.

Final Exit also advised those who used the bag method and wanted the death to appear natural to have the helper remove the plastic bag afterward. It crossed my mind that Muriel might well have been the one who'd done this last service for Harry Silverman. It wasn't Judy, not if she'd been at the movies while it happened. . . . Suddenly I felt less friendly toward Judy Silverman.

"That group isn't still meeting, is it, Muriel?" A more conciliatory tone from Hairpins.

Muriel shrugged, waved a dismissive hand.

"Well, I think it went too far," Doris said. "Trying on plastic bags!"

"It was very educational, Doris," Plaid Blouse explained. "It's easy to believe you'd put an end to it if there was no hope, but five seconds with my head in a plastic bag was enough to change my mind. Sitting there for all the world like a turkey ready to go in the oven." She shuddered. "Very undignified."

Her voice was familiar. I closed my eyes, trying to place her, and realized she was a member of the Middle Ages book group. Lil, that was her name, Lillian Blau.

I didn't have to look to know Muriel was frowning. "Undignified! People are always talking about 'death with dignity'! Let me tell you, there's nothing dignified about death! It smells bad, it sounds bad, and it feels bad. Better to go while you're still able to make a choice than to force your children to cater to a foul-smelling heap of bones and bodily fluids."

Neither of her companions had anything to say to that.

I was surprised at her ferocity myself. I would have expected Muriel to espouse more New Age beliefs on the release of the soul. Her outburst carried the undertone of deep emotion that usually came from personal experience, and I wondered if her parents had died lingering deaths, at home, tended by Muriel.

"Where do ashtrays go?" someone addressed the room.

"Over there, that table by the pillar."

Talk about subliminal suggestibility. "Ashtray" brought me to "smoke."

The nice thing about cigarettes is that they give you an excuse to take a break. I decided my blurring eyes were just as good a reason, and stepped out the basement door for a taste of cold air. It had been in the fifties earlier, and I didn't bother with a jacket. The sky had lowered, however, along with the temperature. The smell in the air, impending moisture with a freshness about it, might have meant snow, but it was still early November.

Self-deliverance. I'm not a fan of euphemisms, although, as Benno says of stereotypes, they've gotten a bad rap. The word *suicide* has the connotation of a desperate act rather than a reasoned choice. Calling it self-deliverance made it sound like the end-of-life equivalent to home birth, with hospice nurses playing the midwives' role.

I wondered if they'd really tried on plastic bags in Issues of Later Life, and whether Susan had facilitated that particular exercise. It would certainly have been prudent for the nurse to be on hand, in case anything went wrong—had Diane been there? And how much did Vivian know about what the group had been up to?

I had to agree with Doris, things had gone too far. I didn't like where this was leading, not one little bit.

I walked the long way around the building to the front entrance, heading back to jewelry duty. When I stepped into the elevator, there was another passenger: Trudi, carrying a glass plate with a bundt cake swathed in plastic wrap.

"Are you joining us?" I asked. Judging by her outfit, a royal purple shirtwaist with a silk scarf in swirls of lavender and yellow tied around her neck, she wasn't exactly dressed to lend a hand with the grubby work of sorting secondhand junk.

The elevator doors bonged open in the basement. "No, I

don't get involved with the pricing. I will cashier tomorrow, but now I just bring a poppy-seed cake."

"It looks good." I was tempted to ask Trudi if she knew anything about all this *Final Exit* stuff. She was devoted to NAN and its good name, maybe she'd help me lay the nasty whispers to rest.

"It is." Trudi deposited her cake on the food table, and brushed past me to the appliance corner.

So much for that option. Well, I knew Muriel had been in the ILL group. I'd just ask her about it.

At the jewelry table, no one had picked up pricing in my brief absence. I asked Muriel if she could spare me a minute. She grumbled about leaving the linens, but she followed me to the far end of jewelry, where we'd have the most privacy.

"I wanted to ask you about a group that used to meet, Issues of Later Life?" No point in beating around the bush with Muriel.

"What about it?"

I had a neat cover story prepared. "While I was going through old newsletters, I saw a notice about it, but it's not still meeting, is it?"

"No."

She wasn't making this easy. "Well, I wondered if you know why the group was discontinued? I think it's a great topic. I'd like to offer something similar, and it would be helpful for me to know what happened so I could tailor a new version more closely to people's interests."

Muriel scowled at me. "I can't speak for the others who attended. I found it timely and pertinent, but I was in the minority. Susan Wu decided not to continue with it."

"A dollar?" Doris called. She held up a bag of embroidery floss so Muriel could see it.

"Two," Muriel told her, then turned back to me. "Was that all?"

"Would you be willing to meet with me next week to talk

about how we might make a group that would be more responsive to NAN's membership?"

Muriel scowled in the direction of the appliances, where Trudi had joined the lone male volunteer in the room. In his sixties maybe, still trim in jeans and a blue oxford shirt, he bent his head toward her, paying polite attention. Trudi rested her hand on his arm. Although his posture said she was too close, he stayed put.

"I don't think I want to be involved." Muriel turned back to me. "It would be better to ask Vivian about that particular group. Yes, Doris, I'm coming."

From anyone else, it would have been rude, but I was accustomed to Muriel's abrupt method of ending a conversation.

Trudi let go of the man's arm and picked up one of the throw pillows arrayed along the edge of the platform. She studied the needlepoint design, then glanced up and contemplated the women gathered around Muriel. As if she felt me noticing her, Trudi put the pillow down. With a wave for the woman slicing her cake at the food table, she left.

In her wake, I pricked my ears toward what the crones had to say about her.

"Poor Russ" was Doris's tart observation.

"Poor Russ nothing," Muriel said. "Now Grace is gone, he's free to pursue other interests."

"Muriel!" Lil pretended to be scandalized. "You don't mean he and Trudi—"

"Oh, don't I?" Muriel hefted a handful of brown yarn and stared meditatively at Russ. "He took good care of Grace, I'll grant you that, more than most men would have done for a wife with Alzheimer's. But you know she was quite a bit older, and if you want my opinion, her suicide was a convenient thing for him. He was ready to put her in a home."

"Wasn't Russ Corbo in that group, Muriel?" Doris inquired. "Trudi, you know, Trudi's mother was a good friend of theirs. They used to play bridge together. Do you think he and Trudi—"

"I have no idea. Russ has some good years ahead of him, and don't think la divorcée Voss is the only one who's taken notice." Muriel jerked her head toward the appliances.

Indeed, Russ was no longer alone; a heavyset woman with light brown hair and a musical voice had joined him. Russ gestured at a row of steam irons. The woman put a hand to her throat, laughed, held his gaze. Flirtation, recognizable at any age.

"Grace to Faith—a neat transition," Lil observed. "What should we do with all these buttons?"

She took the top off a shoebox and gave it a shake. I took the rattle of loose buttons as my cue to go over and inspect a potential treasure. Mostly plastic, from the 1950s by the look of the cards some of them were still sewn on, but right up my alley. I took the whole box.

Corbo. Another name on Mr. Neville's list, not the man with Alzheimer's, obviously, so a file I hadn't yet read. Had Russ taken his wife to the ILL group, where they'd tried on plastic bags?

Euthanasia cult, indeed. The germ of rumor was sprouting all too quickly for my taste.

22

A T three o'clock, I took some comp time and went to the doctor with Barbara. One thing about a small agency, it's easy to flex the schedule. I'd be working at the flea market over the weekend anyway, which would be a pleasure.

Unlike where I was going.

Dr. Andras was in the 1090 building, on Amsterdam across from St. Luke's, where half the medical practices in the neighborhood seem to have their offices. It's a cheerless place, the public areas strictly utilitarian: dark linoleum floors and land-lady-green walls with no attempt at decoration, the elevators small, slow, and creaky.

The doctor's waiting room was no better, a grim little space with four nubbly upholstered chairs that looked comfortable but were too low and too soft for elderly or aching patients to rise from easily. An end table held an unlikely assortment of magazines—*Newsweek* to *W*—in two sliding piles. A window on an airshaft did what it could for an unhappy begonia.

The receptionist stayed bent over her computer as we entered. Barbara sank into one of the low chairs and handed me her insurance card and a $10 bill for the copayment. We were the only patients. The room was loud with the clicking of fake nails on the keyboard. I stood and waited for attention.

From the back, all I could see was that the tapping nails were bright red, with a diagonal slash of black and a line of sparkly dots on the left ring finger. I had no idea if the receptionist was black, Hispanic, or something in between. Her skin was light brown, and her shoulder-length black hair had been processed into a cascade of curls.

When she eventually turned to me, with a glance over at Barbara on the way, we got more of a welcome greeting than I'd expected. "Ms. Baker! I didn't realize it was you coming in."

Barbara raised her eyebrows in a "yeah, right" expression and introduced me. "Connie, this is my friend Anita."

Connie. No trace of an accent, and the name gave no clue to her origins.

It's one of the things I like best about New York, how you can never tell where a person is from by appearances alone. Myself, when I've got a summer tan, I'm frequently mistaken for Dominican. Hispanic gentlemen of a certain age tend to make approving comments on my figure, in Spanish. I'm enough of a New Yorker by now to walk on without deigning to acknowledge I've even heard let alone understood what they've said. I prefer the way the *abuelitas* mistake me for one of their own and look to me for protection crossing the streets.

I handed over Barbara's card and cash.

Connie thanked me and hit a button on her phone. "I'll tell Dr. Andras you're here, he should be with you in a moment."

At my HMO, the seats are always packed, and waits of over an hour are common. Things at Dr. Andras's office seemed to run so smoothly that he never had patients stacked up. Five minutes with the magazines, and we were in.

Barbara had a litany of small ailments and complaints. Her palms and the soles of her feet had turned a sooty black color, like coal dust, that didn't wash off. Her urine smelled bad, and she spent half the day on the toilet. Sometimes the pain in her side was so intense she couldn't stand straight.

Dr. Andras leaned forward in his chair, his elbows on the desk, hands steepled together with his chin resting on his fingertips. Today's starched shirt was oxford blue.

"For the pain, I can provide an oral supplement, OxyFast, a few drops directly on your tongue as needed. The discoloration is caused by the chemotherapy. It's not serious, but since it bothers you, there is something that will counteract it." He put the glasses back on, consulted a loose-leaf binder, and wrote out two prescriptions. "This medication may cause a tingling in your hands and feet."

"What?" I said. "The cure might be as bad as—" I stopped. Yeah, that's about the size of modern medicine. Sick? Side effects? We'll give you something to make you feel worse before the symptoms go away on their own, and then you'll feel so much better by comparison.

Dr. Andras shrugged and went into an explanation of the experimental chemo Barbara was on, how different people responded differently. It made sense, in the way that Western medicine's slash/burn/poison approach does. What do you do when there are no options? Accept the experimental alternative and take it one day at a time.

Barbara brought him back to the situation at hand and asked if the odor in her urine was also a side effect. Good thinking, I told her silently. That was theoretically what I was there for, to keep her from being distracted by doctor-speak.

"Yes, the urine. You may have a bladder infection. Why don't you give me a sample, and we'll send it to the lab." He left the room for a moment, returning with a paper cup and a small plastic vial with a white snap-on cap.

With Barbara in the lavatory, I took the opportunity to see if he'd tell me anything he hadn't told her. "How is she really doing?"

And got the predictable answer. "About as well as I expected. It's not an easy disease. If there's anything she wants to do, she should do it soon."

"How soon?"

"I'd say in the next month or so. As I've said, I'll make a referral for hospice care whenever Ms. Baker feels it's time."

When Barbara came back and lowered herself into the chair, Dr. Andras's next remark, in spite of the compassion in his eyes, made it clear he was done with us.

"We should have the results on Monday. You can call the office, and if the culture is positive, I'll phone in a prescription for you."

"Monday?" I asked.

Dr. Andras stood up. "Yes. It's too late for the lab to do anything today, and they don't work on the weekend."

Assuming the test was positive, that meant three more days with an infected bladder. It seemed like a long time for anyone to go untreated, let alone a woman with liver cancer, and I said so.

Dr. Andras frowned at me, but give the man credit, he considered my objection. "Well, there is a preliminary test I can do right here. It's not proof, but perhaps—excuse me, please, I will be right back."

Barbara and I looked at each other, exchanging a question that didn't need to be spoken: How come he didn't think of that himself? A whole weekend—it wasn't right. I didn't want to think he was treating Barbara differently than any other patient, but expecting her to wait like that—and then when I spoke up, suddenly there was a solution?

I don't go mining for racism in every casual comment, but since I've become the white mother of a black child, I do pay more attention. To examine every interaction, to develop the kind of radar that lets you know when you're being deliberately slighted . . . it was something I profoundly hoped I would not have to teach my child.

Barbara may have shrugged it off, but I experienced the

sting of Dr. Andras's behavior as if it had been my face he'd slapped.

He was back with results in two minutes flat. "There were some white cells in your sample. Although it is not definitive, I think we had better start treatment." He wrote out another prescription and handed it over.

Barbara thanked him. I wouldn't have been so gracious, but then, I hadn't had a lifetime to practice turning fury into the deadly sweet politeness she larded her words with.

In the elevator, Barbara clutched my arm and held on. She took short, deep breaths to keep the pain under control. I matched my breathing to hers and bore the weight as she leaned on me.

Two floors down, we were joined by a young man on crutches, his right leg in a cast from ankle to mid-thigh. A round woman who came up to his elbow was lecturing him nonstop in a language that was neither English nor Spanish.

The teenager hung his head and let it wash over him.

When mother and son were out of earshot on the side-walk, Barbara tried a joke. "It could be worse. I could have my mother riding me, and a broken leg so I can't walk away from her."

"There is that." I forced a laugh. If her mother were alive, Barbara'd take all the hectoring she could dish out.

23

ocusts was an accurate description of the horde that showed up Saturday morning for the flea. When I got to the Estates at nine, a full hour before the doors would open, thirty people were already waiting outside. It had rained in the night, but luckily for them the temperature was in the fifties and the sky looked to be clearing.

At five to ten, Vivian shooed us into our places and reminded us of the rules.

No bargaining; if anyone insisted, send them to her. Keep our eyes peeled for people pocketing things, and alert the security guard at the door rather than confront the miscreant directly. All items to be paid for at the cashiers, except jewelry, which had its own cashier. If an item had no price, we were free to make one up on the spot.

As the swarm filled the recreation room and settled around the tables, the resemblance was more to magpies than locusts, or even better, to pigs rooting for truffles. In ten minutes flat, my artful arrangements of pins and earrings were in chaos. The tchotchke table looked like an earthmover had plowed its way through, tossing everything up in its wake. The neatly stacked linens were a rag pile. The volunteers did their best, rearranging, refolding, reordering their wares. It was an uphill task.

I'd been assigned to pitch in wherever necessary, and to empty the cash boxes periodically so that the cashiers wouldn't have to be responsible for more than a hundred dollars at any time.

Robbery wasn't a real concern, with an Estates security guard at the entrance and people all around; it was more a matter of not wanting to take chances. Vivian had provided me with a money belt to wear strapped under my sweatshirt. Every few hours, I was supposed to unload the contents of the belt in the NAN office.

The ace cashiers, Addie Collins and Trudi Voss, had the busy first shift. By one, when the crowd of purchasers had thinned out a bit, I had close to $3,000 in the pouch. Trudi's replacement showed up first, so I transferred all but $50 out of her cash box.

Out of her work attire, in black slacks and a heather blue Fair Isle sweater, Trudi seemed more approachable. Appearances were deceiving, however. My attempt at conversation about the morning's take got no more than a brief response. I might like her, but I clearly hadn't earned the privilege of being admitted to Trudi's inner circle.

Diane McClellan, with a cut-glass vase and two brass candleholders, was the last one to pay in Addie's line before I emptied her cashbox for the new cashier. Diane had resisted visiting the sale to put anything aside before it was open to the public—a scrupulousness I didn't share.

I contemplated inviting Trudi and Diane to lunch. While I was busy with Addie, however, Trudi disappeared. Then I saw that Diane was having her ear bent by Muriel.

So much for making nice with my colleagues. I pulled my sweatshirt down to conceal the money belt, which was now uncomfortably bulky against my stomach, and headed upstairs. The Saturday video had been canceled, since all the volunteers were busy with the flea market. Expecting the NAN office to be locked and alarmed, I had my keys in my hand.

It didn't occur to me to be nervous with all that cash on me until I heard the thud of the lobby's metal door close behind me and I was alone in the short hallway outside NAN. Up to that point, I'd been surrounded by people. The light in the hall seemed gloomy in contrast to the fluorescent-lit recreation room. It was much too quiet for a lone woman packing $3,000 on her person.

Nonsense, I told myself. It's one o'clock in the afternoon, in a safe, well-guarded apartment complex, and nothing bad will happen to you.

Nevertheless, my brain was on alert, a city person's precaution when alone in a semi-public place in poor light. I put the round key in the alarm and glanced back over my shoulder. There was no one there, which soothed my nerves. I unlocked the lower lock, pushed the door open, stepped over the wide handicap saddle, and turned to shut the door behind me.

At least I thought I did.

I had the sensation of being horizontal rather than vertical, in a dark void, weightless yet heavy, my body moving without volition. Rolled onto my back, then back to my stomach and left that way.

Something metallic clicked above me, followed by hurrying footsteps. Another metal-on-metal sound; the hall door closing. I got my eyes open. The blackness in front of me tilted. Afraid I'd slide off, nothing to hold on to, I closed my eyes.

That was worse. I was in free fall, stars swirling around me. Benno's the one who wants to travel in space, I thought, so why is it me all alone out here?

"Houston, we have a problem," I whispered.

"Damn straight we have a problem." I knew that voice, and it wasn't mission control. A hand supported my cheek, an arm under my waist flipped me belly up. "Anita! Do you hear me? Anita, earth to Anita!"

I didn't like being on my back. I curled involuntarily into a fetal position. This was earth, definitely. I retched.

Nothing came up. A hand patted my back.

"Is she all right?" A woman's voice. Anne?

"All right enough to try puking on me. Better luck next time, kid."

"Michael?" I opened my eyes. Yup, Michael and Anne. A blanket drifted down and covered me. The equator of my immediate world resolved itself to the joint between the black linoleum floor and the baseboard.

"What am I doing in the hall?" I thought I said it out loud, but the voices paid no attention.

"Looks like she got conked on the head." Fingers probed the scalp under my bun. "Got a bruise starting on her forehead, too."

"Ouch!"

The fingers were replaced by something soft. I let my head rest on it before I could name what the object was. Pillow. Oh, oh. Pill-Oh. The word pounded at the back of my head.

"I'm calling nine-one-one," Anne said.

I grabbed for her pant leg. "No."

Nothing like the threat of a ride in an ambulance to make a girl feel better. I tried to sit up, but four hands held me down.

"You've got a nasty bump here, Anita. You should see a doctor," Michael supported Anne.

"Am I bleeding?"

That seemed to be a negative.

"Can we just hold off a few minutes, please?"

"What's your name? Do you know where you are? What day is it? Who's the president?" Michael shot me the standard mental-status questions.

"I'm on the freaking floor, what does it look like?" Idiots, I was surrounded by idiots. "It's Saturday, and no one in the whole damn country knows who the president is."

"Oh, yeah, she's gonna live."

"Damn straight," I told him. Then I remembered the money. I scrabbled at the bottom of my sweatshirt, trying to get it up over my stomach.

No surprise there, Sherlock. It was gone.

Anne softened up an ice pack and slid it under my head. At least the internal blood drummers took a break. In their absence, I remembered a tickle of hands fumbling at my waist.

"I was robbed," I told Michael.

"Yeah, you and Al Gore."

"No, I mean it. I had the cash from this morning in a pouch around my waist."

That got him interested. "Tell me what happened."

"I'm not sure." I wasn't. I looked around the hall. "I thought I unlocked the door and went in, but then everything just—" I wiped a hand through the air in front of my face. "Blacked out."

"You don't remember being hit?"

"No." This time I made it to sitting. It wasn't so bad.

Michael squatted next to me and pressed the ice pack to the back of my head. That was better. I put up a hand to hold the pack in place myself.

"I had about three thousand dollars on me."

"We should call the police," Anne said.

"I am the police." Michael reached into his jacket, fumbled out a cell phone. "Yeah, yeah, I know I'm off. Don't get your undies in a bundle, I'm calling the precinct. It's a mugging, the uniforms can take a report."

"Can I get off the floor now?" I asked.

Anne helped me up. The blood drained to my feet, lending them the solidity to walk into the office, where Anne settled me on the floor again with my feet elevated. After applying a second ice pack to the bump on my forehead, she took off downstairs for reinforcements. Diane McClellan could try persuading me to be sensible, but there was no chance she'd succeed—I knew the inside of St. Luke's ER all too well.

Michael contented himself with pacing around the office while he waited for the troops.

I rolled onto my side and closed my eyes. Maybe a little nap would clear my brain.

But it didn't last long. Diane checked my blood pressure—130 over 85, nice and normal—palpated the lump on my head, asked the same questions as Michael, offered the same advice as Anne: A blow to the head was nothing to fool with, and I should go to the hospital.

I gave them a line about how many concussions Steve Young had suffered and still went back on the field to quarterback for the 49ers.

"Yeah, right," Michael muttered. "All those hits knocked the sense out of him. Besides, they never let Young go back into the same game. He had to be CAT-scanned and rest a week."

I appealed to Diane. "I was only out a few minutes. I'm alert and oriented, my speech isn't slurred, I'm not seeing double, and my pressure is fine. If I rest and my husband monitors me for twenty-four hours, there's no problem, right?"

"In my medical opinion, Anita, you should be examined by a doctor. You could have a hairline fracture—"

Saved by the uniforms. Diane kept her long fingers on my wrist while Michael filled the cops in on what had happened. I fought the urge to close my eyes and drift off while the cackle of voices flapped like a flock of disturbed pigeons in the air above me.

Anne made another trip down to the flea to find Benno and, at Michael's suggestion, Vivian Brownell. After all, it was NAN's money that had been stolen.

By the time Vivian joined us, I was finished reciting my story, what there was of it, for the cops, a sensible, middle-aged black woman who introduced herself as Officer Runyon, and a young white guy with an unpronounceable name full of

*K*s and Zs, who deferred to her. I left out the part about thinking I'd opened the door and gone into the office. Too confusing, and I wasn't at all positive that I'd actually done it.

Vivian started into the living room with her usual aplomb, then stopped abruptly at the sight of me on the floor, Runyon kneeling on one side, Diane seated cross-legged on the other.

The color in Vivian's face faded, and she swayed backward. Anne guided her to a chair.

Diane was on her feet in one limber motion, checking Vivian's pulse, ready to whip out the blood pressure cuff again. Vivian shooed her away.

"I'm all right, I'm all right. What happened here?"

I let Anne tell the story this time.

"You were by yourself, Anita? With how much money?" Vivian tried to dial down the anger in her voice. "You were supposed to ask security for an escort. Carrying that amount of cash—"

"You didn't tell me that," I accused her right back. Never argue with the boss, I could hear Benno thinking it as clearly as if he'd been there. But she *hadn't*.

Had she? It didn't matter, I should have thought of it myself. All that money!

"I'm so sorry, Vivian. All the work everyone put in, and—" I sat up.

"The money," Vivian said it with a sigh, and shook her head absently. She'd looked mad enough a minute ago to fire me on the spot. Now her attention seemed to be somewhere other than in the room with all of us.

I felt like an idiot. I was an idiot. Broad daylight, isn't that always when it happens? Night, alone, your guard is up. One o'clock in the afternoon, blindsided by overconfidence.

From the way her questions went, Officer Runyon had much the same opinion: It was my own damn fault.

And she hammered on the other question I'd been asking myself and hadn't come up with a satisfactory answer to. Who knew I had the flea market proceeds on me? Who saw me come upstairs?

Everyone and no one, were the short answers. Any number of people had seen me taking money from the cashiers during the morning, but I definitely hadn't told anyone I was heading up to NAN to unload it.

My brain was starting to kick in. "I did actually think about asking the guard to walk me upstairs." I spoke mostly to Vivian. "Then I decided it would be just as well to be casual about it, and not draw attention to myself."

You could have erected a circus tent on all the raised eyebrows that greeted my explanation.

"Yes, it was stupid," I acknowledged. "But the last thing I expected was to get mugged!"

"Obviously," Runyon said, heavy on the sarcasm. Her knees cracked when she stood. "Guess we'd better have a look at this flea market. Do you remember anyone in particular who was there when you got into the elevator?"

I'd seen so many people, all morning long, coming and going. To focus on that last time I'd left the recreation room—"I think there were several older women just going in, not anyone I recognized as clients or volunteers. The security guard, Cummings." I decided not to mention the home attendant he'd been flirting with, a lovely woman who freelanced for several residents. I'd seen her with Cummings before, the two of them billing and cooing at various spots while he made his rounds in the Estates.

"Diane was there when I collected the last of the cash, and of course the cashiers—Addie Collins and Trudi Voss. I think they left right away when the next shift came on?" I looked to Diane for corroboration.

She nodded. "Yes. Muriel Dodge stopped me as I was leaving, and we went back in for a cup of coffee. I remember seeing you go out, Anita."

A nod from Runyon was enough for Kzykz to take Diane

aside to get the names of everyone she could remember who'd been in the area at the time.

Then Benno and Clea joined the party, precipitating another discussion of a trip to the hospital.

Clea sat next to me, stroking my arm, and took my side.

"Mama just needs to go home." She put all the authority a ten-year-old could muster and then some into her voice. It stopped the adult discussion raging over me. "We could take her in a taxi." Softer this time, not wanting to step on grown-up toes and be told off for being fresh.

I appealed silently to Benno: Get me out of here.

God bless him, he did.

24

By Sunday afternoon, other than an extreme tenderness when I brushed my hair, the headache was gone. I felt terrible about the stolen money. It crossed my mind to offer to repay it—an idea Benno quickly quashed. No way were we coming up with a spare three thou.

Then I wanted to head back to the Estates and help close up the flea market; it seemed like the least I could do to make amends. Benno nixed that idea, too, flat out refusing to let me out of the house, let alone participate in anything as strenuous as packing boxes for donation to Harlem Restoration, the thrift shop of choice for unsold items. I made a strong enough case for the elderly people needing some younger muscle, however, that he offered to go in my place.

"And take Clea with you?" If I wasn't going to work, I might as well have some peace to watch football. Yes, the Jets were tanking, but the Giants were starting to make a good run.

Clea didn't even grumble; I've failed to instill a love of the game in her. "A bunch of guys start running, then they all fall down" was her assessment of football.

I stretched out on the couch to catch the last quarter of a Buffalo-Patriots game I only cared about because they were both Jets divisional rivals. It was a foregone conclusion in favor of Buffalo. I turned the volume down and opened the City section of the *Times*.

Between the hissing radiator and the sun flooding in from our south windows, I felt swaddled in heat. Nothing in the paper held my interest.

I found myself making home visits, transported from one apartment to the next like jump cuts in a movie. At each stop I asked the same question: Why did you do it?

Harry Silverman lay in a hospital bed, his skin yellow as a lemon against the bleached sheets, his arms crossed on his chest, a huge white lily clasped in one hand. "This is the country of the old," he said.

I went closer, meaning to lay a hand on his shoulder. He lifted the lily and shook it twice, warning me to stay back. A dust of vivid orange pollen fell from the anthers, spotting the blanket.

I knocked on Lucille Dolan's door with my keys. The waves of metal-on-metal sound spread through her apartment. I pushed the door open and found Lucille on the floor, her face green and melting. When I asked my question, she went up in a puff of smoke, cackling, "You'll never know, my pretty, you'll never know."

The Stringers were in bed together, naked and holding hands, with a flowered sheet covering them to the waist. Thank heaven for small favors, I thought, about to leave them their privacy. Ora pointed an admonishing finger at me. "Hold your horses, young woman. If you'd loved me, I'd still be alive."

The last visit I made was to Susan, who sat lotus-style in Katsu's crib. She favored me with an enigmatic look and answered my question with another: "Don't you think it's time you woke up?"

As abruptly as if she'd snapped her fingers, I did. The sun

had traveled behind the building across the street, draining light and heat from the room. I was cold, and I needed to pee.

Emptying a full bladder is one of the best bodily sensations, right up there with taking off a bra at the end of the day.

My personal source of wisdom, Bob Dylan lyrics, advised me not to try to shovel a glimpse into the ditch of what the dream meant.

Blue Monday's weather did nothing to raise my spirits. The whole world was gray, the sky low and overcast, the big apartment buildings of Riverside Drive looming like bullies over the sidewalk. After I dropped Clea at school, I forced myself to cross over and walk through the park. The workfare crews in their charmless navy coveralls swept up the last of the leaves. The trees stretched dark limbs that met overhead in a tangled canopy, a grim tunnel through which I headed to my fate.

I was worried that Vivian would fire me. Losing such a substantial sum of money was not something to be glossed over, and with less than a month on the job, I had absolutely no security. I could be sent packing immediately, with no notice, and no reason given.

And if I stayed on—well, I knew how rumors spread in the small-town atmosphere of the Estates. What if people thought I faked the robbery and took the money myself? That could blow the fragile sense of trust I'd begun to develop with the NAN regulars right out of the water. Even more insidiously, people might hold me responsible even though to my face they reassured me it wasn't my fault. Either way, I'd be too compromised to be effective.

By the time I got to the Bread Shop for my coffee to go, I'd come to the realization that offering to quit was the only honorable course open to me. I didn't like the idea; it would be as financially hard for us to do without my salary as it would have been to cough up the money as restitution. Still, I'd been derelict in my duty, and cost NAN $3,000. The least

I could do was relieve Vivian of the need to let me go, and tender my own resignation.

What Anne had to say when I arrived at NAN strengthened my intentions.

"Anita, are you sure you should be here? I think Vivian expected you to take a few days off, and I was hoping—" Anne put a hand over her mouth to shut herself up.

"Hoping what?" I asked.

She tried to distract me by pointing out a pot of rusty orange mums wrapped in gold foil, accompanied by a "best wishes" card signed by several names I recognized from among the flea market volunteers. Four other envelopes had been slid under the door, all with cards conveying similar sentiments, and there'd been several messages on the answering machine from people asking after my health.

I allowed myself to be cheered up, but I didn't let her off the hook.

"Come on, Anne, spit it out. What's going on?"

She hemmed and hawed some more before admitting that she'd heard Vivian and—"I don't want to name names, because you still have to work with her, but a certain person was pressing Vivian to fire you. I was hoping you'd stay home a day or two so all this talk about letting you go 'for the good of the organization' would have time to die down. I'm sure they'll come to their senses and realize what's good for NAN is to keep functioning, and they need you to do that."

Anne wasn't happy to hear about my plan to fall on my sword.

"I know you feel responsible, but I don't think you should be worried about the money, Anita. If the amount of mail we've been getting from the fund-raising drive is any indication, NAN isn't hurting. And come on—it's not like you to let one old crab run you off. Seriously, that woman has a problem. I've never worked with anyone so fussy."

"Trudi Voss thinks I should be fired?" It had to be. Along with Vivian, Trudi was the person who took NAN's interests most to heart, especially when it came to finances. Of course she'd see the loss of even a relatively negligible sum as a firing offense.

No matter how much I liked prickly Trudi, or even how much she liked me, in her book NAN came first, and a mistake was a mistake. It was exactly the reaction my grandmother would have had. Of all the people I'd let down, Trudi was the one I most hated to disappoint.

I closed the door on Anne's protests and went to my desk. It might be my last day on the job, and I wanted to thank my well-wishers for their concern. They weren't easy calls to make.

As it turned out, all my noble resolve was absurd. Vivian, it seemed, had had opposing worries of her own over the weekend: She was afraid that the mugging would terrorize me into quitting. She absolutely refused to hear more than a word of my offer to resign before turning it down flat.

"NAN needs you, Anita. We do not hold you responsible for what happened." Vivian practically wrung her hands. I was touched.

"I would understand, of course, if you felt you couldn't continue on here because you felt it was too dangerous, but I assure you, this was an isolated incident. I've spoken with Mr. Neville, and he's already increased security in the Estates as a whole."

So it wound up with me graciously agreeing to stay on, without having to admit that it hadn't even occurred to me to be scared off by a mere bump on the head. Even Benno, the chief safety enforcer of our household, hadn't been worried about me being at risk of another attack.

Anne had just shepherded Vivian into the smaller office to start scheduling interviews for the executive director's position when the doorbell rang. I answered it myself, expecting the absentminded Olive to be sorry to bother me. What I got instead was Lil, the woman in the plaid blouse who'd been talking to Muriel during the flea market preparations. She handed me a small Macy's shopping bag packed with crumpled newspapers and a thermos.

Homemade chicken soup. "I heard you got mugged. I don't know if you bring your own lunch, but you try this. You have to keep your strength up. We need a good social worker around here."

Before I could manage a proper thank-you, she was off.

My next visitor, not surprisingly, was Mr. Neville.

Although he brought no flowers, he was solicitous about my well-being. "Ah, Mrs. Servi, I am relieved to see you were not injured so seriously as to have stayed at home. You are fully recovered?"

"I guess I've got a thick skull." I held the door open, not sure if he was making a real visit or just wanted to set eyes on me himself.

"May I, ah, may I come in?"

That answered that. "Of course."

Several plates of baked goods, swathed in copious amounts of plastic wrap, had been left on the counter. I offered Mr. Neville a cup of coffee, which he accepted, and something to go with it. "Chocolate chip cookie, poppy-seed cake, brownie, or apple square?"

"Ah yes, the ladies who bake. I will take a small piece of cake, if you don't mind."

I went for a chocolate chip cookie, myself. It was almost the size of a small paper plate.

We sat in the same places as we had on Neville's first visit to me at NAN. Then, his bulk had seemed solid, assured, filling the chair. This morning he was more tentative, moving in his seat like he couldn't get comfortable.

"I, ah, I understand Detective Dougherty was at the scene of the, ah, the unfortunate occurrence." He held the plate of cake balanced on his knees.

Of course, the old cops network. I nodded.

"Mrs. Servi, I must apologize for my staff. The man on duty should *not* have let you come upstairs unescorted."

I assured him it was my own stupidity, not the guard's fault.

That didn't make Neville sit any more easily in his armchair. "Yes, well, no, perhaps. I am responsible for the safety of the Estates, for all who set foot here, and an attack such as this is not acceptable. I have read the police report. If you don't mind going through it again, I'd like to hear what happened for myself."

I had no problem with that. Neville not only had a cop's training and experience, he also had an insider's knowledge of the Estates and its resident miscreants.

And he was much more interested than the officers on the scene had been in the issue of where exactly I'd been standing when I was hit.

Going through it again, the one thing I felt sure of was that there hadn't been anyone behind me in the hall. I'm enough of a New Yorker to have developed stranger-radar, the sixth sense that alerts you when you're not alone. No way I wouldn't have heard the door from the lobby open, or noticed someone lurking in the hall—not that there was anywhere to hide.

So either the mugger had managed to rush me in the seconds between when I unlocked the door and turned to close it, which I didn't think was possible, or he'd been waiting inside the office.

"If I had to swear to it in court, I'm not positive, but I think I was turning to close the door behind me, and that my forehead banged into the door when I went down." I closed my eyes and tried to see it. "I have this sensory memory of being dragged, too, but whether that's real or I've just imagined it, I honestly don't know."

When I opened my eyes, Neville appeared to be stifling an urge to laugh out loud.

"What? You think I'm making it up?"

"No, no, not at all, not at all. I was admiring your technique of recollection. I've noticed it's very effective when television detectives ask their witnesses to close their eyes, and now I see that it works in actuality also." He was definitely amused.

I wasn't. It was hard enough trying to get it straight in my own mind without being twitted about it. "So is there anything else I can invent for you?" I asked.

Which got me a stumble of apologies, and a bit of explanation. According to Neville, Anne had been positive that when she went to get the ice pack, she'd had to unlock the door *and* turn off the alarm. If I'd been mugged inside the office, and found outside in the hall—

It meant that the person who'd ambushed me had keys to NAN. Which narrowed the pool of possible suspects considerably. Sure, plenty of people had keys to NAN, but plenty was still a finite number, and they could all be checked out.

I rattled off the names of everyone I could think of who legitimately had NAN keys—Vivian Brownell, Trudi Voss, Diane McClellan, the video volunteers passed a set around, I had one, there was a set hanging in the Security office, Anne Reisen.

The taking of information seemed to satisfy Neville; a slight, contented smile made brief appearances in the corners of his mouth. Not surprising, I supposed, that he missed police work. Up until now, the Estates had posed no particular challenge, and as Michael'd said, the old man was bored.

"Thank you for your help, Mrs. Servi. You have my word, I will see that the person who perpetrated this theft and assault is identified and charged." Neville leaned forward and set his plate on the coffee table. "There is the, ah, other matter."

Neville glanced toward the door, making sure no one was there. He lowered his voice anyway. "In light of our conversation regarding the spate of recent deaths here in the Estates, I, ah, I wanted to say that I have perhaps allowed myself to be distracted from my responsibility here, which is the personal safety of our residents. I would appreciate it if you would put my previous concern on that subject out of your mind."

Without meeting my eyes, Neville levered himself out of the chair, thanked me for the coffee and the cake he'd barely tasted, and took himself off.

I dumped the cold coffee from our mugs into the sink. Okay, I could leave the attack on me to the law-enforcement professionals. What I couldn't do was forget about the too-many Estates residents who'd died in the past months.

For all Neville said he'd shifted his attention away from those deaths, I didn't believe him. A dog may drop an old bone for a new one, but he doesn't forget where it's buried. There were still old case files to read, and I badly needed to find someone willing to talk about what exactly had gone on in the ILL group.

It occurred to me that I could've asked Lil about it. She'd attended the meetings, and seemed somewhat ambivalent about the experience. If she hadn't been in such a hurry, and I'd had my wits more about me . . . Well, Muriel had pointed me to a source of information closer at hand. Although I still wasn't feeling any too secure in my position—Trudi carried a lot of weight on the NAN board—I took the chance.

Vivian was no more eager to discuss Issues of Later Life than Muriel had been, but she did let loose with a few facts.

"The group met for approximately two months. Susan intended it initially as a forum to discuss practical issues, such as health care proxies, as well as the more psychological adjustments inherent in the aging process."

I gave her an A for jargon. "Why was the group discontinued?"

"It proved to be somewhat—controversial. Our residents can be quite opinionated."

Now there was an understatement.

"Several people violently disagreed with what they termed 'the namby-pamby view of accomplished elders' put forth by Betty Friedan—Susan began the group with Friedan's book on aging—and they felt the group should confront the main issue of later life, death. The core of NAN's philosophy is that older people themselves should determine what services and activities we provide, so Susan allowed the group to take its own direction. When it became apparent that there was a good deal of dissension among the participants, Susan felt it best to call a halt to the entire enterprise."

"Susan led the group herself?"

"Given the sensitive subject material, Susan served as facilitator for the first few meetings, and continued to attend after the group members took charge. Why are you interested in this, Anita?"

I gave her the same story I'd worked up for Muriel, about wondering whether it might be worthwhile to revive the group in some altered incarnation.

Vivian's response to that was as negative as Muriel's.

"Did you attend the group yourself?" I sidestepped.

"No. As a rule, I don't have time to participate in NAN's recreational programs."

I made an effort to phrase my next words as an open-ended question. "I've heard that after Friedan, the group read a book put out by the Hemlock Society, *Final Exit?* And that some people were interested in exploring the issue of self-deliverance?"

What I got in answer was an extremely appraising look. If I'd been a prospective donor to her congressman, I had no doubt Vivian would've calculated to the minute how much time I'd need with the man, and to the penny how much I'd contribute for the privilege.

Since there was no such quid pro quo involved in our exchange, I thought she was simply going to turn away without replying.

"I see you have a talent for winning the confidence of our residents, Anita." Said with a smile that almost made me miss the frost in her next sentence. "I agreed completely with Susan's decision to terminate the group, and as I said, reviving it is not appropriate."

Dis-missed! Off with you and your questions!

25

I HAVE a ritual to accompany *Monday Night Football*—ironing. It allows me to be productive while I waste time in front of the tube, and now that I was working again, I had to keep up with my wardrobe. Benno got bored and went to bed at halftime. By then I'd done enough blouses to get me through another week.

I was still stiff from the fall. Standing at the ironing board hadn't helped any, so I decided to apply my grandmother's remedy for sore muscles, a tub of hot water with Epsom salts. For reading material while I soaked, I picked up *Amsterdam*, by Ian McEwan. It had been on my list of books to be read, and when I'd seen it lying on Susan's desk in the apartment, Katsu had let me take it home. There was a bookmark stuck about halfway in, and the thought that Susan might have been reading it before she died had kept me from starting it sooner.

I spent thirty pages in the tub and felt like a new woman. Wrapped in my terry-cloth robe, I stretched out on the couch and went back to *Amsterdam*. I'd saved my place with the same bookmark Susan had been using, a long slip of pale orange paper printed with the logo and address of Papyrus, the bookstore around the corner. This time, when I took it out to slide into the back half of the book, I noticed writing on the blank side.

In Susan's small, neat printing, so familiar to me from the endless progress notes in the client files, was a list of names.

Eight of them, then a thin horizontal dividing line, then four more. Twelve. Six were followed by numbers in the thousands, ranging from one to fifty.

I snuck into the bedroom to retrieve my purse. Benno snored right through the squeak of the door hinges and the hammer beat in my chest. I took the envelope from Neville to the couch.

I knew I was right even before I unfolded the note. All the names above the line were also on his list. And all of them were dead.

No way was this a coincidence.

Which meant Susan must've had the same suspicions as Neville. Or that she knew something about how these particular individuals had met their deaths.

Deaths. The phantom file name from the disc drive of Susan's computer.

Of the four names below the line, three belonged to people who'd died recently: Stringer, Dolan, and Silverman. The final name was Patterson. As in, Olive sorry-to-bother-you Patterson? Who as far as I knew was still among the living.

Wait a minute. When Susan had written those names on her bookmark, all the people below the line were still alive—so what were their names doing there?

Above the line, below the line. The dead and the living. The living beginning to die. Had Susan known they were planning their own deaths?

My chest felt tight just thinking about it. I picked up *Amsterdam* and tapped the book with my fingers, like a medium hoping for a message from beyond.

I turned my attention to the numbers. They were too big

to be dosages; those would've been given either in number of pills, 40, 50, or followed by amounts, gm, mg.

Follow the money. It came out of the ether. My subconscious, speaking in clichés.

Next to Stringer, Susan had written "50,000." Extrapolating from the fact that they'd willed $50,000 to NAN, let's assume the numbers referred to bequests. I did some quick addition. Eighty-four thousand dollars. A nice little nest egg to hatch into NAN's endowment fund.

I was impressed. Lucille Dolan and her millions notwithstanding, most retired people in the Estates got by on social security and pensions. A thousand dollars, okay, that was a generous gift. Silverman, now, Silverman was down for five thou. A hefty chunk of change by anyone's standards.

Well, with donations, you give what you want.

Sure, Vivian was actively soliciting testamentary contributions, but NAN and Susan had to be doing a hell of a lot right to inspire gifts of that size.

I mean, I've had clients offer me stuff like a decades-old bottle of Cuban rum, Chanel No. 22 in its original box, unworn silk scarves, the odd twenty-dollar bill, tchotchkes from painted wooden eggs to cut-glass ashtrays. And that's only the items I might've been tempted by, as opposed to plastic tissue-box covers, ancient tins of tea, stale cookies, a moth-eaten fox stole.

Susan must have been providing an extraordinary level of service to inspire that much concrete appreciation. I closed my eyes and let the sums dance around in my head. Come on, Anita, get real. What social service is worth five thousand dollars, let alone fifty?

I opened my eyes and swore.

The answer was appallingly obvious.

Deliverance. Release. A final exit, the ultimate service.

Those pill bottles stashed in Diane's office, one of which had come from Dorothy Norris's apartment. On the list, she was down for four thousand. And Diane had lied about retrieving the medication, even though I'd seen her do it.

All those people dead.

Not to mention Susan herself.

I wanted a cigarette so badly, I almost got dressed and went out to buy a pack.

The look that had passed between Diane and Judy Silverman in the kitchen, in hindsight practically an admission that Susan was supposed to have been involved in Harry's self-deliverance. Then a five-thousand-dollar donation to NAN.

What did we have here, NAN's own homegrown Kevorkian, MSW, and her loyal assistant, Nurse McClellan? United in high moral purpose, one to prepare the way emotionally, the other to provide technical expertise.

And the profits to NAN, so their consciences would be clear.

Diane seemed to have strong opinions in favor of self-deliverance, and she certainly had access to the drugs. Access, nothing. Diane had a stockpile of drugs. *Final Exit* may not have included OxyContin and OxyFast, but I'd bet my button collection they were every bit as effective as anything Derek Humphrey mentioned.

What were they *thinking*?

Damn it all to hell. The living room was too small to get a decent pace going, but I had to move, so I tried it anyway. Back and forth, a full seven steps in each direction.

Slow down, Anita. Consider the alternatives. Maybe it started in all innocence, out of conviction, even. Working with the elderly, after all, means that death is never far from anyone's mind. What could be more natural than a desire for your clients to be able to die with dignity?

Yeah, sure, but what about the money? You don't just come right out and offer to put people permanently to sleep for a fee.

No, you eased into it. Susan started a group, Issues of Later Life. In response to client requests, of course. Suggested books to read, *Final Exit* casually included among them. And under NAN's auspices, intimated that if they wanted to really explore the matter, a practice session with the plastic bag method might be in order.

In an elderly population, there's always someone close to dying. Word would get around, and sooner or later there'd be a taker. Someone who requested assistance from a trusted social worker or nurse known to be open to the idea of self-deliverance, willing to lend a hand. And then said social worker or nurse would delicately allude to a concrete way of expressing thanks for the service they were providing.

I could hear my own response to grateful clients who persisted in offering me presents. "No, really, I'm not allowed to accept anything myself, although if you'd like to make a donation to the agency, that would be appropriate. Not in exchange for my services, just to say thanks."

If you stretched it, yes, I could see how such a thing might happen. And their reasoning: a good thing for the person in pain, to prevent suffering; a good thing for NAN, to build up the endowment and relieve Susan from fund-raising so she'd have more time to devote to caring for needy clients.

Uh-huh. It's called rationalization. And amounts in the thousands could provide incentive to rationalize pretty much anything.

Trudi's mother's name was on both lists. According to Mr. Neville, and what Trudi herself had told me, she'd died of a stroke and been found a few hours later by Trudi. On Susan's list, her name was accompanied by only a one-thousand-dollar amount. More in line with what you'd expect someone to give, although in comparison to the other figures, it seemed chintzy. Especially from a woman whose daughter was so dedicated to the financial well-being of the agency.

I wondered how much Vivian or Trudi really knew about the sizable contributions NAN had been receiving. Were they simply grateful for the money, or had they played a more active role in encouraging its donation? I've never been a big believer in the ends justifying the means, and I didn't like to think I was working for an agency where that was part of the culture.

Conviction and altruism are fine motivations, but Susan and Diane were taking an awfully big risk. If anyone found out, they stood to lose their licenses, not to mention doing jail time. If they were charged with premeditated murder, now that New York had the death penalty again—

I sat down. No one takes that kind of chance simply to be noble. Derek Humphrey made a big thing out of how to skirt the law, but people did get found out and prosecuted. Take Dr. Kevorkian—but he was blatantly challenging a law he thought was wrong. And he was a man near the end of his career. Susan and Diane were young women.

Then I had a more sinister thought.

What if the dead, while they were still alive, had expressed their appreciation directly to Susan and Diane? An advance payment, so to speak, as well as a bequest to NAN? The dead, the grateful dead.

I tried to stomp out the spark of that thought before it started burning. Little as I knew either Susan or Diane, neither of them seemed like the type to profit on the side from providing any kind of service, let alone one like euthanasia.

That got a malicious little inner imp going in my amoral unconscious.

You could definitely afford a Bendel's charge card on a nurse's salary, if you augmented it with a percentage of fifty thousand dollars, it whispered.

For a few cashmere sweaters? I don't think so.

That silenced it, but not for long. *Have it your way, then. But what about Susan? If she wanted a child badly enough to undergo in-vitro fertilization treatments, maybe she'd do almost anything to pay for them.*

Right, and after she'd given up on trying to get pregnant, then she'd kill herself?

I told the imp to shut the hell up and started pacing again.

But it had a point. What *about* Susan?

When the in-vitro didn't work, she had an attack of scruples coupled with depression over her failure to conceive, and took the final exit herself?

Maybe Diane got tired of sharing the wealth, and removed her sister in crime? the whisper suggested.

Because it hadn't stopped with Susan. Four more people had died after she did.

Yeah, right, that sounds like the Diane you know. Get a grip, Anita.

But I couldn't stop seeing that supply of OxyContin and OxyFast in the nurse's closet.

Tell Michael, you have to tell Michael what you know. This is a prime example of when to let the police do their job. You should've told him about the pills when you found them, Anita.

The mantel clock chimed midnight. I wasn't the least bit tired.

I had a Tuesday ahead of me, though, with all its attendant groups, so I put my wildly speculating brain on mute, brushed my teeth, and headed for bed. Horizontal in the dark did nothing to silence the devilish little voice clamoring about the possibility of Susan and Diane running their own personal version of Murder, Inc. I slid a hand along Benno's hip and down, stirring him awake. That did the trick.

26

W HAT had seemed like a simple idea the night before—turn the whole problem over to Michael—
grew complications like Spanish moss as I walked to
work. It was a foggy, foggy morning, but the urban wildlife
could still be spotted. A border collie pulling a woman in gray
sweats emerged like a wraith from Riverside Park. A black lab,
off-leash, sniffed my crotch before trotting off in answer to an
eerie whistle. A scarlet-breasted jogger flashed by, vanished. I
wondered if the Audubon Society had ever documented the
species.

In the muted light of day, my cotton-shrouded brain was
unable to come up with why Michael should care about a
cache of perfectly legal prescription drugs that might have a
perfectly logical explanation for being there. Like that Diane
had removed them from the apartments of the deceased in order to dispose of them properly.

Uh-huh. So why hadn't she done that by now? I devoutly
regretted not having found the right moment to ask her that
question.

It had also occurred to me that the medications could have been hidden in the nurse's closet by Susan, and Diane not even aware of their presence. Maybe there really hadn't been anything for Diane to find in Dorothy Norris's apartment; maybe Susan had already removed it before Diane went looking, and that was what she'd used to tranquilize herself so the plastic bag could do its work. Was I really prepared to accuse Diane to the police before I'd had a chance to talk to her myself?

That raised the other horn of my dilemma, a lose-lose situation rising from the mist. If I was right, okay, it would ruin Diane's career. If I was wrong, though, the suggestion alone would have the same result. Not to mention wrecking my own career in the process.

Not enough caffeine. I left the park and detoured past the Bread Shop, past the Estates and Grant Houses, to the restaurant on Broadway that served the strong, milky Spanish coffee Michael was addicted to, and got myself a container to go.

It didn't do much to clarify my thoughts. Sitting at my desk, staring at Susan's jade tiger, I was all too aware that Tuesday was Diane's day off. I might be a dithering idiot, but at least I could grab the opportunity and make sure I had the bird in hand.

I made an excuse to Anne about needing to consult one of Diane's client files, and took myself off to the nurse's office. Once I had the box, we could sort out the consequences later.

"What do you mean, 'we,' civilian?" I could hear Michael ask. Up a canyon with no way out, Indians thundering toward them from all sides, the Lone Ranger asks Tonto, "What do we do now?" and Tonto answers, "What do you mean *we*, white man?"

I was definitely the cowboy in this scenario, riding off half-cocked to steal evidence. A squirrel skittered up the wide steps ahead of me, flicked its tail, and disappeared.

Gone as completely as the locked green box on the top shelf.

Why was I not surprised? No key pinned to the wall, no box in the closet, no way to prove Diane had provided anything other than nursing services to any of the now-deceased people named on Susan's bookmark.

No problem. Dilemma resolved. I'd jumped to some pretty big conclusions, and maybe I had it all wrong.

I searched the small office anyway, invaded the privacy of the credenza, the medicine cabinet, Diane's desk drawers. And of course, in the shallow center drawer, amid the pens and paper clips, there was a small key just like the one that had been held by the pushpin. In fact, there was the red pushpin itself, jumbled in with a whole family of other colors.

So where was the box? Three of the four desk drawers were unlocked. I hit pay dirt in the large bottom drawer on the right, behind the hanging files of health education information. I didn't even need the key to get it open.

Yup, you got it: empty.

As if the whole thing had been a figment of my imagination.

I went looking for the key to the one locked desk drawer. Nowhere to be found. I even pulled the center drawer all the way out and felt underneath in case Diane had taped the key nearby. Nothing. I was so frustrated, I kicked the drawer.

When I left, I locked Diane's door and added its key to the ring Vivian had given me when I started the job. The one thing I was sure of was that NAN's security measures were way too lax. Sure, there was an alarm on the office door, but that only protected us from outsiders.

I kept banging into the brick wall of Susan's death. If she'd started the whole thing, why had people continued to die after she was no longer on the scene? Was it all Diane? Some? None? But then who?

Something about what was going on here had the smell of insider. The Estates, for all how neighborly people were, was full of petty rivalries, gossip, jealousy. In my opinion, altogether too many people had keys to NAN. And the key to the nurse's office had been kept, clearly labeled, in Susan's desk. Where anyone at all could have borrowed it.

The next item on my agenda was to have another look at the case files of the people on Neville's list, especially those whose names had also showed up on Susan's bookmark. I didn't have a free minute until the sing-along started. Tuesday after lunch, the least cosmic time of the week. After the second chorus of "Mairsie Doats," Anne fled, leaving me almost an hour to browse the files.

I closed both doors to Anne's office, as much to block out what the blended voices of those who could carry a tune and those who couldn't were doing to "Goodnight, Irene" as for privacy, and sat myself on the floor where I had easy access to the closed cases in the bottom drawer.

Mr. Neville had told me that the man who died shortly before Susan was a textbook example of the *Final Exit* technique. I figured a person who'd done things properly would be a good control subject, so I started with him. His diagnosis had been pancreatic cancer. Interestingly, he was also a patient of Dr. Andras, Barbara's physician. Not that it meant anything; half the Estates probably saw doctors with practices in the 1090 building.

As I glanced over the intake sheet, a casual note under "Other Interests" caught my attention: "Plays bridge with the Corbos and Mrs. Voss."

Corbo. Grace, Alzheimer's, dead by plastic bag with no note. Her husband, Russ, the appliance-testing man from the flea market, object of flirtatious attention from Trudi and that other woman. And donor of five thousand dollars to NAN.

Mrs. Voss could only be Trudi's mother. Several small strokes, then a massive one that killed her.

A nice foursome, Grace with Alzheimer's and Mrs. Voss stroke-impaired. They'd probably played their best bridge when they had the dummy hand.

I moved on to the Corbos' file.

It appeared that Russ had taken devoted care of Grace. The month before her death, however, he'd filled out an application to have her admitted to the Jewish Home and Hospital on 106th St. From the progress notes, it wasn't clear what exactly had led to Russ's decision to place Grace in an institution. She wasn't incontinent of bladder or bowel. Nor was there any indication that she'd become abusive, physically or verbally, to Russ—the two most common breaking points that got Alzheimer's caregivers to consider placement. One of the things they teach you in social work school is to pay attention to the precipitating factors when a person seeks help; knowing the why can help you tailor the solution to the underlying problem. Often it's obvious—the loss of a job, a home, a loved one—but for Russ Corbo, none of the usual applied.

Except maybe for the universal motivators: sex and money. Judging by the attentions of the women during the flea market, a love interest wasn't out of the question, although there didn't seem to be anyone in particular who'd succeeded in replacing Grace. Unless it was a liaison still kept secret? But why, since he was a widower? Because he'd hastened his wife's death in order to be with someone else?

As for money—a glance at the copies of financial records in the file revealed that the legal process of transferring joint assets into only Russ's name had been completed less than a year ago. The timing meant that, for an immediate placement, Russ would have had to pay full freight for Grace's care for at least the first several "penalty" months. It was also clear that he could easily afford the expense. So much for that motive.

When indignant politicians get going about welfare cheats, there's one group that never gets mentioned: elderly Medicaid abusers. Or rather, the well-off children and spouses of elderly people who make paper paupers of their incapacitated relatives so that Medicaid—no, not Medicare, which doesn't pay for nursing homes—will pick up the tab for the $100,000-plus per year it costs to keep a person in an institution.

For me, this is one of the biggest ethical quandaries I face in my job. Although it's all legal—divesting assets in order to become Medicaid-eligible is a subspecialty of elder law—I'm not comfortable with faking poverty in order to receive a government benefit. On the other hand, the cost of skilled nursing care is so prohibitively high that paying out of pocket eventually bankrupts all but the wealthiest. Medicaid was intended to provide health insurance for low-income families and children. At this point, most of its budget is spent on long-term care for the elderly.

The holy grail of universal health care would not only put a stop to the practice of transferring assets, but also, not incidentally, drive the elder-lawyers out of business.

I know, enough already. Benno's not the only one capable of a good rant.

What did emerge from Susan's notes was Grace's terror of what the disease would do to her. A fear I'd felt myself, on the rare and unsettling occasions when my memory had been completely unable to recall a familiar word or name. As I replaced the file in the drawer, I remembered hearing someone mention Russ in the context of attending Issues of Later Life. If only I could find the sign-in sheets.

I decided to give up on the subjectivity of case files and try to get a handle on some more objective information. Trudi Voss was right; my key to the client file cabinet also unlocked the financial files. I didn't expect to find the checkbook, since Trudi'd said she'd be paying bills from home. It didn't take a forensic accountant, however, to notice that the past six months' worth of NAN's bank statements were not in the drawer.

The endowment fund had its own manila folder, which contained early drafts and a sample copy of the brochure that had gone out with the direct mailing to drum up testamentary bequests. I knew from Vivian that Trudi was working on the

fund from home, too. I didn't like it much, all that bank information in someone's apartment rather than the office, but
I trusted Trudi's financial rectitude implicitly.

If there was anything wrong with the bequests, Trudi
would spot it. And do what? Bring it to Vivian's attention. And
Susan's. Or Susan's. And if there was something wrong, and
if Susan was involved, and if Susan knew Trudi knew—would
suicide have been her way out?

Way out, indeed, Anita. You're getting a bit far-fetched
with this scenario. If, if, if.

I pushed the drawer shut just as Anne opened the office
door.

"What do you think about mercy killing?" I asked.

Anne put her hands on her hips and stared at me. Well, it
was an abrupt beginning to a heavy topic.

"They shoot horses, don't they?" Anne answered with a
question of her own.

"No, seriously."

"If it's good enough for my dog, it's good enough for me."

"Anne!"

"I'm serious. Have you ever had to put an animal to sleep?
It's no different than a person. Maybe worse, because a dog is
dependent on you, you're her whole world."

I perched on the windowsill. "I didn't know you had a dog."

"Before I knew you. The longest relationship of my adult
life was with Tippy. We were together more than fifteen years."
She reached for her purse, got out her wallet.

"She was mostly mutt, with a lot of spaniel mixed in. That
was her personality, too."

It was an old photo, the colors fading, of a knee-high
black dog with an elegant white chin ruff.

"Cute," I said.

Anne snapped the wallet shut. "I noticed the first tumors
when she was twelve. I paid for the operation and nursed her
afterward. Two years later, the cancer came back. She just
wasted away. I couldn't bear the way she was suffering."

I handed Anne a tissue.

"The vet let me be there when he put her to sleep, and she died in my arms." Anne blew her nose.

I was sorry I'd asked, and I said so.

"I know, you're thinking it was my misery I was putting an end to, not Tippy's, but it's what I'd want someone to do for me, Anita. So to answer your question, yes, I believe in mercy killing. Now if you don't mind, some of us have work to do."

27

UST before five, Michael showed up. To collect Anne, but also to see me.

A hatless head poked itself in my door. "Hey, Social Worker, how you doing? Still orbiting the planet?" He settled himself in the client's chair next to my desk.

"Nice to see you, too, Michael. Come on in, have a seat, make yourself comfortable."

"I'm not interrupting anything?"

I'd been doodling around the edges of my blotter, staring at the next week's schedule. "Yeah, I'm reinventing the wheel. I thought I'd try square this time, to make it more stable."

It didn't even rate me a smile. Michael stretched his legs out and considered the room. It wasn't much to look at. I'd already drawn the venetian blinds against the early dusk. The walls were empty except for a poster of Matisse dancers and several lighter squares where Susan's diplomas had hung; the furniture was generic office-supply-catalog modern. Trust Michael, he went for the one quirky item in the room: Susan's tiger.

"Nice piece. Your guardian angel?"

"Susan's, actually."

That got his attention. He drew his legs up and sat forward. "It wasn't here when she did herself, was it?"

"No, her husband gave it to me as a memento." I let the crude reference to Susan's death ride.

Michael reached over and picked up the little figurine. "Yeah, so, that's what I'm here to talk to you about, the boss's death. Not that I think I should, understand, but I said I would." He held the tiger so it faced him, and addressed his words to it rather than to me.

"We just got the toxicology report in on the Stringer couple. Seems they used Seconal. Not your most common sleep aid these days, but according to the pathologist, it's not unusual to find people of a certain age with doctors who still prescribe it. People who've been hooked for decades, it's easier to keep them on than put 'em through barbiturate withdrawal." Michael, I knew from past experience, had a dim view of people who used drugs, legal or otherwise.

"I went over the report on Ms. Wu, too." He waggled the tiger at me, like it proved his point. "Seems she had this synthetic morphine stuff, oxycodone, in her system. ME thinks she took the liquid form, trade name OxyFast, dissolved in a glass of wine. A teaspoon of the stuff would've been enough to knock her out so cold she'd sleep right through suffocating to death. And make my job easy, CSU documented an empty bottle in the trash."

OxyFast. What had been hidden in the nurse's office. And now was missing.

"Where did it come from?"

Michael shrugged. "We're checking out whether she had a prescription for it. The stuff comes in a bottle with an eyedropper to dispense it, and the bottle comes in a box—that's where the pharmacy puts its label." He nodded, pleased by the neatness of what he was laying out for me. "Suicide, pure and simple. Doped herself up, then let the plastic bag contraption do the rest. So what with the bag business being the same in both cases but the medications used in conjunction with it being different, I'd say what we had was coincidence."

"Okay." I didn't know what else to say. My brain was scurrying around to ten other places.

"Neville asked me to let you know. So you won't go around thinking there's something linking the two deaths. Now, why he'd think you'd think that, I don't know, but if you were going anywhere along those lines, I'm here to let you know that you can stop."

"So I won't—" I narrowed my eyes at him, trying to figure out why all of a sudden Neville was putting his whole conspiracy thing on my shoulders. Then I got it. "You mean Neville didn't give you a copy of his list?"

"List?"

Great. Neville was suspicious enough to get me rooting through client files, but not so suspicious that he'd used his connections to get autopsy reports. And now I'd put my foot in it. Heck with him, then. I'd tell Michael myself.

"When I first started, Mr. Neville came to see me. He said he was concerned that more people than were statistically probable had died using the plastic bag method in the Estates in the past several months. He gave me a list of names, and asked me to read through their case files and see if anything jumped out at me. I just assumed that after Susan and the Stringers died, he would have told you what he was thinking. I know the deaths were ruled to be suicides, but Neville seemed to think that someone actively assisted in them, or at least provided encouragement. I don't mean to be telling you how to do your job—"

"Yeah, right."

"—but couldn't you call up whatever paperwork there is, like death certificates and autopsy reports, and take a look at it all together?"

Michael squinted at me, a look that said "not on your life."

"I mean, maybe there's a pattern, or something that connects them all that no one's noticed because their deaths weren't linked in any way."

"Look, Anita, sure, assisted suicide is a crime. My personal opinion, it's not one we should be prosecuting. Somebody with a terminal disease wants to check out early, that should be their right. Plus it's damn hard to prove. So unless we've got a family member raising the roof, we don't look too close."

"No harm, no foul?" I asked, sweetly.

"There you go again! For Pete's sake, Social Worker, get off it. I don't need to be making homicides out of closed cases just because you've got an itch any more now than I did when that old lady died in your building."

"That *was* a homicide." Idiot.

Michael reached over and put the tiger back on my desk. "Yeah, right, okay. It was, and you showed Detective Neville up pretty good. So spit it out, I'm listening. What's making those blips on your radar screen?"

"Neville's radar," I told him, pissed. "You better ask him."

We had a staring contest. I got tired of it and let Michael win. Damned if I was going to say another word about Neville's list, though. He was a grown-up, he could speak for himself.

Michael stood up. "Listen, I'll talk to Neville. But I'm serious, don't let him get you all revved up just because he's bored with his new job."

I tilted my head back to look at him. "He's the one whose motor is racing, but I wouldn't worry about it if I were you. He told me he shifted his gears to finding out who mugged me."

"Okey-dokey. As long as we're clear on that."

"Michael—" I had one more question.

"Yeah?"

"Does OxyContin get sold on the street? I mean, if I wanted to score some without a prescription, could I?"

"What makes you ask?" I had his full attention, focused as a flashlight beam.

"Could I?"

"Yeah." He sat back down and rubbed the top of his head

while he answered. "This drug—it's got the potential to be the crack of the new millennium. Some parts of the country, Ohio, West Virginia, they call it hillbilly heroin. The stuff's supposed to be time-release, but your ever-resourceful drug abusers figured out if they smashed the tablets, they could snort it or inject it, have themselves a nice pure high. And it's easy to get—forged prescriptions, pharmacy break-ins, or better yet, just steal grandma's. It works so well that it gets used for all sorts of things. Fake yourself some back pain, and you're in clover. Except the stuff's so pure and potent, there're starting to be OD deaths associated with it."

"So it's available on the street?"

"Sure." Michael nodded. "You won't find the NYPD making a big thing of it, though—don't want to publicize the stuff, give anyone any ideas they don't already have."

The dilemma of drug-abuse prevention: The line between education and advertising is awfully thin. You tell people about illegal highs, what drug has what effect, how to recognize it, and you're also telling them what to look for and how to identify it when they've found it.

Anne knocked on the open door between our two rooms. "Ready to go?"

"Absolutely." Michael bounced up from the chair, released.

After the door closed behind them, I had a word with the jade tiger myself. "So where do *you* think Susan got her stuff?"

The tiger had no answers for me.

28

W HEN my brain starts to resemble one of Clea's gerbils in its wheel, the only solution is derailment. Diane took Wednesday off to study; Thursday, as usual, she had classes. I filled the days by taking care of living clients. Starting with Olive, sorry to bother me, but a welcome interruption in my frustrated state. I escorted her back to her apartment, where I did some more productive detective work and located a phone number for her son, who it turned out lived in Connecticut.

I didn't know for sure what Olive's presence on Susan's list meant, but the other people scribbled down there were all dead, and I didn't want to take any chances with her safety. The woman had a son; I intended to speak with him. If he couldn't take her in himself, at least I'd encourage him to hire a caregiver.

It felt good to get back to basic social work and earn my salary.

Although I was burning to ask Trudi about the endowment fund, I didn't dare. I might trust her completely when it came to safeguarding NAN's finances, but the feeling was not mutual. Anne thought it was irrational of Trudi to want my head on a platter after the flea market robbery; I, on the other hand, saw her point. I'd been careless, and cost the agency money dozens of volunteers had worked countless hours to raise.

Doing my job was the least I could do to make amends— and in the process, I hoped, win back Trudi's confidence.

First thing Friday morning, however, I was sitting on the bench outside the nurses' building with a cup of coffee and a bummed cigarette that was making me slightly dizzy. It was cold, clear; my breath made plumes in the air even without the exhalations of smoke. I'd decided to confront Diane head-on, get it over with before the distractions of the day intervened.

"Good morning, Anita." I'd been watching the elegant woman in the full-length fur coat sweep down the broad steps from 123rd like Norma Desmond, but until she spoke, I hadn't realized it was Diane.

The sight of her in that coat took the indignant wind right out of my sails. It was gorgeous. I'm neither pro- nor antifur, although if you pushed me, I'd admit to being antitrapping. Farm-raised mink, well, what's the difference between a mink and a chicken, when you get right down to it? And a vegetarian I'm not about to be, much as my sympathies are with the animal world. Eat and be eaten; the tigers are welcome to my carcass.

"Wow," I said. "Nice coat."

"Thank you." Diane's smile let me know she was pleased by my reaction. "You were waiting to see me?"

I stood up and stepped on the cigarette butt. "Yeah." I couldn't resist petting her shoulder. What could win me over to fur is the way it feels, the lush softness. "What is it?"

"Black mink. Isn't it wonderful?" Diane stroked her own arm. "This is my ultimate weapon to combat the stereotype of the black home health aide."

"I'd say it works pretty well." If my reaction was any guide, at least. Blew the stereotype of underpaid nurses clear out of my mind. What replaced it was the thought of Diane supplementing her income by selling her patients' unused prescription narcotics. Or taking a cut of donations from grateful elderly clients she'd agreed to help into an early grave. Nice work if you can get it.

Diane took a padded hanger from the shower rod in the bathroom and shrugged out of the mink. As if I hadn't felt like enough of a frump, in my democratic cloth winter coat, the flash of Diane's cherry-red silk blouse, tucked into a narrow black wool skirt, did the trick. My lavender cotton turtleneck couldn't hold a candle to that level of elegance.

"Who was it who died yesterday?" Diane asked.

"What?" I shot the word at her. My first thought was, So that's where the drugs went—used up on another victim of your mercy. "You expected someone to die?"

If Diane was offended by my tone of voice, she didn't show it. She took her seat behind the desk, leaving me the client's chair. "You were waiting for me outside my office. I assumed you had news you wanted to deliver in person."

"No one died," I said. "That's not why I'm here."

I tried to get a grip. Diane waited me out.

I went back to the speech I'd been rehearsing on the bench. "I don't want you to think I'm prying"—which was exactly what I'd done—"so I'm going to be blunt. Do you collect unused prescriptions from people?"

Her smile was polite, baffled. "You know that I do, Anita. It's part of my job to ensure that unused medication is disposed of properly. You saw me do it when we met in Dorothy Norris's apartment. There's an enormous potential for abuse with some of the things that my patients take."

"I thought you didn't find anything in the Norris apartment." This wasn't in my script.

"I didn't say that." Diane met my accusatory eyes. "You might have assumed I didn't, and I let you think so."

"All right, I'm talking specifically about OxyContin and OxyFast. Isn't that what you were looking for?"

"Dorothy used both of those medications. As I said, they are among the drugs I am the most careful about. If they fall into the wrong hands, the potential for abuse—" She stopped. "Why are you asking me about this, Anita? You think that I have done something wrong?"

"You tell me." I waited. Diane didn't answer, so I went on. "I admit I was out of line, and I didn't intend to snoop, but—a few weeks ago, I noticed a box on the top shelf of your closet."

"What were you doing in my office?" Her voice was level, but I could've sworn I saw a shimmer of tension disturb the smooth red silk of her blouse.

"I came to get the wheelchair, on election day. But that's not the point. What I want to know is why you were keeping those drugs, and what you did with them, since they're not in the closet now."

"You have searched through my office *twice*?"

I almost blushed. "Yes." Nosy I might be, but I wasn't the one with something to hide.

"Then you also found the supply of Coumadin, Lasix, and Lopressor I keep locked in my desk?"

There I was, going off half-cocked. At the memory of kicking that drawer, I did blush.

"No?" Diane unlocked the drawer with a key from her ring. "There is one shred of my privacy you have not invaded?"

Several brown plastic prescription bottles thudded onto the desk. She explained each one as she set it down. "Coumadin, blood thinner. Lasix, diuretic. Lopressor, blood pressure. Prescription drugs are expensive, especially for elderly people on fixed incomes with inadequate insurance coverage. Many people will cut the recommended dosage in half to stretch their supply of pills. Sometimes I need to provide extra medication—in accordance with the prescribing doctor's specifications, of course—from what I keep on hand."

How was I supposed to know that? I thought. "Why didn't you tell me?"

"This is a matter for the nurse, Anita." Diane swept the pill containers back into the drawer and relocked it. "Stockpiling prescription drugs was Susan's idea. She thought of it as taking from Peter to help Paul. It is my responsibility to be sure that people take their medications properly."

I wasn't shocked by the concept, but I couldn't believe how abysmally idiotic Susan and Diane had been. Not to mention possibly being criminally stupid as well.

"What about the OxyContin and OxyFast? What did you use them for?"

"I already told you about those drugs." Her tone was fierce. "OxyContin is a time-release form of oxycodone. People can take large doses, and it doesn't make them high like a narcotic. OxyFast is a liquid, for quick relief of breakthrough pain. For terminal cancer patients like Harry Silverman, those drugs helped him to pass his final months without pain."

I wondered if Diane was speculating on my willingness to pick up where Susan had left off, the Robin Hood of pain relief.

Not a chance. I may bend a few rules, but I don't mess with the line between life and death. We sat there long enough for me to realize that I had nothing to say to Michael. Susan had killed herself. One way or the other, Harry was dead, and so were the others. However she'd been involved, the accounts Diane had to settle would be with her own conscience.

Mine, however, still needed to know a few things.

"Didn't it occur to you that that might be what Susan used to kill herself?"

"Of course it did. But I don't know that it was, and neither do you."

"Well, it was. They got the toxicology report yesterday."

Diane couldn't meet my eyes. "When he came to my apartment, the detective mentioned that they'd found an empty bottle of OxyFast in Susan's wastebasket. He asked if I knew where she got it. I told him no, because I didn't."

"But you suspected."

"Yes. Susan, she was aware that it was one of the medications I kept on hand. I *did* check my supply after her death. All of the bottles were there."

"And did they have the right amount of liquid and the right number of pills in them?" I was getting hip to Diane's lawyerly way of answering only and precisely what was asked.

"Now how would I know that, Anita? I don't have time to measure exactly how much is in each vial. There is no way to tell whether what Susan took came from my supply."

"Not now, there isn't. But if you'd told the police—"

"Well, I'm sorry, but I didn't. Now I have disposed of the rest, poured the liquid out and flushed the pills down the toilet." Diane rolled her chair back, turned it sideways, and stared out the window. "I should never have kept it."

You got that right, sister. "Why did you?"

"In case. Someone else in Harry's situation might have needed it. It can be difficult to get."

"So all of a sudden, you decided to dump the stuff?"

This time she stared right back at me. "What difference does it make now? Susan is dead. I could lose my job, if not my license." Diane's voice was matter-of-fact, as if I should have understood without asking.

And maybe I should have. You set out to do good works, with no idea of the moral thicket it can lead you into.

"Why didn't you get rid of it right after Susan died?"

Diane glanced across to the closet. "I don't know. I had a lot of things on my plate, and I thought it was safe where it was."

Pretty lame, if you ask me. "When did you dump it out?"

"The week of the election. On Friday, I think."

"That would be right after Harry Silverman died? He'd

built up a tolerance, so he would've needed quite a bit more than what he was taking—"

"I have nothing to say about Mr. Silverman, Anita. He had a terminal illness, and now he's passed away."

"Okay, then let's talk about the rest of them. If you include Susan Wu and the Stringers, six people in the Estates have died using plastic bags. I'm sure once the police start putting things together, they'll find most of them used some form of oxycodone in their 'self-deliveries.' If you had anything to do with it, it's all going to come out."

"I don't know anything about that!" It was immediate and indignant. "I know one man, he had pancreatic cancer, who went that way. I am sure that he had his own prescription. Whatever Ralph and Ora Stringer ingested, I didn't give it to them."

She was right about that; they'd used their own Seconal.

"What about that group, Issues of Later Life, where they read *Final Exit*? How involved were you in that?" Go ahead, Anita, get it all out. I sort of felt sorry for Diane, on the receiving end of my suspicions.

All of which, I have to say, she deflected quite neatly.

"I knew about it, but I didn't have time for that." She gave a pointed look at the blinking light on her answering machine.

Thrust, parry. Still nothing that connected Diane to any of the deaths. Except—

"Are you aware that many of those people willed substantial amounts of money to NAN?"

"No, how would I know about that?"

That denial didn't sound quite so confident to me.

"Susan could've told you."

"Susan and I provided those medications free of charge, as a service to our clients. If you always abide by a strict interpretation of the rules, it can lead to a great deal of unnecessary suffering."

We stared out the window. A shaft of light landed in Diane's lap.

"Who else besides Susan knew you kept extra medications on hand?" I asked. "Vivian Brownell? Any of the NAN board members?"

"No, of course not. I told the people when I supplemented their prescriptions that the drugs were given to me as samples."

"Did Susan tell anyone?"

"Susan knew we were taking a chance. I'm sure she would not mention it to anyone."

Confident words, but in my opinion Diane looked less than certain. I had a feeling that NAN's clients wouldn't be getting any supplemental medications from our nurse in the future.

Diane consulted her watch. "Isn't it time for both of us to start work?"

"I thought that's what we were doing." I stayed put in the client's chair and let the silence be between us. "You did really throw it all away, didn't you? You won't start collecting medications again?"

"No." Diane's voice was unreadable, without emotion, but she faced me straight on. "Not anymore."

I had to believe her, even though the whole situation made me nauseous. If there was mercy in it, well, there had also been killing.

29

WHAT is it about Tuesdays after lunch? The least cosmic time of the week, and yet the most insignificant impulses tend to have extreme consequences. Lillian Blau, of the plaid shirt and chicken soup, appeared in my office right after the *Family in the Western World* book group ended. She leaned on her cane, waiting for me to look up and notice her.

I almost had a heart attack—it was like the ghost of Susan, a sudden apparition I hadn't even heard enter the room.

"Hah," Lil greeted me. "You're awfully busy."

"Just paperwork." I closed the case file I'd been updating and thanked her for the soup—which was, honestly, the best I'd ever eaten, my grandmother's included.

Lil blustered with pleasure. "Ah, my son calls me the Jewish gourmet. You wait, when it comes Passover, I'll bring you soup with matzo balls. Now, that's real Jewish!"

I believed her.

"I want to talk to you." Lil sat herself down in the client's chair. "Could we have a little privacy?"

"Of course." I got up and closed the doors.

Lil sighed, pursed her lips, sighed again through her nose. She looked around the room, making sure we were alone, her gaze landing everywhere but on me.

I clutched my hands together in my lap so I wouldn't start tapping with impatience. Whatever it was, I had to let her say it in her own time.

"You haven't changed much in here, have you?" She still wasn't looking at me. "I don't blame you for not setting down roots, with all that's happened."

"All that's happened?" I prompted.

"It was my idea that we should hire a professional for NAN, you know. I convinced the others. Vivian, Claire, Edith . . . we were all volunteers, and it got to be too much. Some of us needed help ourselves. I asked Trudi to do the books—her mother and I were friends, I knew her since she was in college—and Vivian raised the money."

I nodded encouragingly.

"I tried to warn Vivian, but she only wants to know abou it if it has to do with her fund-raising. I shouldn't be sui prised. That's what she did, you know, in her career, raise money. For a politician." Lil sighed again. "You don't know what I'm talking about, do you?"

I shook my head. I didn't have a clue.

"All right. It was trouble from the start. Well, almost from the start. I thought it would be interesting, that's why I went. But Susan was busy, and she let that Muriel take over."

"I'm sorry, Lil, take over what?"

"The group. Something about 'later life,' they called it. Okay, we all live with one foot in the grave. Preparing ourselves for the inevitable, fine. I filled out one of those living wills when the lawyer was here. Betty Friedan, I liked her book. That's my generation. Muriel's, too, but she had different ideas about what we should read. So, it was something to do on a Thursday afternoon. I read that other book she wanted, *Final Exit*. Me, I don't believe in cheating God, but I could see the value in it for those who don't feel about things the same as I do. If you ask me, though, Muriel pushed people too far."

"What do you mean?" Now she had my attention.

"That Hemlock Society, she joined. Some of the others, too. They wanted to make a pact, agree to help whoever wanted to 'deliver' themselves. Like we were Chinese food! Someone brought a box of those bags they cook turkeys in, and a lot of big rubber bands." Lil shook her head in disgust. "So we could see what it felt like. That book said it was a good idea to practice."

I saw Susan's face, the fright mask of her mashed features in the plastic bag. Practice! If they'd had any idea what real death looked like, I couldn't imagine a room full of elderly people would ever have put their heads in bags with elastic bands around their necks.

"I don't know why anyone went along with it. I didn't. One look at those bags was enough for me." Lil shivered. "I went to Susan. She had no idea how far Muriel had gone, and when she found out, she put her right out of business."

Good, I thought. That's what Susan should have done, and I said so.

Lil tapped her fingers on the arm of the chair, considering what to say next. "Well. Now I'm asking you to put a stop to it once and for all."

"I thought you said Susan—"

"Sure, from meeting here in the office, she stopped it. But Muriel didn't give up. Invited people to her apartment instead. I want you to find out who made those agreements and make those people stop what they're doing."

Those people. It's an expression my social work professors warned us not to use; it sets up a group who can be criticized: them, the others, outsiders. We're taught not to judge, but it can be useful to be able to make distinctions. As in, people who help other people die. A group that might include Muriel, Susan, Diane?

"That Muriel has me worried." Lil continued as if she'd read my thoughts. "She has a look in her eye whenever death comes into the conversation. She's on a crusade, and I don't trust crusaders. I tried to tell Vivian after Susan . . . and then that couple upstairs—you know about them?"

"Ralph and Ora Stringer? Were they in the group?"

"Not him. Ora, she came to everything. She went along with it when we did that with the turkey bags, but I don't think she kept up with the group when it moved to Muriel's apartment." Lil lowered her voice. "Muriel didn't care for Ora."

Good. Because if Muriel had had anything to do with the Stringers' deaths, I'd wring her neck. "Who else attended the group, Lil?"

"Addie Collins was sensible enough to drop out when we began that *Exit* book." Lil thought about it. "Other people came from time to time, I don't remember who-all. I'm sure there are attendance sheets somewhere. They're very big on taking attendance over here."

Yes, they were. I didn't share with Lil the fact that I'd been unable to find any sign-in sheets for that particular group. Nor was it listed in the statistical tabulations Susan kept to verify the number of people who participated in NAN activities. Call me suspicious, but I wondered if the records of the group had disappeared on orders from higher up.

"I don't believe in banning books. I'm sure that *Final Exit* is a comfort to some. I know, you can't stop people dying, but why you'd want to encourage them!" Lil sniffed.

"Did Vivian attend?"

"Not her. Money, that's Vivian's concern. A good thing, too. Vision is all very well, but reality requires funds. Vivian deserves the credit for NAN being what it is. Take this endowment. I don't know beans about that kind of thing, but Trudi was all for it."

"What about Russ or Grace Corbo?"

"That's right, they were there. Only the one time, though.

He liked to take her out and do things, but she couldn't always follow along." Lil paused. "You know Grace died that way, too? I can't believe she understood enough to use what she heard, but you never know, do you?"

No, you don't. "I'll have a talk with Muriel."

Damn straight I would, and this time I wouldn't let her wriggle out of answering.

"That's all I can promise you, though." I wasn't happy about what else I had to say to Lil. "There really isn't anything I can do, officially, about any private arrangements that may have been made." It was embarrassing to have nothing better to offer than the standard right-to-privacy, cover-your-agency's-ass rap, even though it was true.

Lil didn't have to say anything; the disgust she felt was clear in the downturned corners of her mouth.

"If you remember anyone else who might have been involved, will you let me know?"

Lil nodded grudgingly. "If that's the best you can do."

Heaven help me. At the time, I thought it was.

It was 4:42. I should've called it a day, but Clea was set at the after-school until 6:00, and I knew, with Thanksgiving the day after next, that if I didn't talk to Muriel right away, it would be Friday at least before I had the chance. I didn't bother calling, just headed over to her building.

Muriel's apartment was the same cookie-cutter layout as all the other studios, but her decor was unique. She'd grown up in Panama, where her father was an engineer who'd worked on the canal. Her place was a slice of Central America—walls painted a sunny yellow and hung with *huipeals*, chairs covered by hand-woven fabrics in bright colors. Folksy candelabras and animal figurines littered every available surface. The wrought-iron furniture could have come straight out of a Pottery Barn catalog, but given her background, I assumed it was genuine.

If Muriel was surprised to see me at that hour, when I should have been on my way home, she didn't show it.

"Come in, Anita, come in." Her giggle sounded pleased, and I let her tour me around her collection for a few minutes before I got down to business.

"I hope you don't mind my bringing it up again, but I've come to talk about that group, Issues of Later Life?"

Muriel stiffened.

I plowed on. "I understand that the group didn't stop meeting when it was supposed to, that you kept on with it here."

"There's no law against that, is there?"

"No." I paused. In my hurry to see her, I hadn't thought out the best angle to approach the subject. "No, there isn't. What I'd like to know is who attended, and what you talked about." Might as well be direct.

It didn't work. "It had nothing to do with NAN, and I don't see that it's any of your business."

"It's NAN's business if you're encouraging senior citizens to take their own lives."

That got her back up but good.

"Are you accusing me of something, Anita? Because if a group of us were interested in exploring ways to die with dignity, that's our right as individuals."

"Did those individuals include Grace Corbo, Ora Stringer, and Harry Silverman?" I shot back.

"I don't know what you're talking about. Several like-minded friends and I gathered to discuss a book. Neither Russ nor Grace Corbo was ever in my house. And Ora Stringer! I wouldn't have anything to do with that woman if you paid me." Muriel sat back, satisfied that she'd shut me up.

"What about Mr. Silverman? You and Judy are friends, aren't you?"

"What's that got to do with the price of tea in China?"

"You tell me."

"As far as I know, Harry Silverman died of liver cancer. After, I might add, a long illness, and under the care of hospice."

Confrontation didn't do it, so I tried flattery. "Muriel, I know you believe in a terminally ill person's right to die, without pain, at a time of his choosing, and I agree with you that physician-assisted suicide should be legal. What I'm concerned about is people dying long before it's medically inevitable. Do you know how many people in the Estates have—"

"Chosen the alternative to a slow, painful, degrading death? Made peace with their illnesses in the privacy of their own bedrooms?" Muriel spit the words at me. "Whatever you're after, you can forget about it. I have every right to invite people into my home without having to name names to a nosy social worker."

And that was that. I tried to make a placating, graceful exit, but Muriel refused to say another word to me. So much for my vaunted interviewing skills.

When I got to downstairs to the lobby, Trudi was shouting into the intercom. "Muriel, this is Trudi Voss! Buzz me in, please!"

"You're going to see Muriel Dodge?" I held the door open so Trudi could enter the building. "She probably thinks it's me, trying to get back in. I was just visiting her."

"Thank you." Trudi stepped around me. "You're here late, aren't you? Is something wrong with Muriel?"

Damn. Talk about unprofessional—I'd just breached confidentiality by naming the person I'd been to see. "No, everything's fine."

Trudi hesitated, as if waiting for me to elaborate.

It was an awkward moment. We hadn't been face-to-face since the flea market. I was still distressed about the lost money, and knowing that Trudi had wanted me fired didn't help.

Nervous small talk isn't usually something I do, but I was anxious to get back into her good graces. "It seems like the direct mail appeal is having great results."

"Yes." She softened. "Naturally, you've seen the envelopes

come in. We always have a good response. This year I think the amounts people give are larger. I'm just bringing Muriel the most recent list of donors so she can keep up with the thank-you notes."

"Trudi—" She'd already turned toward the elevators. "Did Lucille Dolan leave a bequest to the endowment fund?"

As soon as I'd said it, I realized I'd blown it with Trudi. The endowment fund wasn't my business, they'd made that clear enough. Before Trudi could open her pursed lips, I made a show of consulting my watch. "Oh dear, it's later than I thought. I'd better run."

And I did.

30

THE only conventional feature of our Thanksgiving is that we eat turkey and mashed potatoes. It's a long story, but I met my father for the first time two years ago, and whatever we do together is along the lines of starting rather than continuing family traditions.

Since my father's rent-controlled apartment is three times the size of ours, he got to host the holiday. The guest list included Lavinia, the live-in aide who'd tended my father's mother during her slide into the long death of Alzheimer's. She'd stayed on with him, keeping house in exchange for room and board, and now took care of my neighbors, Elizabeth and Catherine Wilcox, five mornings a week. The Wilcox sisters, naturally, had been invited. Also along for the meal were my father's friend Maude, who lived in the building, and Katsu, honoring us on his last day in New York by coming for dinner. Clea was the token child.

Benno went over in the morning to help my father cook, while Clea and I cabbed down later with the Wilcoxes. The ride exhausted Elizabeth, who was in her early nineties, and she nodded off as soon as Lavinia settled her in an armchair with her purple afghan over her knees. Catherine, a former singer, was thrilled by my father's collection of old blues LPs, and kept Lavinia busy playing disc jockey while she treated us to a running commentary on the personal lives of the performers she'd known. Clea performed briefly herself, boogying to Etta James, before she disappeared into the guest room with her book.

Maude poured sherry all around. I got a wink along with my glass, to acknowledge our mutual pleasure at how we'd tweaked this most American of holidays. The women were drinking in the living room while the men presided over the stove. Add to that the various ages, races, and classes we represented—the Wilcoxes, elderly, black, on Social Security; Lavinia, fiftyish, Trinidadian, a service worker who'd made herself a comfortable life; Maude, white, same age as Lavinia, a sculptor who scraped by on her art; me, forties, professional; Clea, nine, almost adopted.

In the kitchen, my father, a well-off lawyer who'd taken up cooking as a hobby; Benno, a cabinetmaker, a working-class trade with a barely middle-class income; Katsu, Japanese, cabinetmaker, shiatsu practitioner. Your basic, all-American *mischegas*.

I took my drink in to see what was going on with the food.

My father mashed sinful amounts of butter and whole milk into the potatoes while Benno made matchsticks out of carrots for his brussels sprouts and toasted almond specialty. Katsu stood at the stove, sautéing the sprouts in a cast-iron frying pan. The countertop TV was tuned to the football game, but the men were more absorbed in talking politics than watching. I wasn't much interested, either; the main thing I want from Thanksgiving football is always for the Cowboys to lose. So far, so good; the Raiders were up by ten. The election talk was too depressing, so I wandered out through the door on the opposite side of the kitchen, meaning to see whether my father had done anything with his mother's room yet.

She'd died almost a year ago. Other than replacing the hospital bed with a computer console, he hadn't changed much. The room looked unused, like a place two stray armchairs and a floor lamp had come to have an awkward social encounter. The shades were half drawn, obscuring the sky part of the view south down the Hudson. I pulled their strings and sent the shades flapping up. The room filled with a pearly light.

"Anita." A tap on my shoulder. For a split second I thought it was my grandmother's ghost.

Katsu stammered apologies for startling me before he held out a small package wrapped in a square of green silk with a pattern of red maple leaves. "I have this for you."

I thought he meant it was a present, since he'd tied it up in a *furoshiki*, but Katsu waved away my thanks. "No, no. It is what you ask me to find, from the computer. When I am cleaning in her desk, I feel it under the drawer."

Katsu turned to the computer and pulled out the keyboard shelf. "Like this, here. With tape." He ran his hand under the top of the table, showing me where the disc had been hidden. "I don't know is it what you want. I don't use the computer."

A dinosaur, like Benno.

He left me alone with the packet. I sat in the desk chair and booted up my father's computer. It was a PC, and it had Word. I put the disc in the A drive, and called up its contents in the Open menu. There was only one file, and it wasn't called "Deaths."

No, its name was "Baby."

I opened it. Twenty pages, single-spaced, of dated entries that started over a year ago and ended the month before Susan's death.

It seemed to be a record of how she'd felt during the two attempts at in-vitro fertilization. Some of it was factual—her reactions to the ovulation-inducing drugs, what the doctor had said. The rest was sheer emotion, a roller coaster of hope with sharp descents into despair. Reading as a woman, I recognized all too well how the hormone-induced level of intensity made an abyss of every low moment.

In the last few months, after Susan had given up on Western medicine's assisted reproductive technology and switched to Chinese herbs, the tone of the diary leveled out. Not that she'd had any more luck with the Eastern approach, but she seemed more resigned to the possibility that she would never bear a child. The last entry stated simply that Katsu had brought home information on adopting a baby from China.

NAN didn't come up at all, other than a passing mention of how difficult it was to be at work while she was affected by the hormone regimen.

Nothing about Issues of Later Life, or bequests, or a file named "Deaths."

I stared out at the river, debating whether I should print it out for Katsu. Would it be kind or cruel for him to know how distressed Susan had been? A tugboat escorted an ungainly tanker toward the Jersey docks. I decided reading the diary would provide more reasons for him to lash himself with guilt, so I ejected the disc. As I straightened, I noticed Katsu leaning against the door frame.

In the moment before he came toward me and took the disc from my hand, I thought of the phrase "the hollow men." Katsu seemed thin, insubstantial, a shell whose animal has abandoned it. He reached for the *furoshiki*, folded it around the disc, and knotted it.

"This told you the reason why Susan—" He couldn't say the words, *killed herself*.

"No, Katsu, it didn't." As I said it, I realized that the disc had given me an altogether different feeling. Maybe it was because I'm an adoptive parent myself, but I didn't think anyone contemplating that hopeful step would give up the way Susan had.

"The disc was a kind of diary. She was sad, depressed even, about the failure of the in-vitro and the herbs. But the last entry was about the adoption. Hormone therapy does strange things to emotions, and it's natural to grieve when a treatment doesn't work."

"She wrote down that she was sad?" Katsu's black eyes seemed like windows into the void.

"A diary is where a person puts all her most negative thoughts. It's not an accurate record." I hesitated. All I had to go on was my intuition. The disc was hardly proof that Susan hadn't been suicidal, and whatever suspicions I was having about the other plastic bag deaths in the Estates, they were just that, suspicions. I felt like I'd just turned a kaleidoscope and created an entirely new pattern from the same shards of information that had been tumbling around in my brain for weeks.

Because if what I was beginning to sense was correct, that Susan hadn't committed suicide, it meant someone had killed her. And that led to a whole other can of questions. Like Who? and Why?

Questions that were not going to be answered before Katsu left for Japan in the morning.

If ever. He had his own life to get on with. I kept quiet, but I made him an internal promise to find out what, really, had happened to his wife.

I wanted to put my arms around Katsu, to ease his sorrow as he'd so often eased my physical aches with his strong fingers, but he turned away, leaving me to stroke the air behind his shoulder.

I followed him down the long hall, bypassing the kitchen. Katsu stopped at the coat closet to put the disc in his bag. I continued on into the dining room.

Lavinia had managed to pry Clea away from Madeleine L'Engle, and had her helping set the table. Clea placed a fork carefully in the center of each folded napkin. I felt my heart fill with the pride of a mother whose child is behaving properly for a change.

From the French doors, I studied the women in the living room. Catherine, animated, in an indigo pantsuit, her hair dyed a youthful black, sang to Maude. Elizabeth, her gray Afro like a halo around her small face, sipped sherry and nodded along to the music. This is how aging should be, a long process of slowing down, punctuated by new friends and new experiences to which you contribute from your store of memories.

It was a wonderful meal. We held hands for a silent grace, and I gave thanks for the decisions that had led us to Clea. If I'd grown her from my own blood and bone, I couldn't have loved her any more than I did.

Since Benno had come early to cook, he was on the first shift home with Clea and the Wilcoxes while I drew cleaning detail. Maude headed over to the East Side for a second dessert at her sister's apartment, and my father disappeared into the back room with the computer.

Lavinia was restful company. She didn't need to make small talk, and she worked with an economy of effort that I found calming. I cleared the table and loaded the dishwasher. Lavinia packed a shopping bag of leftovers for me to take home, enough to feed us for several days, along with an extra sweet potato pie she'd baked especially for the sisters.

"Anita, will you join me for a cognac before you leave?" my father asked.

"Sure." I was glad of the invitation to spend a few minutes alone with him. He handed me a snifter, and I settled into the window seat. The lights of Manhattan glittered like a necklace flung along the dark river, ending in the twin pendants of the World Trade Center. If I'd known what he was going to ask of me, I wouldn't have been so eager to linger.

We don't look much like each other, apart from being on the short side and having long, agile fingers, but I've learned that we share certain habits of mind. My mother is like a knife; to her, every issue has a right side and a wrong one. Benno also has a finely honed sense of what's moral and what isn't. He calls it spinning, the way I can explain a position from any side.

I see it as the response of a trained social worker. Every transgression has not only a cause, but also a reason. I need to understand motivation to find the most effective way to intervene. For my father, the ability to argue the opposition's point of view as though he believes it wholeheartedly is the primary tool of a defense attorney; he has to be able to build the prosecution's case to defend against it.

It occurred to me that my problem with Susan's death was that I didn't get the why. Sure, suicide is unfathomable to those who would never contemplate it, but once you look, there's always a reason. From one angle, Susan had more than enough reasons—despair over failure to conceive, lack of desire to adopt, guilt over her possible role in the "self-deliveries" that had been going on in the Estates. I just wasn't convinced that any of them, individually or together, added up to her particular death.

I realized my father was waiting for me to come back to the here and now.

"Sorry," I told him. "I've had a lot on my mind."

"Yes, Benno was telling me about the difficulties of your new job."

That was an unfamiliar feeling, my husband and my father talking about me.

"Which is why I realize that this may not be the ideal time to bring up such a serious topic." My father studied me, and seemed to decide that I could handle it. "If you would, Anita, I'd like you to take this home with you and read through it at your leisure." He tapped a large manila envelope that he'd placed between us on the window seat.

"What is it?" I was thinking, Will. I drew back from the envelope like it had a snake in it. I had no desire for this man to leave me anything; what I wanted was for him to stick around.

For all he'd missed my formative years and then some, my father read me right.

"It's not what you think." There was a twinkle in his smile. "That is, not exactly. Following my mother's diagnosis of Alzheimer's, I have as you can imagine been concerned that I might myself have inherited the disease. Of course, a certain absentmindedness is to be expected at my age."

He was only sixty-six.

"According to Lavinia, I have not yet stored any dishes in the microwave or put canned goods in the oven."

It was a stab at comic relief, and I gave him the grin he was after.

"My doctor gives me a clean bill of health. Since my mother's death, however, I've felt it incumbent on me to make certain arrangements in advance of whatever infirmities of age life has in store for me. You are my closest relative, Anita, and I hope I'm doing more than flattering myself to think that we share a similar outlook on life."

I nodded agreement to that.

"In this envelope you will find a living will, a health care proxy, and a durable power of attorney. I would like to appoint you as my representative should I ever be unable to make medical decisions for myself. I've included a letter that states clearly what I do not under any circumstances want in terms of heroic measures."

"Okay." This time I was genuinely amused, as well as touched. "You and my mother—she did the same thing with me, right after your mother died."

"That's Rosemarie, beating me to the punch again." My father got serious. "There's more, Anita. In the event that I do fall victim to my mother's disease—" He held up a hand to keep me from interrupting. "I do *not* want you to do what I did for her. It would bankrupt you financially, and the emotional toll . . . No. Please, hear me out. It's not how I would choose to die. I am a member of the Hemlock Society, and I've made arrangements for an alternative. In the event that the disease takes me over before I am able to carry out my plan entirely without assistance, I'm asking you to help me."

I shook my head. "I—"

My father stopped me again. "I understand from Benno that you are familiar with a book called *Final Exit.*"

He waited for me to acknowledge having read it. Thanks, Benno, for paving the way for this request.

"There is a chapter in *Final Exit* titled 'When Is the Time to Die?' It sets out very clearly the situation I may find myself in at some later date. I've also written a personal letter to you that explains my feelings and my reasoning." His voice took on the measured, reassuring tones he used on his clients. "I fully expect to be able to take care of matters without assistance. I am, however, familiar with the ways in which Alzheimer's can cause sudden and unanticipated lapses in memory, which is why I'm telling you this now. There is no need to respond immediately, Anita. Take this home. Think about it. Talk it over with your husband."

He put the envelope in my lap. I swallowed the last sip of cognac. It tasted like ashes.

I hate November. Of all the months, it has the least to recommend it; after the leaves have fallen and before there's a chance of snow to soften the gritty gray city. The wind off the river bit through my wool jacket. Give me rain, sleet, hail, thunder, snow—anything but wind.

It dug under my hat and reached into my collar. Without gloves, the hand carrying the bag was instantly frozen to a claw. If an empty cab had passed, I would've treated myself, but none did.

I turned my back on the river and let the wind push me along to Broadway. The last shreds of turkey-induced tranquillity had blown away with my father's request. That I might lose him to Alzheimer's—not that it hadn't crossed my mind. And yes, the fear that I might be carrying the seeds of that devastating degeneration myself has visited me in sleepless hours.

But my father's mother, my grandmother, had died what I

think of as the best possible death. At home, free of pain, well tended, in her own bed, and in her own time. I know, she was basically comatose for the last months. What it meant for her I have no way of knowing, but it gave me the chance to meet her, to sit by her bed and stroke her hand. Not that I could say I knew her, but still, it was more than nothing.

I bought a pack of cigarettes and a lighter from the newsstand on the corner. The old trick didn't work. I had to smoke a whole one, waiting in the bus shelter, before three M104s lumbered up and I rode on home.

31

THE day after Thanksgiving brings my second favorite of the twists New York City puts on its holidays. Nothing can touch green bagels for St. Patrick's Day as a prime example of how the city, you'll pardon the expression, celebrates diversity. When the evergreen forests of Canada and Vermont descend on the city sidewalks, they bring a pagan magic with them.

I always think of Birnum Wood coming to Dunsinane— the rooted trees seem to lift their feet and replant themselves hundreds of miles away. Every few blocks on upper Broadway, Christmas tree vendors set up their rows of balsam, pine, blue spruce. The best thing is the smell, a piney aroma that overrides the prevailing city scents of exhaust, coffee, concrete, rubbish, and hot dogs. Next is the way the trees add shadow to the sidewalks, the feel of a forest dark and deep on familiar streets. Last night's wind had blown the November sky to a bright, polished blue. I could have been in the Maine woods, if it hadn't been for the traffic on Broadway.

I was almost happy to be going in to work. Benno didn't

view the day after Thanksgiving as a holiday, and Vivian agreed with him; she insisted NAN be open. "Four days is too long for our seniors to be without recourse," is how she explained it to me.

Clea was spending the day with Benno at the shop. Anne and Michael had had long-standing reservations at a B&B in Woodstock, so Vivian granted Anne the Friday off. I would have the office to myself, and I was hoping for a quiet day.

I saw the flashing lights as soon as I turned the corner of LaSalle Street. When you work with very old people, you don't need a sixth sense to dread the appearance of an ambulance in front of a building where dozens of your clients live.

I bypassed the NAN office and headed over to see if I knew the person the EMTs had been summoned for. What I got was a faceful of Michael.

"Yo, Social Worker, I think you better change your title to Angel of Death." He wasn't amused, and neither was I.

"Who is it?" I asked.

"Woman named Muriel Dodge. I was just on my way over to talk to you."

Muriel? "I just saw her two days ago, she was—" Fine. Just great. Healthy as a horse. "What happened to her?"

"Come on, I'll show you." Michael bowed and made a sweeping gesture with his arm, inviting me into the lobby.

I had no desire to start my day by viewing Muriel's body, but in the face of Michael's savage tone, it was easier to go along than protest.

"Stuck her head in one of those damn turkey bags, just like your friend Susan Wu and that couple upstairs." Michael pounded the elevator button like it was to blame.

"Suicide?" I had to ask. Unlike with the others, I felt responsible for Muriel's death, implicated somehow, after the hostile tone of our last conversation.

"What it looks like."

"When did it happen?"

"How the hell should I know?" He hit the elevator button again. "Eight o'clock this morning, the neighbor lady called Neville. Seems the two of them had a system, some plastic card they passed back and forth under the door to keep tabs on each other. Neighbor slid it under the Dodge woman's door before she went to bed, and Dodge was supposed to return the favor when she woke up. Only today she didn't. Neighbor called her. No answer, natch, so the neighbor let herself in with Dodge's spare key." He glowered at me. "Nobody should have to see someone they know like that."

So why do I have to? I wanted to ask. It felt like Michael was punishing me. But what, exactly, had I done? Another question to keep me awake at night.

"Michael. What's going on here?" I said it gently. Then it occurred to me—"What are you doing here? I thought you and Anne were in Woodstock."

"Yeah, well, she is, and I'm not. Pigheaded—" But he smiled. The elevator came, and we got on. "I was held up on a B&E Wednesday night, never mind the pun, so Anne went without me. I'd've gone up yesterday morning, but I got noble and took a couple shifts so Graffo could spend some time with his family."

"You mean you got pissed because Anne didn't wait for you."

Michael laughed. "Yeah, and for my sins, I got this." The elevator door opened on a hallway crowded with uniforms of various sorts. Two cops, a cluster of EMTs ready to occupy the elevator we'd just vacated, a pair of orange-jumpsuited crime scene officers, Mr. Neville.

"Ah, Mrs. Servi, good morning," he greeted me.

What's so good about it? I wanted to ask, but I simply nodded to him. "What happened?"

"See for yourself." Michael prodded me along the hall, his hand on the small of my back. "Excuse me. You fellows done in here?"

"Yeah." An orange jumpsuit nodded. "Hey, don't go in there!"

I stopped at the threshold and glared at him. "I wasn't going to." I didn't need to. I could see just fine from the door, mannequin Muriel in the recliner, feet crossed at the ankles, hands folded in her lap, head encased in a beige bag. My stomach lurched. I stepped back.

Michael gave a satisfied nod at the color of my face. "Where's the note?" he asked Jumpsuit, who handed him a clear plastic bag with a sheet of blue-lined white paper in it.

"Well, Social Worker, it seems you were in her thoughts right before she took the final exit." He flapped the bag at me.

"Let me see that."

Michael held it up so I could read what was inside. The wavery handwriting slanted downward on the page.

"You were right, Anita, I got carried away" was all it said.

"Right about what, I wonder?" Michael, snider than he needed to be. Mr. Neville leaned close to hear what I had to say.

Right about her getting carried away, obviously, you idiots. I bit down on the words. "There's no need to antagonize the cops, Anita," my internal Benno reminded me.

"I think—can we—" It felt like all the air in the hallway had been used up.

Mr. Neville came to my rescue, got me to unbutton my winter coat and take it off, then ushered me into an elevator that came as soon as he pushed for it. Michael, not about to let me out of his sight, came along for the ride. By the time we hit the fresh air in the lobby, I knew what was wrong with me.

I'm usually on the objective side of shock rather than the subjective, and I know how to treat it. I lay flat on the floor and put my legs up on the armchair. Neville folded my coat and tucked it under my head.

The dizziness would have settled down a lot sooner if

Michael hadn't still been looming over me, and if one of the security guards hadn't taken Mr. Neville, my protector, away on some other business. I closed my eyes, but it had no effect on Michael's voice. He settled in the armchair by my head and started in.

"So here's the deal, Social Worker. Quid pro quo. I'm going to let you in on a few things, then you're going to give me the whole story on Ms. Dodge upstairs. Okay?"

I opened my eyes to listen.

"Sitting on my desk Wednesday morning was the ME's report on one Lucille Dolan. Found dead in her bed, an apparent heart attack. Neville asked me to request it, is the only reason they did a tox analysis on her. Humor the old man, I figured, why not?" Michael stretched his legs out, his feet inches from the left side of my head. "I've got a copy for him, right here in my pocket."

I sat up and rested my back against the armchair. From the amusement in his eyes, he enjoyed torturing me, dragging out the information so I'd have to ask. I didn't give him the satisfaction.

"You don't want to know what killed your Ms. Dolan?"

I kicked his foot and got a grin in response.

"Our old friend, oxycodone. Liquid form again, that Oxy-Fast. Her last meal was apparently a piece of poppy-seed cake saturated with the stuff."

"She didn't use a plastic bag, did she?" I asked. A buzzing started up in the back of my head, and I lay down again.

"I always said you were a smart cookie, Anita. No plastic bag, and according to the photos the ME's office took of the scene, no empty bottle of OxyFast right to hand. No plate of cake lying around, either." Michael leaned over to look in my eyes. "You know, it's a funny thing. When they found this Lucille Dolan, no one saw any reason to inventory her kitchen. Time Neville went up there Wednesday afternoon, the dishes had all been washed and the fridge cleared out. I suppose one of your do-good *yentas* took care of that, not so much as a jar of mayonnaise or a pickle left."

Mayonnaise. Harry Silverman's last word. Judy, I should talk to Judy.

"Now we got another death. Textbook case of bagitis, what it looks like. Except I got Neville's take on the overall situation here, and a list of names so long I'll never tunnel my way out from the paperwork. So save me some time, Social Worker, and tell me what you've dug up so far."

The sight of him upside down, features distorted like a cheap Picasso, was too much for me. I sat up again.

This time I made it onto the couch. If he wanted the whole story, he could have it. I started with the list of names on Susan's bookmark, which Michael confiscated from me.

"What's with the numbers?" he wanted to know.

"It's only a guess, but based on the fact that Ralph and Ora Stringer left fifty thousand dollars to NAN in their will, I think they might refer to bequests."

"Uh-huh, and I'm guessing you've had your grubby paws all over NAN's financial records, tracking down who donated exactly how much."

I felt like the little girl who cried wolf. "All right, I confess. I did try to look at the bank statements, except they're not kept in the office. The treasurer, Trudi Voss, she works on them at home."

"Why is my life never easy?"

So I told him about Issues of Later Life, and the conversations I'd had about it with Vivian, Lil, and Muriel.

"Let me see if I've got this right now. Your Muriel Dodge was advocating self-deliverance, death with dignity, a plastic bag as the ideal way to shuffle off the mortal coil? And she helped, what, five, six people make their final exits? Jesus, Mary, and Joseph, you need a scorecard to keep up with all who's been dying around here! Anyway, after you called her on it, she had an attack of remorse and took the easy way out herself?"

It wasn't exactly what and why I thought happened, but laid out nice and neat like that, it made a certain kind of sense, and I said so.

"Yeah, that's what bothers me." Michael leaned back in the chair and tugged the knot of his tie loose. "I don't like my answers wrapped up all nice and neat, especially when the questions are as messy as what we got here in the Estates."

"I thought you lived for the simple solution, Michael."

But I didn't like it either. Muriel as crusader for death with dignity was fine as far as it went, but if she was going to take that way out herself, why not leave a note that told the whole story? What better opportunity to proselytize her belief in self-deliverance?

"Some ADA's going to propose to me, when she finds out this won't be landing in her lap. Assisted suicide is a bear, and this one didn't even have a wisp of what you'd call evidence." Michael flipped his notebook closed.

I could have told him right then about Diane McClellan's secret cache of medications. I should have. The only reason I held off was that I wasn't willing to put her career in jeopardy without more consideration than I was capable of at the moment.

And he'd mentioned something about Lucille Dolan that stuck in my mind. I needed to be someplace quiet where I could concentrate.

"Do you think I can go to work now?" I asked, meek as a lamb.

I got the one-eye squint again. "Yeah, just don't leave town anytime soon."

"Did Anne ever tell you you're a walking cliché?"

"If that's French, I'll take it as a compliment."

Back at the NAN office, luck hadn't deserted me altogether; no messages on the machine, and no Vivian to answer to. My knees were a bit on the wobbly side, so I made a pot of coffee and drank a cup heavy on the milk and sugar. I wasn't quite ready to swallow a particular bit of the information Michael had given me, not yet, but it was definitely something to chew on.

32

J UDY Silverman offered me coffee and a slice of pumpkin pie. I declined both. This wasn't a social call, and for what I was about to do, I didn't want to like her. We sat in the living room, in matching armchairs angled toward the household god, a television in a sleek wall unit.

I hitched my chair around to face Judy directly, and just said it. "Muriel Dodge was found dead this morning, an apparent suicide by plastic bag."

Judy's head snapped back against the chair as if I'd slapped her. Her face went red, then white. It was a reaction, all right.

"I need you to tell me how exactly Harry's death happened." I said it gently, but I looked straight at her to make sure she understood that she had to answer.

"Not with a plastic bag!" That brought color back to her cheeks.

I didn't let it bother me. "Then how?" I let her stutter out some objections before I said it again. "Just tell me exactly how Harry died."

Judy closed her eyes for a moment. Her hands clenched and unclenched in her lap.

I waited until her breathing settled, then insisted. "Tell me."

"It was an overdose of OxyContin. We crushed ten pills and mixed them with applesauce. I went for a walk, and Muriel fed it to him. He ate less than half, and he was already comatose when I got back. It took another four hours for his breathing to stop. I sat with him the rest of the time. Muriel wasn't here."

"Where did you get the extra pills?"

Judy shrugged, puzzled. "Extra? I'd just renewed the prescription, so we had plenty. In fact, I donated the unused tablets and a bottle of OxyFast to Diane for NAN's people."

Oh, did you now? I thought. That would be after I found Diane's original supply and before she said she dumped it all, so—so what?

I must have looked skeptical, because Judy started explaining. "I don't want you to get the wrong idea about Muriel, Anita. What she did was simply a kindness, feeding an old man some applesauce. Harry was tired."

They shoot horses, don't they? "You mean she didn't know what was in it?" Unbelievable.

"Of course she knew. I would never ask anyone—it was just that I couldn't do it myself—hold the poisoned goblet to my own husband's lips—no, Muriel offered."

"Did you go to that group at NAN, Issues of Later Life, or any of those meetings Muriel had at her apartment?"

"When they talked about the book? No. I'm too young for most of what NAN offers, and I'm not much of a joiner. Harry and I went to their movies now and then, but that's all. I met Muriel in the pottery workshop, that's how we came to be friends."

"Was Diane McClellan involved in any way?"

"She wasn't here. She didn't know what we were going to do. That's all I'll say."

"Okay." I could respect that. As far as I was concerned, they hadn't done anything so very wrong, and I said as much.

Judy was grateful, and relieved. I had to refuse the pie and coffee again, although I could have used the jolt of good caffeine.

I sat on a bench outside the Silvermans' building before I headed back to the office. Bare tree limbs scratched the blue blue sky. Something was happening here—I got Dylan lyrics again—and I didn't know what it was, any more than Mr. Jones did.

I'm not a believer in conspiracy theories. In my opinion, a blind man with a gun is all it takes to create chaos. From where I sat, though, Muriel as a lone actor just didn't wash. Plastic bags don't do the trick by themselves; it takes medication to induce a sleep deep enough to prevent a panic response to being smothered. And where would Muriel have gotten the drugs from?

For all both Judy and Diane had refused to talk about it, I was sure Diane had played at least an advisory role in Harry's death. Someone had to have provided them with the information on crushing the pills. I didn't really have a problem with Harry's death; his cancer was terminal, and he'd clearly chosen his time to go.

Maybe it wasn't what I'd want for myself. Or for Barbara, or even my father. I did, however, have to respect their decisions.

A flock of leaves skittered across the path and wrapped themselves around the skeletal chrysanthemums.

What nagged at me was that the deaths had continued even after Susan's. If it had ended then, the blame could have been laid at her door, and her suicide been explained as an attack of conscience—the deeper meaning of what she'd started had gotten to her, and she wanted out.

Or maybe Susan had been taken out. Because she knew too much, and the others had too great a stake to let her simply bow her way off the stage.

Look at them. Vivian, with her place in an upscale retirement community. Diane's wardrobe of cashmere, leather, and mink. Trudi and her excursions to Foxwoods. Muriel—I hadn't known her well enough to know why or if she might have wanted a share of the proceeds, but money is one of those things everyone finds a use for. And Susan, those expensive, futile attempts at in-vitro.

A cabal of people who were helping their neighbors to die. Mercy killing, an ancient and honorable pursuit. Like honor among thieves, it was still theft. And then the financial angle—a bit of altruistic fund-raising for NAN, with a dash of personal profit for those who took the risks.

Next to denial, rationalization is the most powerful defense mechanism. I put an end to their suffering so they could be at peace. I rid the community of undesirables who dump feces down the compactor chute. And if, in the process, I provide funds for the agency that offers services that enable others, more worthy others, to live comfortable, secure lives, isn't that a good thing? Put a belief in doing the right thing behind it, and you can justify anything.

Wait a minute, Anita. Do you really think two or three women were on a mission to lay a nest egg for NAN and in the process rid the Estates of social misfits and line their own pockets?

As a rationale for murder, it did seem a bit extreme.

I peeled back the layers. A group, started in good faith, to inform seniors of their rights and options. Living wills, health care proxies; nothing wrong with that. An open discussion of self-deliverance; nothing wrong with that either, not among consenting adults.

Whatever arrangements individuals made with other individuals, that was between them. So, fine for the terminally ill, like Harry Silverman and the man with pancreatic cancer. Grace Corbo? Ralph and Ora Stringer? Muriel Dodge? Susan? If they had all really committed suicide, okay, fine for them too.

But had they? And if so, would they have without encouragement and assistance from the ILL adherents?

What about the others on the list, those who died of apparently natural causes? Take Lucille Dolan, Dumpster-diving millionaire miser, who turned out to have a lethal amount of oxycodone in her system—without Mr. Neville's insistence on a toxicology scan, her death would have raised no suspicions. Did she dose herself up? Was there a caring friend who came in later and removed the evidence?

And Trudi's mother, a stroke victim; she also left a bequest to NAN.

Well, at least Olive Patterson's son had taken her to Connecticut for the holiday weekend, which was one worry off my shoulders.

Was Mr. Neville turning molehills into murder, or was it me?

It was really too beautiful a day for all this speculating, and I decided to walk myself over to Met Foods for a soda to go with the turkey sandwich I'd brought for lunch.

On the way back to NAN, I paid a visit to the Security office. Being a former cop, Mr. Neville wasn't thrilled with the proposition I laid out for him. He'd been in Lucille Dolan's apartment both before and after someone had cleaned it up, however, and his training also told him that my plan might be the best shot we had at proving anything.

There was one other person I needed to talk to. When I got back to the office, Vivian and Trudi were adding up the week's take in contributions. Getting permission to come in the next day after the video program to catch up on my own paperwork was no problem.

Just before two on Saturday, Clea and I headed for the Estates. It was Tamika's eleventh birthday, and brave Carla had agreed to a sleepover. Nine preadolescent girls for twenty-four hours—talk about a Valium-inspiring event. Clea carried her pajamas and a change of clothes packed into the smallest of my grandmother's set of nesting, zippered suitcases. I had my arms wrapped around a sleeping bag with a koala bear and a pillow rolled inside.

We were the fifth to arrive, and the apartment was already bursting at the seams. Between 'NSync blaring from Tamika's bedroom and the jumble of sleeping bags and pillows in the living room, it was bedlam. Carla was stirring spaghetti sauce, much calmer than I would've been without a dose of mother's little helper. I didn't linger.

I'd timed my arrival at NAN to coincide with the end of the afternoon's movie. The person I wanted to see wasn't among those on their way out, so I helped Addie fold chairs. She was surprised to see me.

"Working on the weekend, Anita?"

I explained about Clea's sleepover, and wanting some quiet time in the office to get caught up.

"So you're sticking with us, are you?" Addie adjusted a knit cap over her thinning hair.

"Of course." I shot her a smile. I had no idea who would be hired for the executive director's position; it would be up to my new boss, first, to see if he or she wanted me to stay on, and second, to me to decide whether I could work under whoever it was. So I filled in with platitudes, how nice everyone was, how at home I felt in the community.

Addie raised her eyebrows and considered me. I hadn't fooled her one bit. "Well, I hope the person they hire for Susan's job has enough sense to see that you're kept on. We old folks need continuity. Too many upheavals recently. It takes time to warm to someone new. I hope you realize how much people like you here."

"Yes, Addie, thanks. I do, and I'd like to stay."

I held the door and watched her walk down the hall. From behind, she could have been a girl of ten, the red tassel on her beret bouncing with each step.

If I succeeded in proving what I suspected, I wasn't so sure Addie or anyone else would still want me around.

I turned on the lights in my office as well as Anne's, where the file cabinet was, but I didn't open the blinds. No sense in advertising my presence; if someone saw me from outside, they might stop in. That's the thing about a small community, people do drop by. There was only one person I hoped would come to see me that afternoon.

I also had an invited guest, and it didn't take him long to ring NAN's bell.

Without the boxes of envelopes that had been stored in the bathtub, there was plenty of room for a bulky man to lurk behind the shower curtain. I'd snagged a bath bench from Diane's office for Mr. Neville to sit on. Which he did, but not without complaint. It took all I had not to giggle at how undignified he looked, overcoat folded on his lap, shiny black shoes against the white porcelain.

"All you need is a ruffled shower cap to complete your outfit," I told him.

"Yes, well. Perhaps I'll, ah, I'll sit elsewhere while we wait for your visitor to arrive."

I left the head of security looking marginally more comfortable but no less ridiculous perched on the closed toilet seat and went to work pulling files.

I arrayed them all on my desk, fifteen green case files, the name tabs clearly visible to a person sitting in the client's chair. In the center of the arrangement, I placed my copy of *Final Exit*. The gate through which all of these people had passed. And Susan. I moved the jade tiger to the right of the display, where it could witness the proceedings.

By the time a key turned in the door, I'd picked up *Final Exit* and started on the chapter my father had asked me to read—"When Is the Time to Die?"

33

'M glad you're still here, Anita." She walked right into my office and proceeded to hang her coat in the closet. Good thing I'd convinced Mr. Neville not to hide in there. "I was hoping to catch you."

I couldn't have said it better myself.

"Let me just put these away." She tapped the accordion file that was tucked under her arm. "I have just checked over the past six months of NAN's bank records to be sure that Susan left everything in order."

"Did she?" I asked, genuinely curious. What if I was wrong, and it had been Susan all along?

"Yes. Susan was very conscientious. I am the one responsible for oversight, and I will make a full report to the board." She went into Anne's office. I heard her key click into the lock and a file drawer screech open.

I tried to go back to Derek Humphrey, who wasn't advocating that elderly people should take their own lives but rather "speaking up for tolerance, compassion, and understanding for those who do make a deliberate final exit." He went on to make exactly the argument my father had—if he ever became incompetent, he'd want someone to do him in. I could see how he felt that way, I just wasn't sure I wanted to be the one to carry out his wishes.

I looked up at the sound of a metal drawer banging closed. She stood in the doorway between the two rooms, in the same spot where I'd been when I'd seen Susan's body in the chair by the desk.

"Would you like a glass of wine?" she asked.

The last thing I was about to do was let this woman feed me wine, but I had to admire her nerve.

"No thanks, I've still got work to do." I nodded at my desk.

"Well, I think I will. There is something I need to speak with you about."

I rubbed my palms along the arms of my turtleneck to dry the sweat and petted the tiger for courage.

She came back with two glasses and set one on the desk for me. "If you change your mind." She settled herself in the client's chair, still without so much as a glance at my deliberate arrangement of file folders. Maybe she did take client confidentiality seriously.

"What's up?" I asked.

"This may be a delicate matter. That's why I thought, perhaps, a little wine . . . ?"

Not a snowball's chance. I waited. Let her show her hand first. I stared at the files, silently inviting her to have a look.

She shifted her head slightly, unable to resist a glance at what I found so interesting. When I looked up, she gave a slight nod, as if confirming to herself that she'd come to the right decision.

"It concerns Anne Reisen."

"She's doing a great job, isn't she?" I tried to cover my surprise at this tack.

"Do you think so?"

I did. I launched into a list of all the wonderful things

Anne had done for NAN. She heard me out, but it didn't sway her.

"Yes, I know she is your friend, Anita, and you asked her to work with you. Are you sure you won't have a sip of wine? This isn't easy."

I shook my head, politely I hoped.

"I'm afraid we have to let her go." Then came a little speech about how NAN appreciated, on such short notice, but what with budgetary constraints—and Anne herself seemed unhappy here, unable to adjust to the constraints of working within the parameters that Vivian had established for the staff.

Bullshit, bullshit, bullshit. I couldn't keep the anger out of my face.

"Understand me, please, this is not personal. It's about what is best for NAN." She nudged the glass closer to my hand.

I actually touched it, reflexively, before the awareness of what might be in it shocked me back to clear thinking. It was time for me to take control of this interview.

I pushed the glass away. "I'm sure you always have NAN's best interests at heart, don't you, Trudi? That's why none of these people"—I waved at the files—"are still around to need our services, right? And why they made such nice bequests when they died?"

This time she made a show of reading the names spread on my desk.

I helped her out, lifting the case files one at a time and slapping them back down on the desk. "Ira Rosenstiel, dying of pancreatic cancer, what harm in giving him a little push? Poor Grace Corbo, lost her mind to Alzheimer's, put her out of her misery. Dorothy Norris, lung cancer, living in a pigsty. Ralph and Ora Stringer, a hazard to the community, dumping feces down the compactor chute, how nice that they had lots of money and no relatives. Lucille Dolan, another wealthy woman with no close family, committed the sin of Dumpster diving at Met Foods."

Trudi let me get it all out. "Yes, as you say, these people re- ceived services from NAN. Naturally, it's gratifying that they chose to express their appreciation with a contribution to the financial security of the agency. I don't understand why you are so upset."

Smooth.

Breathe, Anita. Reason, not emotion. Be direct. "I think you helped them die."

"Yes, I am among those who believe in the right to death with dignity, in a manner and at a time of one's own choos- ing. This is not a secret." Her voice was patient, reasonable. I noticed she kept her hands tightly folded in her lap. "As did several of those people." A nod at the files on my desk. "Your accusation that I am responsible for their deaths is ridiculous and offensive. There are others in the Estates who believe as I do. Perhaps an overzealous individual got carried away—"

That did it for me. "You killed Muriel Dodge."

"Anita, you are across the line." Trudi stood, glared at me.

Finally, a sincere reaction. I almost believed her. "You just quoted her suicide note, 'I got carried away.'"

"It's a common expression. A figure of speech."

The woman had an answer for everything. The memory of Muriel's slanted, drugged scrawl got to me. "You dictated it, and Muriel was so out of it, she wrote whatever you said. You were the one who went too far, and she wanted you to stop." Things were beginning to clarify in my mind. "Susan Wu was onto you, too, wasn't she?"

"Susan was despondent over her failure to conceive a child," Trudi reminded me. "She also left a note."

"Uh-huh. On the computer, which anyone could have typed in. That still doesn't explain how you knew what Muriel wrote." I almost reached for the wine again. "You had to shut them up. Just like you're trying to do with me, a nice Bor- deaux laced with OxyFast."

"I see you are the one who is not happy here, Anita. There

are easier ways out of a job than accusing one of your bosses of murder, don't you think?"

Before I realized what she was going to do, Trudi had snatched the glass and left the room. By the time I got to the kitchen, she had the faucet running and the glass rinsed out. Which left me with shit for proof.

I blocked her route back to the closet for her coat. "The police already know that what killed Lucille Dolan was a slice of poppy-seed cake, your specialty, soaked in OxyFast. Now they're looking into the autopsy reports of every elderly Estates resident who died in the past six months."

"I'm glad to know my tax dollars are being put to such use, wasting civil servants' time. There is nothing to find. I baked my cake for the flea market. I think Muriel purchased several slices for her friend Lucille."

All good bluffs are built on at least a pair of deuces. "Next they'll be going through all NAN's financial records, to see how much of the bequests went into the endowment fund and how much into your pocket," I added.

Trudi saw right through me, and raised me one. "They will find that every penny left to NAN is where it was intended to go. Now, your keys, please, Anita. I will make your excuses to Vivian on Monday. I wouldn't bother coming around for a letter of reference, if I were you."

I ignored the hand she held out. There was still a card up my sleeve. "You thought that computer disc was the only place Susan kept track of the deaths, but you're wrong."

Trudi's hand dropped. It was the first time she'd looked remotely worried. "I don't know what you're talking about."

Not even an ace high, but she toughed it out.

"How do you think I figured it out? She left a list of names, people who were already dead and what they'd willed to NAN, as well as a few who were still alive when she died. I had to ask myself, how did she know these people were going to die and leave bequests to NAN?"

"People often inform us when they've remembered NAN

in their wills." Trudi's voice was scornful. She thought I'd shown my hand too soon.

"Maybe they did." Good, lulled into overconfidence. "At any rate, I gave the list to Detective Dougherty, the one who's investigating Muriel's death."

"You have already cost us much more than you're worth, you silly woman!" I thought for a moment she was going to slap my face. "I should have insisted that Vivian let you go when you didn't have enough sense to resign after you were attacked."

"You were the one who hit me."

"I!" She had the nerve to be amused. "You think I would do such a thing!"

Trudi reached for the wine bottle.

I stepped back, out of reach, ready to holler for Neville if she swung at me.

"I won't hurt you." She laughed at my reaction. "Come, let's have some wine, and I will tell you a story. Perhaps you will understand why bringing the police in will destroy NAN." She held out a cup and poured the wine right in front of me, as if to say, "Look, Ma, no drugs."

She'd used my favorite mug, the one with a crackled silver glaze. I waited for her to pour her own and sit down before I chose a chair closer to the door. Being curious didn't mean I was going to let down my guard. I raised the cup to my mouth and didn't sip.

Trudi began by explaining Susan and Diane's personal prescription drug benefit plan for NAN members. To my ears, it was a tacit admission that she herself had also known about the supply of oxycodone.

"So you see, the police are not necessary. The nurse has already disposed of all medications and tendered her resignation. In exchange, I have agreed not to inform the authorities of her complicity."

I should have expected Trudi would try to hang it on someone else. "You mean Diane McClellan was the one who helped all these people die? By herself?" I gave her a length of rope.

Trudi used it. "I believe Ms. McClellan was an unwitting accomplice. By taking their own lives as they did, Susan and Muriel have acknowledged their parts and done their penance. As both of them are now deceased, I hope you will respect my decision to close this situation without further damage to NAN's reputation. The people whose files are on your desk—all of them chose their own deaths."

I pretended to take another sip of wine while I considered the logic of what she'd said. It could even be true. "Carried away by good intentions, that's how you see it?"

"Yes, exactly."

I wanted to believe her, this woman sitting in front of me, who spoke with a trace of my grandmother's accent.

The day before, Mr. Neville and I had gone over the list of deaths, and agreed that Susan Wu and Muriel Dodge were the most troubling. With the others, a case could be made that at the most Trudi's involvement had been to assist in a suicide. That, I might be able to understand. Susan and Muriel were the two I was supposed to focus on.

"Wait a minute," I said. "Before, you said Susan killed herself because she was depressed over not getting pregnant. Now you're saying it was remorse. Which is it?"

"Both." Trudi frowned, trying to see why I had a problem with this. "She had a double motive. Personal and moral."

"So what was Muriel's personal reason?"

"I—perhaps she was ill."

This wasn't getting me anywhere. It was time to press what I hoped would be Trudi's Achilles heel.

"Tell me about your mother," I said. "Why was her name on Susan's list?"

"I know nothing about this list. My mother left money to NAN in her own will."

"Not very much, though, was it? Only a thousand dollars.

In fact, of all the bequests, hers was the smallest. Not what I'd expect from—"

"I took care of my mother. I have all the bills to pay!"

That's right, Trudi, get defensive. Get careless.

I rubbed my head, trying to think how to push further. My fingers touched the lump that hadn't totally disappeared yet.

"You have your little gambling hobby to finance, too. I thought you hit me to scare me away from NAN, but that was only the secondary reason, wasn't it? You were really after the flea market money. Tell me, do you prefer Atlantic City or Foxwoods?"

"Puh!" Trudi exhaled in disgust and turned her face away.

"Your mother left all her money to you, didn't she? You made sure of that, just like you made sure she wouldn't have any more strokes. I read her file, you know. There was no way, with her left side impaired like that, your mother could have taken any pills without help."

"Pills! How did you know my mother—" As we stared at each other, I watched awareness of what she'd admitted dawn on Trudi. "She was in misery. I did only what she wanted me to."

"Mercy killing." I nodded encouragingly. "All of them, suffering, their miserable lives not worth living. You provided a way out."

"I gave them what they wanted. Ira Rosenstiel begged me to help him. Begged. No one else would do a thing. His doctor was a hypocrite. Pills for pain the doctor gave him, but never enough." Trudi's eyes glittered. "You won't prove anything."

"Yes, we will. You've just told me that there's a reason to look. You killed Susan and Muriel, and you killed your own mother."

I hoped Neville was getting an earful.

"I helped them to find peace." Trudi put a hand to her heart. I could see her reliving the experience. "Death was very gentle to them. It came like sleep. The breathing slowed as

life released its hold. Then the body is free from suffering."
Her face was transformed, beautiful even.

I didn't hear his footsteps in the hall, but when the lights
flicked off and on, off and on, I knew it was Mr. Neville's
hand on the switch.

Trudi shot to her feet. "What is this?"

"Please stay calm, Ms. Voss," Neville said. "The police are
here to see you."

He opened the door. There was Michael, and two uniforms right behind him.

Trudi managed to keep control of her face, but the rise
and fall of her chest showed how agitated she was.

Michael cuffed Trudi's hands behind her back, went
through the litany of Miranda rights. I got her coat from the
closet. Trudi allowed me to drape it over her shoulders, but
she didn't say a word.

34

WHEN the lawyers got their hands on it, things got so convoluted that no one had a clear idea about what or if Trudi would be charged with. The assistant district attorney was furious with Michael, who in turn was furious with Neville, who . . . It wasn't fair.

Without my confrontation with Trudi, they wouldn't have had anything whatsoever to go on.

Which was the problem in a handbasket.

Yes, Lucille Dolan had been poisoned; no, nothing other than the circumstantial evidence of a slice of her cake being the vehicle of delivery pointed to Trudi Voss as the culprit. Same with Susan Wu—for all the police dug through everything again, they uncovered nothing that proved she hadn't committed suicide. Ditto for Muriel Dodge. With the earlier bodies either embalmed or cremated, the medical examiner's office had nothing to work with there, either.

Although they'd found a bottle of OxyFast in her purse, there hadn't been any in the second glass of wine Trudi had poured for me. Since she'd washed out the first glass, there wasn't any solid evidence to support an attempted murder charge. Everything they investigated turned out to be like that: suspicious actions that added up to a certainty of guilt unprovable in a court of law.

The forensic accountants confirmed that, true to her word, Trudi had been scrupulously honest with NAN's bank records. Not a penny had gone astray or been misspent on her watch. When the wills of people who'd left bequests to NAN were examined, it turned out that Trudi had been the executor on all but two of them. Suspicious, yes, but not illegal. The closest she'd come to fiscal impropriety was that she'd billed each estate for her services. Again, not illegal—all of the wills had made provision for the executor to be paid. Maybe she'd compensated herself much more generously for the time and effort involved in probating the estates than was called for, but of course she'd kept meticulous track of every minute and minor expense she'd charged for.

Seen in the larger context . . . there was still nothing that would stand up in court.

In spite of exhaustive canvassing in the Estates, the police turned up no one who could definitively place Trudi at the scene of any of the deaths. Rumors, sure, there were plenty of those. Especially about Grace Corbo. In the end, that was the one they charged her with.

Trudi had sat with Grace regularly when Russ needed to go out. In fact, the reason Russ had left his wife alone on the morning she'd died was that Trudi had canceled on him at the last minute. Trudi had keys, though, and could have let herself in after Russ went out. Coupled with the questions raised by the Alzheimer's—Where did Grace get the medication she'd used to tranquilize herself? How did she know what dose to take? Could she have been organized enough to carry out all the steps involved in using the plastic bag without help?—the ADA got a grand jury to indict.

True to her concern for NAN and her promise to Diane, as well as out of sheer self-interest, Trudi denied all knowledge of

Susan's Peter-to-Paul prescription drug plan for NAN's clients. Although I realized the prosecution would need to advance a theory about where Trudi had gotten the oxycodone she'd fed Grace, it wasn't in Diane's or my interest, either, to volunteer the information. In any case, the medications were long gone.

The lack of tangible evidence protected several reputations: NAN's, Susan's, Diane's, my own. Was it worth the chance that Trudi would get away with what she'd done? No, but still, I dithered over whether and what to admit.

In the end, Michael told me, Diane had spoken to the ADA herself.

"Brought along a high-priced mouthpiece who drove a hard bargain. Made sure she wasn't going to testify unless she got immunity. Lawyers." Michael snorted. "Prosecution wants to make a point and hopes she'll cave. Defense has their own show to put on. It'll all come down to theater, you watch."

The stickiest part of the whole mess for me personally had to do with my father involving himself on Trudi's behalf. A woman charged with murder for doing what he'd asked his own daughter to do—the case was right up the great Wertheim's alley. He'd actually called her attorney and offered a consultation, which was eagerly accepted. When he was reviewing the files and came across my name, however, he withdrew. To my great relief.

Diane went through with her request for transfer to another placement. By the second week in December, NAN's new executive director had been hired. Although I had no desire to continue working in the Estates, I agreed to stay on until the twenty-second to familiarize her with the caseload and membership. Anne was offered a full-time position, which she declined.

So when Christmas rolled around, I was out of a job again. It was good timing. We do all the holidays, eight nights of

Hanukkah, six nights for Kwanza, the big enchilada of Christmas in the middle. I had plenty to occupy me.

A tree is Benno's one concession to my pseudo-Catholic upbringing. We chose a seven-footer, balsam because it smells the best, from the Vermonters who spend every December living out of a small trailer parked on Broadway at 111th Street. A beefy young woman in a sap-stained down jacket patched with duct tape ran the tree through a metal hoop from which it emerged swathed in a net of plastic, a long, neat, heavy package to haul home. Good thing we only had to carry it half a block.

I love everything about the tree ritual, from the two days we wait for it to warm up and unfold before adding lights, ornaments, the shiny silver tinsel. It feels pagan to me, this seasonal presence that takes over a corner of the living room, dominating the apartment with its scent. We're no better than primitives, celebrating the solstice with little fires lit against midwinter's early night.

This year's tree was crowned with our own angel, courtesy of Clea's new school, where the lobby tree is decorated with hundreds of paper-plate cherubs, a photograph on the face of each one, every child in the school represented. Three strands of red chile lights, my mother's contribution, nestled deep in the branches. My grandmother's rainbow of delicate glass ornaments shared space with Benno's favorites, a dozen jewel-tone globes big as navel oranges, from the Museum of Modern Art.

The holiday observance that's all our own is an annual Christmas Eve party, attended by a mix of stray Jews and various other friends close enough to be family. I do Benno's mother's *cholent*, a Sabbath dish that's become a party tradition, and everyone else brings whatever they want.

My father came early, so he'd be there when we lit the candles for Hanukkah. He brought the tiniest of Tiffany's famous turquoise shopping bags for Clea. It held a silver chain with a sterling starfish, and she twirled off to change her outfit to something that would show off the necklace. Benno went to put the finishing touches on his killer eggnog, an artery-clogging concoction that includes a dozen eggs, three pints of cream, and you don't want to know how much rum and cognac.

I sat in the living room with my father. We watched the candles flicker, stars of flame reflected in the dark window glass.

"Is anything happening with the adoption?"

I thought he was just making conversation. "We're still waiting for a date from Surrogate's Court. They keep asking for more information, like old transcripts from the paternity hearings. The transracial aspect never came up before, and the judge evidently wants to know why."

"It's a little late for that, isn't it?"

"You'd think so," I agreed. The lesson I've taken from the whole drawn-out process is that the wheels of the system would rather stay locked in place than move.

My father reached into his pocket and took out a square black velvet jewelry box. "I have another gift for Clea. I'd like to give it to you now, Anita, so that you'll have it for her when the adoption is finalized."

I opened the box. A pair of diamond studs set in platinum winked in the light. "Why don't you hold on to them? It shouldn't be much longer."

"They were Mother's." He nodded at the earrings. "The only good piece of jewelry she had left. I want Clea to have them, and I'm afraid I won't remember when the time comes."

We looked at each other for a long moment, both of us aware that I hadn't yet responded to his Thanksgiving request. Not that it hadn't been on my mind; chief among the thoughts that woke me up in the small hours was what I would do if my father did develop Alzheimer's.

"I thought you said you were fine."

"Please, Anita, humor me. Keep them for your daughter."

How could I refuse? The same question I asked myself

when I considered his end-of-life wishes. All I was certain of at the moment was that I wasn't ready to give him an answer just yet. When in doubt, play for time. I was abetted by the door buzzer.

Michael and Anne were the first to arrive, followed by Lavinia with a hand-knit sweater for Clea, then the Wilcox sisters with a fruitcake. After that it was a constant stream. Diane McClellan even stopped by, in a swirl of mink and on the arm of a man in an extremely well tailored cashmere overcoat. They didn't stay; they had theater tickets; she just wanted to drop off a small gift.

It was a huge, ornate selection of cookies from Neiman Marcus.

"He works for Merrill Lynch," Anne whispered. "Diane told me the mink was last year's bonus. Did you notice her left hand? That's this year's, a ruby the size of a pea."

So much for getting by on a nurse's salary.

By ten o'clock I realized that Barbara wasn't going to make it. Suddenly my face hurt from smiling. I needed a break from the people I loved, the cookies and guacamole, cheeses and dips and carrot sticks, the opulence of presents tucked into closets and drawers waiting for Clea to go to bed so they could emerge for their brief moment under the tree.

I filled a plate with food, tucked a coat under my arm, and drifted unobtrusively out the door.

It took Barbara a full minute to answer her bell. Every time I saw her now, it was a shock. The extreme weight loss had hollowed her cheeks. Her arms were sticks, sinew and bone and snaking veins. Hardest to look at was her belly, swollen to the size of a full-term pregnancy from fluid retention, and growing by the hour.

When she smiled back at me, though, I recognized my friend.

"Hey, Anita, just in time. I want to go out back and see if I can catch Santa." Barbara laughed. "George always used to take the girls outside on Christmas Eve to look for him. When a jet flew over, he told them it was Santa coming, so they better hurry inside and get to bed or no presents!"

Barbara put on a red hat trimmed with a band of white fur that made the sunken planes of her face seem even deeper. I left the plate of Christmas Eve treats I hoped she'd at least pick at on the kitchen table.

Between my arm and her cane, we made good progress down the hall and around the corner to the yard. "Pills are working fine tonight," Barbara said. "If I were still drinking, I'd toast to OxyContin."

It did seem like a miracle, for her to be up and moving, as wasted by disease as she was. The hospice nurse had been trying all month to get her to accept a hospital bed, but Barbara wasn't having it. "Thinks I'm ready to go," she'd complained only a few days ago. "Well, I'm not about to lie down and die for that nurse or anybody else, either."

We sat on the wrought-iron bench that gets left out all winter and looked up. No planes flew over.

Everybody does it differently, I thought. Here was Barbara, so close to the end, and all she wanted was to keep on living. My father, in perfect health and all his faculties intact, was preparing to short-circuit the process should he become ill.

Barbara took a pack of cigarettes out of her pocket, and I bummed one.

The sky glowed an odd, apricot color, the reflection of city lights on the underbellies of low clouds. Snow wasn't predicted to start until dawn, but it had already begun. White flecks floated steadily down. The advance guard melted as soon as it hit the concrete; on the frozen garden, snow clung like a downy blanket.

Barbara extended a gloved hand. "How do you like that, snow for Christmas. Hardly ever happens these days."

I stuck my tongue out, hoping to tempt a flake, but they danced away from my warm breath.

"So what's your plan, Anita, now you're unemployed?"

"I don't know. I'm not even interested in reading the want ads." Out of a job. I was trying to remember how good that was supposed to feel. "Social work—my heart's just not in it anymore. This last place, it was too much death and dying."

"I know what you mean." It was the first time I'd heard resignation in her voice.

I could have bitten my tongue.

"No, don't worry about it." Barbara caught my embarrassment and changed the mood back to optimism. "Me, I got no intention of going anywhere. Except maybe Florida. I'm even thinking I should make a few New Year's resolutions."

"Oh, yeah? You finally giving up smoking?"

Barbara laughed. "No, I like to make resolutions I have a shot at keeping. Like eating more bacon. Now, that's one I can get behind."